Oversleeper

by
Matt Mountebank

Published by Accent Press Ltd 2018

ISBN 9781786155542

Accent Press Ltd
Octavo House
West Bute Street
Cardiff
CF10 5LJ

Chapter 1

Monday morning, head throbbing like a sub-woofer, and the goddamn power was out.

Crusty eyes found the unlit bathroom. No hot water. A cold, dark shower. Reluctant muscles woke from their atrophy while my mind remained empty save for the dull ache of a hangover. I stretched and wrapped a white dressing gown around my pale body. No radio or TV to accompany breakfast. The fridge was starting to stink, so the outage must have been a few hours. The milk inside it tasted good, if unusually warm and creamy, sticking in lumps to the cornflakes. I couldn't remember buying full fat. Hadn't had that stuff since I was a kid. And in a glass bottle, too. Hadn't seen those in decades. My sore head was grateful, though. I finished the bowl in silence, slowly bringing the room around me into focus.

The kitchen was my pride and joy. Not expensive, mostly IKEA, but good-looking and all put together by my hands in my spare time. It had everything needed to create a four-course dinner for six guests with ease. I had hosted some great parties in that kitchen. Maybe there had been a party last night? Couldn't have been, though, because it was clean. Too clean. I'd never had it as neat as this. Not even when the old man came to visit. I liked to keep it a little cluttered, homely. This was weird. It was clinical, like an operating theatre. Scrubbed and organised. Everything that I usually wasn't.

A seedy smile found its way onto my unshaven face. I'd scored. I'd had a party, got lucky, and some woman, who right now I couldn't even remember, had cleaned up for me. Trying to impress me with her homemaking skills. Trying to show me she'd make a good wife. That had to be the answer. Maybe she was somewhere in the apartment still? I put the empty cereal bowl in the sparkling sink and explored other rooms. No one else around, but everything was spotless. Everything shone like diamonds in the morning sun. Even the windows had been cleaned. Up here on the eighth floor, that never happened. With my head for heights I rarely went near them on the inside, let alone on the outside. I'm all in favour of having a room with a view of the Hudson River, so long as that view can be enjoyed from the safety and comfort of the sofa. And what was with the sofa? Cushions plumped up like balloons, no sign of the familiar depression shaped to fit my butt precisely. What kind of woman sleeps with a guy, scrubs his apartment, then disappears having risked her life a hundred feet from the ground with a squeegee and a sponge? No woman that I'd ever met. There had to be another answer. I checked the time. Better get to work. Calling in sick with a hangover wasn't an option if I wanted to stay in the running for promotion.

Heading back to the bedroom I glanced again at that sofa. Another oddity struck me. It was covered in a red fabric, but where the sunlight had hit it, the red was faded to orange. And yet it was only a couple of months old. Had it faded overnight? I made a mental note to send a strongly-worded e-mail to the store threatening to retract the five-star review I'd originally given them.

Inside my wardrobe lay the next surprise. My shirts were all pressed, lined up like soldiers, all facing the same way. My other clothes were similarly ordered. Something was definitely up. I looked over my shoulder expecting to see a film crew. I was part of a reality TV show; it was the only explanation. Cleaners had come in the night and I was secretly being filmed to monitor my reaction. Quite insulting to think that my place should have been considered disgusting enough to deserve a television makeover. But there was no film crew, and no cameras hiding anywhere that I could see. In any case, there was no electricity this morning to power them. Now convinced I was in the middle of a practical joke, I threw on my clothes and set off for work, my sore brain steadily churning its way through possible culprits and finding no answers.

After I left the building, I settled into the instinctive groove of a pedestrian commuter, trudging to work, head down, avoiding eye contact. My route only covered a couple of blocks and, before I was even aware of it, I was in the foyer and stepping into the elevator. Another day at the office: e-mails to answer, memos to write, coffees to drink, meetings to fritter away time, invoices to send to clients.

I didn't recognise anyone riding with me, and was surprised when some of them got off on my floor and walked into my company's suite. Some of them half-glanced at me, as if they almost knew me.

I thought I must have looked pretty rough after whatever partying had wiped my short-term memory, but when I saw Josie at reception I figured I'd got off lightly. Hot Josie, the bright and cheery twenty-something graduate, looked terrible. Her supple skin had lost its bounce. Crow's feet pointed to her eyes. I couldn't imagine the water-cooler banter would be the same today. Something had happened to her, something had toppled her status as the most desirable woman in the building. Josie was staring at her cellphone, like she was waiting for an important call. I gave her a smile but it washed over her, unnoticed.

Staff seemed thin on the ground this morning. At least half of the usual crowd of thirty or so was not in evidence. I guessed there was a big early morning meeting somewhere. Maybe I should have been there, but I really couldn't remember. Until I checked the schedule on my PC I'd have no idea what was going on. Those who were at their desks seemed tense. I wondered if redundancies were on the cards. It had happened before, and everyone in the office had been so stressed wondering if they were for the chop that people barely spoke for a week.

Fat Eric always sat at the closest desk to my own. He was passionate about gardening, so what he was doing living in one skyscraper and working in another processing invoices on behalf of an elevator repair company I could never fathom. He'd spent twenty years working in Manhattan, and all he had to show for it was a colourful window box, a few dozen more pounds around his waist than when he'd arrived, and a 401k retirement fund that was still less than a quarter full. His two ex-wives were great pals with each other: he reckoned they conspired against him to milk him for every cent he earned. Mid-forties, single, still had some hair left. Should have been having some fun times. Instead, he always looked as if an invisible chain was dragging him down by the neck. He bounced from one mini financial crisis to the next, always cursing at the price of a coffee, never relaxed about buying a Subway sandwich for lunch if he forgot to make his own.

This morning Eric was gone. Someone else sat in his seat. Skinny, bald, but equally as downtrodden as his predecessor. The man worked in quick spurts, reading reports, sorting papers, checking his cellphone for messages, then repeating the cycle again. I watched him for a couple of minutes before I came to a frightening conclusion: this was Eric. Thirty pounds lighter, smooth as a bowling ball on top, but the same man. He looked crushed, defeated by life, *old* – as opposed to the Eric I remembered: still crushed and defeated by life, but younger.

Eric and Josie had both gone through some kind of terrible weekend. I couldn't figure it out. Eric looked up at me and did a double-take. I guess I looked kinda ropey too. Maybe that was it? We were all part of a reality show together, not just me. One of those shows where everyone in the office does weird shit together in the name of teamwork. Usually they ended up stark naked. Something to do with breaking down barriers between co-workers, they would say. More likely a way to get ratings with some tits and ass. The way I was feeling there was no chance of my clothes coming off in front of any cameras.

Forget Eric, I told myself. I'd find out what the hell was going on eventually. In front of me was a tidy desk. Not at all how I'd left it on Friday. The computer was already on, so I wiggled the mouse to wake the monitor. I was in no mood for real work just yet, and figured a few Facebook minutes would set me up nicely. I clicked the browser button, but an error message came up. Thinking there might be a problem with the company homepage I tried the Facebook shortcut. Same message. The network server must be down. No social networking fix for me this morning. As a backup, I turned to my phone. Apple iPhone. A miracle of modern technology in glass and stainless steel. Fully charged before last night's power cut. Should be able to check in to the world on it this morning.

I pulled the phone from the inner pocket of my jacket. It was dead. I glanced at Eric. He wasn't using an iPhone. Seemed to have replaced it with some kind of brick and was currently arguing into it with a client.

'It's not new,' he was saying. 'The law changed more than ten years ago. In case of fire the elevator automatically descends to the ground and opens its doors. We have to retrofit the sensors and the software in every elevator we service. I don't care if you don't like it, but you do have to pay for it.'

I remembered those chunky phones from the nineties. Great for making phone calls, basic texting functionality, but incapable of any kind of computing experience. Perhaps he was using it out of some fanciful retro notion? I rummaged in my desk drawer for the USB charging cable. The cable wasn't where it was normally kept, and in its place was an old-fashioned phone, just like Eric's. I picked it up: it was fully charged. Must have been new company issue. Useful in an emergency, but a guarantee of social isolation. As I held the phone, it beeped. It wasn't a call. Those primitive beeps meant messages. I looked at its tiny monochrome screen. In highly pixelated green letters there was a message from someone I didn't know. I put the phone back in the drawer without bothering to read the message.

And that's when it started.

'You can't ignore that!' shouted thin Eric, suddenly ending his call. 'You have to check the message as soon as you get it.'

'All right, calm down,' I told him.

'Check the goddamn message. It's important.'

I picked up the phone again and read the message. It told me to climb out of the window and stand on the ledge for thirty minutes. I laughed and shoved the phone back in the drawer.

'What did it say?' Eric gasped, a look of genuine fear in his eyes.

'Nothing,' I told him. 'Just some dumb spam.'

'It's not dumb. You have to do it. Whatever it says!'

No matter how hard I studied his face I couldn't detect any sign of irony. This guy was terrified of something. Again, I took the phone out of the drawer. Someone was playing a sick joke. I typed out a quick reply: 'GO SCREW YOURSELF ASSHOLE'

I had no idea who might be the recipient of my instruction to perform such an act. I didn't care. I wasn't in the mood for anonymous bullshit so early in the day.

'Hey, Eric – I told them to screw themselves,' I boasted, showing him my message.

'Don't press send! I beg you!' He ran towards me, moving with far more fluidity and ease than I remembered him possessing, and lunged at the phone.

It was too late. I'd sent it.

A line of sweat appeared from nowhere across Eric's brow. He spoke deeply now, with authority and with a sombre tone that would have suited a funeral speech.

'You have thirty seconds. Get the hell outta here! Oh God!'

It was a good wind-up. No hint of a smile cracking through his stony face. Very convincing. Others started to gather around me in apparent disbelief at what I'd done. Faces that were familiar, but all slightly different. All looking defeated by life, carrying regrets, bad memories, painful experiences. Suddenly they all shouted at me to go. I couldn't keep a straight face. Someone had gone to a hell of a lot of trouble for this, and I had to show I was game for a laugh. Spurred on by my audience I walked over to the window, phone in hand, and tossed it out onto the street a dozen storeys below. I knew it was a service alley. Chances of it hitting anyone were minimal. Nevertheless, the look of abject shock on the faces that surrounded me was a little unnerving.

Then they started to panic. They ran to reception, piled into the elevators. This was getting beyond weird. I turned to Eric for an explanation. He was gone, already jamming himself into an elevator car. He couldn't explain anything to me. He didn't need to.

A window smashed, a smoke canister exploded on the office floor, and a figure dressed in black burst through brandishing a semi-automatic weapon. A second figure smashed through another window. My sense of humour left me. I looked at the elevator doors that were closing and decided against forcing myself into one of them. The stairs were just as close. I yanked open the doorway and threw myself onto the handrail and began to slide down it in the manner that I'd perfected years before at high school. Other than a quick bounce to change direction on each level, my feet didn't touch the ground until I was twelve storeys lower. Smoke was already starting to fill the stairwell, and it wasn't the canned variety: this building was on fire. It spread fast, spilling down the staircase at high speed, singeing the backs of my legs.

I didn't look back. The building was history. I ran outside, passing a huge billboard that normally advertised Broadway musicals in neon lights. Only today, there were no lights. No musicals to promote. Just a paper hoarding in black and white about the importance of carrying a mobile phone at all times. Beyond the billboard was a checkpoint. Police were stopping pedestrians and drivers, checking something. The fire in my building must have been visible to them, but they didn't pay it any attention. I needed to feel safe. I wanted their protection. I got in line with others waiting to pass the roadblock.

'What are they checking for?' I asked a woman in front of me. She said nothing, but wiggled her cell at me. Yet another brick. Perhaps they were offering upgrades to the latest models? Everyone around me seemed to need an upgrade from where I was standing.

Not having a phone to be inspected, I left the queue and started walking away from the checkpoint. The shouts that followed me were reminiscent of the chaos from which I had just bolted. One of the police officers was running towards me. Instinctively I ran. Around the corner I spied another roadblock and checkpoint, just two blocks ahead. How was the city supposed to function with this lockdown taking place? How could checking phones be more important than a building on fire? There were now two cops on my tail, both hollering at me. I didn't know what the punishment would be for failing to carry a cell, but from the aggravation on their faces, I guessed it was more than a rap on the knuckles. I had to think of something fast. With my mind at once tired, exhilarated and confused, I couldn't think straight. I just needed a miracle.

I didn't know it at the time, but the miracle's name was Tania.

Chapter 2

The basement was sordid, and I don't mean in the dirty movie sense. The place was gross. Filthy. Like it had been abandoned by humanity and left for the rats and the pigeons and the stray cats to call their own. The creatures were gone now, but the ingrained shit, the mould and the stench remained. A fog of daylight fell weakly through a small, clouded window close to the ceiling. The place was furnished with a couple of stained sofas and a bed made from fibreboard that had become swollen from the moisture in the air. A faucet dripped noiselessly into a basin in the corner. Footsteps thumped through the ceiling from the floor of the store above.

Tania obviously wasn't proud of this place, but she appeared to be attuned to it. As I sat cautiously on one of the dank sofas it occurred to me that she must have been waiting for me up on the street. She had spotted my plight instantly, thrown open the delivery hatch in the sidewalk and thrown me and herself inside before the cops had gotten close enough to see where I went. I was off the hook – a hook that made no sense to me.

I didn't know what to say to her. My heart was still beating fast, and I might have been in shock. I didn't even know if I was safe with her. She might have been an undercover policewoman. FBI, CIA, Men In Black – by now I didn't care. I just looked up at the source of the footsteps above me and said, 'Isn't that the record store?'

She smiled and shook her head slowly. I started to wonder if she was attractive. Not really my type, although I was struggling to remember what my type actually was. She wore tatty, black overalls and worn-looking sneakers, and her hair was short in a kind of butch crew-cut. It seemed more likely that I wasn't her type than that she wasn't mine, but there was something in that smile that worked for me. There was a kind of magic going on when she looked at me. Appropriate for my miracle.

'Tania,' she said, offering me her hand.

I held it instinctively, like a child holds his mother's hand for security. She laughed and forced a shake and a release. I cottoned on and mumbled an apology. I think she knew I was having a rough day. I read sympathy in her eyes.

'Ignatius Inuus. Bit of a mouthful, I'm afraid. Call me Iggy.'

'I know who you are,' she told me, flatly. 'We have been waiting a long time for you.'

'You have? Look, sorry I was late. Had a bit of a weird morning.'

She laughed again. Somehow I felt like I was the butt of her jokes. There was something other people seemed to know and that I didn't. I felt green, a new guy, alien to this place. Overnight I'd become a stranger in my own city.

'What do you know?' she asked me.

Big question. Wasn't sure if the answer should include my acquired general knowledge from a decade of Wikipedia searches and the Literature degree I was given after three years at NYU getting drunk and failing to get laid, or whether she just wanted to know about the crazy world into which I had stumbled this morning. I guessed the latter.

11

'Is this some huge reality show or what?' I asked. 'This is like the goddamn *Truman Show* on steroids. You gonna advertise a new chocolate bar to a camera behind my shoulder, huh?'.

'So you know nothing?'

'About what?'

She sighed, but in a patient, sympathetic way. I sensed a story coming, something that would require considerable effort on her part. It took her a long time to start, as if she didn't know how to announce whatever news the explanation would involve. She fidgeted. I looked up at the ceiling again, lost in a surreal morning, listening to the irregular thuds of the customers one floor above me. I wondered if their worlds were any different this morning. I wondered if I could go back to my apartment, sleep off this hangover, and find the nightmare had been and gone.

'I don't live here,' said Tania. 'No one does. It's just one of a network of rooms and apartments that we can make use of. That's why we keep it so disgusting in here: if we clean it up someone's going to wonder why.'

That made no sense at all.

'Why were the cops chasing me?'

'I'll come to that. It's a long story. I, er, guess I'd better start at the beginning.'

Something caught my eye outside the grimy window up high. Just feet, nothing too out of the ordinary, but they weren't going anywhere. I counted two pairs, shuffling, rotating around each other. Dark shoes, dark pants. Tania followed my gaze. We watched the feet head to the store entrance and heard them above our heads, louder and more ominous than those of regular customers. She put her finger over her lips, but I was already speechless. The feet returned to the window. Fear and confusion returned.

The legs began to crouch. Tania threw me behind the sofa and dived on top of me. We couldn't see the window from there, but I guessed that was the point. Someone was probably looking through the glass, down into this cellar. I held her in a tight hug to prevent her sliding off me and into view. I couldn't deny the pleasure the forced intimacy gave me. A speck of warmth in a cold world. Her body was light, verging on underfed, but soft in the right places. She placed her face tight up against my cheek.

'Don't move until I say,' she whispered.

The cellar filled with daylight as the steel delivery hatch opened with an ear-splitting screech.

'Move,' she said, louder this time, her lips brushing my ear as the word was formed, almost as if it were a kiss. She sprang to her feet and ran to the wall nearest the delivery hatch down which I had slid minutes before. I followed and pressed myself tight behind her, watching and waiting. Those same dark shoes appeared again, this time dangling into the hatch. Another pair joined them. Without another word Tania grabbed hold of a pair and yanked them down, and did the same to the other before he could pull himself out of the hatchway. Two policemen now lay stunned at our feet.

Tania pushed me up at the hatch, lifting my leg to help me climb out. One of the cops was already gathering his senses, trying to stand up.

'Run!' she shouted. 'Don't go home. Try to get to the Hudson. There are more of us who can help you there.'

I peered back down. Handcuffs were already being placed around her wrists, while the other cop was trying to climb up and pursue me. But without assistance from his otherwise occupied colleague he kept slipping back. I ran a few steps, then stopped. What would happen to Tania? What would become of my miracle? I couldn't bear to leave her. She was my only source of sanity. A crazy sanity, I had to admit, but right now it was the best I had. I couldn't take on two armed law officers, though. Friends used to say I couldn't fight my way out of a paper bag. In any fight or flight situation I'd ever been in, the latter option always won with a comfortable margin. I'd never even punched anyone. Never felt the need, frankly.

Ignoring my unsuitability for what I was recklessly and foolhardily contemplating, I returned to the loading hatch. My mind was alive. This morning's hangover was an ebbing memory. Ideas crackled back and forth inside my head at the speed of light, and while my body was operating at full revs, the world around me moved in slow motion. I found myself easily pushing the emerging cop back down, then jumped in, landing hard on his back.

My brain remained hundreds of moves ahead of me, making new connections and working out options, lighting up a synaptic path for me to follow until I was out of danger, filling my head with potential futures. And as I clumsily wrestled a key from the other officer, taking advantage of his shock at my unexpected reappearance, I noticed something occur amongst the adrenaline-fuelled thoughts. It wasn't as clear as my visions of the immediate future in which Tania and I would be running along the street, hand in hand, free from persecution: we would make it to the Hudson, others would be waiting, others would take us in – we would be OK. The hazy images that slowly pulsed amongst my imaginings were not as fanciful as this. They were not optimistic fantasies of the future, they were pictures of the past; they were memories. And they were not good.

Chapter 3

Tania was a blur of flailing hands and kicks, a fighting machine running at full power. The cops were pinned down, unable to reach their guns or radios. She had earned us some breathing space. I grabbed the pistols from their holsters and held them outstretched, business end in line with their dicks. Something I'd seen in a movie once, guaranteed to invoke more terror in the victim than the threat of instant death. All resistance ceased. The guys were desperate. Tania calmed down, took a couple of deep breaths, and relieved the cops of their curiously bulky radios, which she duly smashed on the floor.

The memories came back again. I didn't want them. There were more important things that should have been occupying my brain right now. There was a doctor. Painful injections. Concerned faces. Helplessness. Blackness. I recalled hideous dreams like nothing I'd imagined before. Dreams of battles, of suffering, of hunting and destroying. It was like I was one of my own white blood cells, an armed and dangerous lymphocyte sniffing out viruses in my bloodstream, battling to the death in the name of a greater cause.

The recollection of these nightmares left me cold. Tania snapped me out of it. We had to move. The cops would stay down as long as I kept them at gunpoint, but they wouldn't wait more than a few seconds once we climbed out of the cellar.

'What are you waiting for?' she asked me.

'An answer,' I replied. She looked at me quizzically. 'An answer to why I'm here, in this goddamn basement, pointing guns at cops instead of sitting at my desk, pretending to work whilst updating news of my social life on Facebook. How the hell has this come about?'

I looked down at the cops. They didn't appear to have an answer. They were more concerned about wriggling backwards to keep their nuts out of my firing line.

'I meant why haven't you shot them?' she continued.

'Huh?'

'Look, this is no time for old fashioned values. Mercy doesn't belong in this world. Give me a gun.'

The cops looked desperate, pleading with their eyes for me not to hand a gun to the woman. They needn't have worried. I couldn't kill in cold blood. Or hot. It wasn't in me.

'It's OK, guys,' I told them. 'No one's gonna hurt you if you lie quietly while we get on our way. Understood?'

They nodded appreciatively.

'This is not the way!' screamed Tania. 'This is not *their* way. We won this fight. We are the strongest. We won the right to survive. They may not like it, but they expect you to kill them.'

She wasn't making any sense to me. I ignored her ranting and pushed her up through the delivery hatch above. She sighed and reached down to help me up, which I managed with some difficulty, trying not to drop either of the weapons along the way. As I stood up and dusted myself down, I felt a hand in my pocket. In a slick movement, Tania swiped one of the pistols from me. She dropped to her knees and leaned over the open hatch. Before I could say anything, she had pulled the trigger twice in quick succession and closed the hatch.

I didn't need to remember my nightmares. I was inside a real one. I had evaded the sinister cellphone-checking police only to end up with a crazed murderess. In the absence of better options, however, I decided to follow her. I still had one pistol in my pocket, and I knew I had more shots left than she had in hers. One false move from her and ... who was I kidding? I couldn't shoot anyone. I was at her mercy. After what she'd said on the subject, though, I wasn't naïve enough to expect compassion from her.

So when she put her arm around my waist and squeezed me close to her side as we walked, I didn't know what to think.

'We're lovers,' she whispered. 'Keep moving. Head down. No eye contact. I know a route to the river that avoids the checkpoints.'

I did as I was told, secretly thrilled by the unexpected intimacy of her potentially deadly embrace. I looked down at the sidewalk. Nothing odd about it. The buildings looked normal, although some were a little scruffy and neglected. It was the people who were different. I only looked at their legs, but there was something in everyone's walk that concerned me. During the ten minutes it took us to reach the West Side Highway, I didn't see anyone walking in a manner that suggested contentedness. Fair enough, this was New York, which wasn't exactly a giant health spa, but I had never seen feet move with such despondency, such a complete absence of *joie de vivre*. It must have been a hell of a weekend.

The sense of moral outrage within me wanted to demand why Tania had shot the cops, but my fear of her unpredictability kept my mouth shut. There were no heroics in me. I wasn't made for that kind of thing. Maybe she would tell me later. Maybe it didn't matter anyway.

There wasn't a reason on Earth that could undo what she did. Right now it was as much as I could do to hold my nerve and stick by her, sensing her cold, confident fingers press against the soft ridge of my waist. The same fingers that had just fired murderous shots.

The West Side Highway was deserted, like it had been closed off for a bomb scare or a parade. Fifteen lanes of concrete for our silent feet. That's when it struck me that I hadn't seen a single car that day. Somewhere deep below us was the Lincoln Tunnel. The air inside it must have been at its purest in almost a century. To the north and south of me were the piers, some restored to receive honoured visits from ships like the *Queen Mary II*, others mere lines of stumps licked by the waves, pathetic wooden tombstones in memory of an earlier maritime age. Tania took me north, along the jogging track. Only no one was jogging except us. I was instantly out of breath. I couldn't find the stamina that usually enabled me to jog five or six miles with no problems. That knock-out weekend had a lot to answer for.

My eyes filled with tears as my face filled with a fresh wind. Through blurred vision I noticed something missing besides the traffic. We'd reached Pier 86. I'd run this route not more than a week ago. It was a stretch of Manhattan coastline that I knew well and I was certain this pier was the home of the *Intrepid* aircraft carrier, a local landmark for over thirty years. Its cluttered deck should have dominated the skyline to my left with its jumble of decommissioned airplanes and even a space shuttle.

The retired warship was gone. Heavy ropes, and fenders as big as row boats, hung against the side of the concrete pier. I wiped my eyes and looked down at the water, half-expecting to see the ship's bridge poking above the waves, or some other indication that the seventy-year-old carrier had finally sunk. No sign of it. Thirty-thousand tons of steel had vanished. The Philadelphia Experiment came to mind.

Just when I found the strength to keep running, Tania blocked my path with her arm. A security fence sealed the entirety of Pier 86 from public access. She pulled up a loose wire at the base of the fence and held it while I slid beneath. She followed and took my hand. Gone was the warmth of the pretend lover. She was all business again as she dragged me along the length of the pier, heads down, aware of our visibility from the highway. She stopped me again and I stood tall, finding myself now in the place where another of the museum's exhibits should have been: Concorde. I would always take a moment to admire the sleek, white bird when I was out jogging. Concorde had been preserved immaculately, as if always in flight-ready condition. I had never been inside a passenger jet capable of Mach 2, let alone flown in one, but it used to make me feel good to see the majestic plane perched there each time I passed by. Its sudden absence was bewildering. My first thought was Hollywood: they'd moved the carrier and the jet so they could use them in a movie, but there would have been a sign put up to explain that. Or they had needed the pier as a film set. Except there were no lights, no cameras, no people.

'What happened to Concorde?' I asked.

'Recycled,' she said. 'Everything has been recycled.'

'So what now? We wait for a boat?'

My ever-surprising companion shook her head. She scrabbled in the dust and lifted a handle from its recess. A short aluminium ladder led to a service tunnel crammed with sewage pipes, fuel lines, power cables and ventilation ducts.

'Wait down there until nightfall. Others will come for you. They'll know where to find you.'

Without questioning her authority, I climbed into the dank space. The metallic lid closed above my head. The dark solitude was oddly comforting. I had found a refuge, finally safe in my new world. I sat on cold concrete and leaned against what felt like a bundle of pipes. Sleep came fast, as if I'd lain at the foot of a waterfall of dreams and drowned beneath them.

I wanted to wake up, but the weight of sleep that pressed upon my consciousness was more than my weakened mind could resist. Dream scenes orbited me like electrons, too fast to see, too small to interpret. They began a dog-fight, a battle of good against evil. And when evil won, it dragged me to the depths of pain and despair. I was strapped to a steel bed. Plastic tubes emanated from me like spaghetti. Doctors shook their heads. Nurses tried not to cry. I was being written off, fit only for the mortuary slab. I tried to scream at them, but every muscle was paralyzed. I knew I was having a nightmare, but that knowledge was not sufficient to pull me from its grip. Through a window, I could see a doctor arrive at the door of my room. He knocked but didn't enter. I wondered why he couldn't just open the door and walk in, but he kept on knocking. Other doctors joined him in the corridor and knocked on the door with him. I wanted to open it for them, but my incapacitation was total.

It took a determined battering at the door to cause my eyes to open. Instantly the dream world dissolved. I was back in the bowels of Pier 86, and there were footsteps scampering above my head. Occasionally they would make direct contact with the lid above me, causing it to resonate uncomfortably. Was this my cue to open the hatch and announce my presence? Were these the people

20

Tania had said would find me? It was impossible that enough time had passed for the sun to have set. The dreams had come and gone so quickly, it seemed almost conceivable that this was Tania returning to tell me something, just minutes after she'd left. I reached up and felt for the handle. With a stretch, I should be able to open this door enough to climb out without assistance. I braced myself, ready to open it, ready to be received by the smiling faces of those who would take care of me.

I'm still not sure why I hesitated. Whether it was the scattergun directions of the feet or the tone of the muffled voices, I'll never know, but something held me back, made me aware of my vulnerability. On a day when everything had gone wrong, I had to entertain the possibility that something could have screwed up Tania's plans regarding my rescue. A minute later and the footsteps were distant. There hadn't been a direct hit of shoe upon metal above my head for some time. I pushed the hatch open a couple of inches and peered into the gloom. I had slept for many hours. Pier 86 was lit by nothing more than starlight. I could make out the dim silhouettes of skyscrapers. The stars shone brighter above New York than they had at any time since the great power cut of 2003.

I climbed out and closed the lid softly. No one was waiting for me. I didn't know whether to feel relief or fear. I began to think the footsteps might have been a manifestation of my dream. This theory was soon crushed by the sound of voices from the other end of the pier. I wasn't alone after all. The footsteps started up again, coming my way. The only question was whether to trust my life to these indistinct characters of the night. Caution got the upper hand. There wasn't time to climb back into the hole, so I ran to the edge of the pier where once had been moored the mighty navy ship. There had to be some other place to hide. Water lapped against the structure. I was out of options. I recalled the huge fenders that dangled here. Inflatable tubes, tied with rope to protect the side of the ship from damage. I couldn't see them now, so intense was the darkness. I ran my hands along the edge of the pier until I found a metal mooring cleat. A thick rope was looped around it. The footsteps were heading in my direction. I heard the confirmations I had been dreading: the crackle of a police radio followed by the clicking of a gun. I pulled the heavy rope from its cleat and held tight as I slipped with it into the invisible Hudson.

The current was slow at first, but as the voices faded behind me, I felt the fender being pulled by a stronger force. I gripped the rope to keep my head above water. Several times I slipped under and had to fight my way back up, spitting and gasping, wondering if the merciless spotlight of a helicopter would pick me out, followed by the red targeting laser of a marksman's rifle. The police wouldn't lose sight of me for long – they would have night vision equipment of some kind. But when I stopped struggling and found my equilibrium all was silent, invisible, almost calming. I was utterly immersed in the power of nature. My destination, and, indeed, my destiny, lay in the path of this current. I felt like I was being swept from my old life to the new. It was only a mile or two of Hudson, but the separation felt total and I felt at peace. My rebirth was not something to fear. I would embrace all that was to come. When my knees dragged on mud and silt, I knew I was close to a shore. I groped in the black goo for a sign of land. Crumbling wood posts were all around. I released the fender and clung to the decaying piles, convinced I was at the end of a disused pier. A few minutes of uncomfortable scrambling and I was on dry land. Judging from the black shapes of the distant buildings across the river, I had hit the New Jersey bank across from the Freedom Tower.

If this was where I thought it was, I was at Liberty State Park. Ships used to dock here with immigrants from distant corners of the globe, and they would then board a train at the terminal to their destination. The docks and the rail terminal were derelict now, and the surrounding land was a public park. I was away from urban sprawl. I ought to be safe.

But, drenched though I was, I needed water. The window of the park's café at the end of the terminal building broke easily with a sturdy kick. No alarm. I was free to unlatch the door and let myself in. Pitch black inside. I groped my way forward through the heavy dust that covered tables and chairs. At the rear of the café, I felt the glass front of a refrigerated display cabinet. Inside the cabinet was nothing but more dust. The place must have been shut for years. And that, I knew, was impossible.

Behind me I could feel the handles of cupboard doors. All empty. The cooler was turned off and full of mould. All I could think was film sets. There was no other explanation. But no movie company had the budget to turn the whole of New York and a chunk of New Jersey into a film set, devoid of power and people. That was what CGI was for. No one made sets on that scale any more.

The next handle I found belonged to a door that was locked. Several kicks and a painful bludgeoning with my shoulder caused the wood around the lock to implode. Sawdust and wood fragments clung to my wet clothing. I stumbled blindly into another room, which from the close echo of my breathing sounded small, like a walk-in larder. Tentative searches with my fingertips told me it was lined all around with shelves, most of which were empty. But on the highest one I could reach I felt a glass bottle. And another. I pulled them down and found my way back outside where there was at least a tiny amount of starlight, but the shape of bottles and the dirt on their labels revealed no clue as to the contents. By their size and weight I guessed they each held a couple of pints. The cap of the first bottle snapped off cleanly on the corner of a window sill. I smelled the liquid. The aroma of Dr Pepper was unmistakable. But in a glass bottle? I thought they had been phased out years ago. It reminded me of the milk in my fridge, also in glass.

I didn't care. I drank like it was the end of the world. Satiated to bursting, I put the other bottle in my pocket and walked away to find some place to spend the rest of the night. It would have been madness to remain at the scene of my crime and await capture, after all.

My crime. Two words I had never expected to be such close companions. I stopped and thought about it. I was a proper criminal. Now the police had something on me. It felt fairer that way. I didn't much like being on the run for no reason, but after the break-in, I felt that I had crossed the line. Criminal damage, trespass and theft. I'd never been in any kind of trouble before. And could I ever go back? What was it that Tania hadn't had a chance to explain to me? Would I ever see her again? These questions buzzed uselessly through my mind, knowing they would not find answers.

I walked around the decaying buildings to the park. The grass would provide me with something moderately comfortable to lie on until daybreak. I expected to find the well-tended lawns that I knew were always there. Not

24

today. Not in this screwed-up reality where nothing made sense. Where there should have been acres of grass, I found only fields of what seemed to be wheat. Too exhausted to question the presence of farmland in such proximity to New York City, I lay amongst the wheat and curled up.

Chapter 4

Drizzle collected on my lips and ran down my cheeks and into my nose. I sneezed and turned over on my bed of wheat. I was cold to the bone, soaked and filthy. There was no escaping the discomfort at ground level. I stood up and shook the rain from my hair like a wet dog. I could feel stubble starting to cover my face. My feet squelched inside my shoes. I was a mess.

The sky above me was grey, stuffed with dense clouds that threatened to obscure the sun for the rest of the day. I hugged myself for warmth. I jogged feebly on the spot to boost circulation. Above the heads of wheat, I could see Manhattan squatting in the mist across the water like a ship about to depart. There were no ferries plying between the shores and the islands and, although I couldn't see high enough through the cloud, I couldn't hear any airplanes. There were three major airports within a short taxi ride from here, and the sky would normally be buzzing with jets filled with wide-eyed visitors and bleary-eyed business people. Not today, though. Ash clouds from a volcanic eruption, maybe? That could ground all flights. Or, more likely, a complete lock-down due to a threat of terrorism. My country was prone to paranoia, jumpy at the slightest possibility of an attack, so for the moment I convinced myself of this explanation.

It was difficult to tell, but I thought I saw a flash of light bursting from a window in one of those distant buildings across the Hudson. Maybe a camera flash. Maybe a bomb. It reminded me of the attack on my office. Perhaps my experience was not unusual? If so, why was no one doing anything about it?

I turned slowly through three hundred and sixty degrees. The pregnant clouds hung low over a skyline that hadn't changed: the arm of the goddess Libertas still held aloft her torch, though the liberty for which she stood now seemed an empty promise. It was the silence that chilled me more than anything. Where were the people? What had happened to the vehicles?

There was a path around the wheat fields, hugging the coast. I followed it in the direction of the golf course. I had no agenda. No purpose. All I knew was that I had to keep moving; behind me, there were no answers.

There was no golf course. The greens were divided up and fenced in, home to pigs, sheep and horses. Through the drizzle I saw a woman throwing scraps to a pig. She was dressed in dungarees and wore a simple sheet of plastic to keep the rain from her head and shoulders. The animal looked as if it had been on a diet. I hid behind a tree and watched her. Another human. The sight of her warmed me. I felt a sneeze coming, and managed to muffle it in my hands.

Something distracted her. It wasn't me, I was certain of that. She reached into her pocket and produced an old-style cellphone like the one I had been given yesterday. She seemed to read a text message. With no apparent emotion and without pausing, she stripped to her underwear and sprinted to the Hudson. I watched in astonishment as she dived recklessly into the chilly water and started swimming across to a small spit of land, a distance I reckoned to be a hundred yards. She seemed strong, but I knew from my experiences last night that there were powerful currents at work in these waters, eddies and tides that could overwhelm even the most confident swimmer.

It came as no surprise when her bold strokes became progressively less effective as the opposing water sapped the strength from her limbs. She paused and tried to tread water, to save her energy. For a few seconds it seemed to work, and she was able to resume her forward progress. She paused again. This time her head dipped below the surface and she popped up, gasping and choking. I looked around for a sign that anyone else was aware of her predicament. No one. When she slipped below the water a second time, I didn't hesitate. I threw my mud-encrusted clothes to the ground, paying no attention to the bottle of Dr Pepper that smashed within them, and dived into the water. She was flailing her arms and panicking now. The co-ordination needed to keep herself afloat was gone. She had seconds left.

Acutely aware of the limitations of my own strength, I powered my way forward, face down in an aggressive front crawl that only occasionally stopped for air and to calibrate my direction. I could only hope that I would have enough in reserve not only to get to her in time, but to drag her back to shore again.

I didn't. Before I could reach out to her I felt my muscles weaken and my lungs rasp for more air. The woman was just a few strokes away, and I had to tread water and watch helplessly as she gave up her struggle and went limp. Just a couple of seconds of rest gave me the fuel my body needed. I splashed forward and reached her lifeless form. There was no reaction from her as I twisted her over to keep her chin above water and clumsily dragged her back to shore in the way I'd seen done on television shows but never thought I'd have to do myself. I was probably wasting my time, but I was determined not to give up until I had at least attempted a bit of mouth-to-mouth.

On the muddy shore I turned her face-down and tried to shake the water from within her. Not much seemed to come out, so it was time to turn her over again and mix some inexpert mouth-to-mouth with equally inept chest compression, all based on half-remembered scenes with David Hasselhoff and Pamela Anderson. I shouted for help, knowing I couldn't keep this intense resuscitation attempt going for long, and equally sure that no assistance would arrive.

I would give it ten more seconds, I decided. After that, she would be gone and I would be faced with deciding what to do with a half-naked corpse on the edge of a former golf course. Frankly I had no idea what I would do with her, and I had no desire to be in the situation where I would need to find out.

Her eyes opened. I jumped back in alarm as she began coughing and retching. I felt like I was intruding on this private moment of her reanimation, and the fact that we were two wet strangers wearing nothing but our underwear reinforced my social discomfort. At least she would be pleased to see me, I reminded myself. On this lonely new world, I really needed a friend. I waited until her breathing had normalised and she seemed fully conscious before introducing myself.

'Iggy,' I said, holding out a hand to help her up. 'Nearly lost you there. Glad to see—'

'What the hell did you do that for?' she screamed, lunging at me with fists that were fortunately too sapped of strength to be any worse than embarrassing.

'I'm sorry?'

'Shit. Shit. Shit,' she said. Not the elaboration I'd been

hoping for. 'You saved my life?'

'Er, yes,' I replied, almost apologetically. 'You were drowning.'

'Shit. You idiot. What's the matter with you?'

I wondered if her brain had been affected by lack of oxygen.

'You're welcome,' I grumbled. 'Don't mention it.'

She slapped her head in frustration. By now, she was beginning to piss me off. I reclaimed my clothes, shook the glass fragments from one of the pockets, and slid miserably into them. The garments were wet. I was wet. I would have been more comfortable without them, but the instinct to cover myself was too strong to allow for common sense.

'You broke the law,' said the woman, pulling on her dungarees. 'You made me break the law. We'll both be killed now.'

'You were going to drown,' I protested. 'The only law I broke was the law of nature.'

She looked at me as if I was even more of an idiot than she had previously thought.

'The text said I had to swim to the spit and back. I was drowning. That means I failed. Shit.'

'That's why I saved you.'

'If I fail it's because I'm not the fittest. I didn't deserve to survive. I'm getting older. I used to be able to do this kind of thing no problem. Guess I'm slowing up. Guess my time has come. Have to make space. Shit. Now I have to face it all again.'

'I don't understand,' I said.

'You stopped me dying. Now I have to die again. They say the waiting is the worst. Seconds, minutes, it makes no difference. They will catch up with me. They're watching.'

'Who is watching?'

'You really don't know?' she asked. 'Where have you been?'

'Nowhere. Just woke up and suddenly it's the law of the goddamn jungle out here.'

'You should go. They're already after me. If you want to have a chance you should keep away from me.'

I stepped back, as if she were infected by some virulent contagion. She held up her arms and stood still, resigned to dying once again. I could see no one around. There seemed nothing to fear. Then I heard the crack of a rifle. She seemed calm as she fell backwards, the life finally ripped from her by a bullet.

I didn't look back. I was running along the shoreline, a hunted prey once more, guilty of violating laws I didn't know existed and couldn't understand. Where could I go? Where could I find sanctuary in this nightmare? Who could I trust? There was only one person. One place.

The old man. Pops – the only family I had left – lived alone to the north of New York City in a plain, fifties house, almost in the shadow of the Tappan Zee Bridge. The road noise from that bridge was so invasive and incessant that you kind of got used to it. As his hearing started to weaken in old age, he forgot all about the bridge anyway. To him the village was Paradise on the Hudson, and he would often call it by that name instead of its proper title, Grand View-on-Hudson. And he certainly had a grand view from his living room, straight across two miles of the river. He loved the community spirit of the villagers, and would arrange picnics, barbeques and holiday celebrations. Everyone trusted him. I certainly could.

Grand View wasn't far from where I was now, maybe twenty miles north of me. More importantly, it was a crucial ten miles or so beyond the outskirts of New York City, and might just be far enough to have avoided the descent into amorality and the law of the jungle that seemed to have afflicted the urban areas.

Trouble was I was running in the other direction, to the south. Getting to Grand View by car or bus was so routine that I'd never questioned the accessibility of the place back in the days when things made sense, but I hadn't seen a car today, and I was convinced there was no longer such thing as a functioning public transportation network.

Then I hit a problem that focused my thoughts more clearly. I didn't know if the sniper who had shot that poor woman was following me, but I'd reached the peninsular development that faced Half Moon Isle. This meant I could easily be cut off and cornered. I had to assume the worst, that there was at least one gunman on my trail, and that meant I needed a solution fast. Pleasure boats were docked all along the riverside here, some right outside the luxurious waterfront houses and apartments. Most of the boats were in a poor state of repair; some barely managed to keep afloat. I jumped onto the transom of a small sailing yacht with a hull encrusted with barnacles around the water line. The boat probably only measured twenty-six feet. It had a cosy cabin, accessed through a plywood door secured with a rusty padlock. I tugged at the door and it opened without resistance, thanks to screws that had perished within the wood. I climbed inside and closed the door behind me, catching my breath and hoping that, just for a few precious minutes at least, I was safe.

I couldn't be complacent, though. I thought of the fugitive Boston marathon bomber who had hidden inside a boat a few months back. He hadn't lasted long in there thanks to the blaze of publicity. It was the last big news event I could remember before everyone starting obsessing about some tedious bird flu outbreak in Asia, so I knew it would only take one eagle-eyed member of the public to give me away. With hundreds of windows facing this boat it would be a miracle if no one had seen me. If anyone had been pursuing me, they would have reached this spot by now. I couldn't run any more. I just pulled off my wet things and lay down on a thin mattress that smelled of mildew and spread an old sail across me for comfort. The gentle lapping of water against the hull was soothing, and the longer it remained the only sound I could hear, the more confident I became that this latest threat to my being had receded.

Through a porthole no larger than a CD, I peered out at the water and the surrounding properties. There was no sign of life until a man opened a door to a third-floor balcony, just across the waterway on the exclusive Half Moon Isle. I watched as he double-checked a text message he had apparently received on yet another of those bulky analogue cellphones and then proceeded to climb out over the safety railing and down to the balcony below. This continued until he reached ground level, whereupon he reversed the process by climbing up the outside of the building once again until he was back at what I guessed was his apartment. He seemed to wave at no one in particular, then went inside and closed the door behind him.

If nothing else, the bizarre incident would at least have taken people's attention away from my arrival. I felt relaxed enough to focus my thoughts once more on how I could get to my father's house twenty miles upstream without coming under the radar of a police department that seemed to have the whole neighbourhood on lockdown with a shoot to kill curfew. Life without a cellphone was hard, I realised. With my iPhone I could just have called him. If that didn't work, I could have Googled for the news; I could have found the answer to any question that bugged me. Without that overview of the world I was more isolated than I'd ever felt before. How could I know if it would be safe to head inland and maybe look for a car or a bike to take me as far as Tappan Zee? How could I find out whether there were more rebels like Tania, just waiting to help me in their rather weird and unhelpful way?

I ran through the options in my mind. Travelling by day had to be out of the question: too risky. At a brisk walking pace, I might be able to cover the entire distance under cover of darkness in a single night, provided there were no substantial detours necessitated by police roadblocks or other complications.

Next, I considered the boat. I had been a windsurfer once – not expert, but I had a grasp of the basics. Surely a sailing yacht was just a big windsurf board? I shot that idea down immediately. Getting out of this little marina under sail would be the clumsiest and most attention-grabbing thing I could do. Attempting to sail upriver, against the tide, possibly tacking side to side for twenty miles would be like holding up a giant flag saying 'here I am – please shoot me'. No, I had to make this journey on foot. It was the least conspicuous option available to me.

Three times the length of Manhattan. Ordinarily it would be a challenge, but not impossible. With plenty of food and water, I could usually take on a hike of that extent. It was less than the New York marathon, and I'd run that a couple of times, too. I just needed to find sustenance. Then I needed to get past Hoboken and Union City. After that, I would have miles of parkland in which I could avoid detection more easily. With that plan brewing in my head, I slept to conserve energy and waited for nightfall.

Sometimes I wonder why I bother to make plans. All they do is show you where you might have gone, before life inevitably trips you up and drags you off in the other direction.

It was the rocking of the boat that woke me. Footsteps on deck. Whispers. I was defenceless and had nowhere to run. If I'd thought about it earlier I might have scoured the lockers for tools to use as a weapon with which to defend myself, but a screwdriver or even an anchor was not much use against a rifle. My last card was the sail. I wriggled beneath it, hoping the shape of my body wasn't showing through too clearly.

The plywood hatch opened and a weak sun entered the cabin. I could feel the fresh air swirl softly around me. It felt as if the clouds had thinned and the drizzle had stopped. Feet tramped down the steps and paused in the confined space. I felt a hand on my ankle.

To play dead or to kick blindly. The options ended there. Neither had a great prospect of success. The hand poked at my foot through the sail beneath which I was hiding. There was no sense of aggression in the touch. That resolved my dilemma. I would lie still.

It was the right call. When the sail was pulled back I could see who was standing there. A face that I recognised.

35

Chapter 5

'Thought we'd lost you,' Tania said, without emotion.

I looked into her eyes. She was relieved to see me, but not pleased. This was business as usual for her. She offered me a bar of unbranded chocolate and water in a glass bottle. I downed them gratefully.

'Tell me what is going on,' I said. I wasn't prepared to wait this time. If her plans went wrong, as they seemed to have a habit of doing, I wanted to learn as much as I could whilst I had the opportunity.

'Not yet,' she replied, helping me to stand up. 'You're not safe here. Come.'

'Am I safe anywhere?' I asked without optimism.

Her silence on the matter was sufficient answer. We climbed onto the deck and, checking there was no one around, jumped onto the quayside.

'Follow me,' she whispered, and began a brisk walk.

Here we go again, I told myself.

Before we were out of sight of the boat, the walk had finished. Tania darted inside a door of an apartment building that overlooked the water. The place had been built to impress, but years of neglect had turned the tide the other way. Peeling paint and rotting wood. We ran up the stairs to the top floor. I thought I could see rat droppings everywhere. She knocked at a door, and instantly it opened. A stranger with a roll-up cigarette in his mouth ushered us inside.

If this was another of their safe houses, it was much less squalid than the basement to which Tania had previously taken me. Despite the run-down appearance of the building, the interior of this apartment showed signs of having been loved by someone, albeit not very recently. The couches were almost clean; darkened paintings hung on the walls; curtains hung beside the windows, though not with the grace that they'd once possessed. A brown stain in the corner of the ceiling hinted at the reality of neglect in the outside world.

Tania's host held out his hand.

'Pascal,' he said, with an accent that owed more to Europe than it did to the States. I shook his hand and began mouthing my own name when he interrupted, saying, 'it's all right. I know who you are, Ignatius.'

He was tall and thin, with dark brown eyes that were sunken into their sockets. His long sideburns and designer stubble marked him out as a youthful non-comformist, a fashion style that was unfamiliar to me. I wasn't sure if I could trust him, though. I didn't sense that we had clicked in these first seconds of our meeting. There were too many unknowns about him for me to be able to relax in his presence. Not that Tania was any better, of course – I'd witnessed her killing two police officers, after all – but at least with her there was the physical attraction, a cocktail of charisma combining explicit danger with powerful femininity. She was trouble.

Pascal invited me to sit down. He placed a towel on the sofa for me, as if I were a muddy dog. I tried not to take offence. He and Tania sat on the opposite couch, holding hands. An irrational wave of jealousy zapped through my system. At least I now knew where I stood with her.

'How did you find me again?' There was so much I

wanted to ask her, but I had to start somewhere.

'You were spotted by one of the residents here,' Tania explained.

'How come they didn't call the cops?'

'Not everyone is evil,' she said, 'even if it might look that way. Our network is pretty big.'

'Most people would join us if they had the courage,' said Pascal. 'Too many people have too much to lose, that's the problem.'

It was time for the big question. I had to know.

'What is going on?' I asked. Four simple words. I knew it would take substantially more to provide the answer.

Tania seemed about to talk – she had tried to explain things to me at our first encounter, after all – when Pascal glanced at her and shook his head. I took this to mean that whatever was actually going on, he thought I wasn't yet ready to know. Sometimes big news had to be dished out in small pieces, I realised, frustrated. Great truths could be hard to swallow in one go.

'How are you doing?' asked Pascal.

'Fine. Just a little tired,' I replied. 'Tough couple of days.'

'A tough couple of days!' echoed Pascal, looking at Tania and laughing. I hoped to be let in on their private joke, but this desire remained unfulfilled. I was still very much the outsider.

'Sorry it took us so long to reach you,' said Tania. 'Getting about is not easy. And I promise you we will bring you up to speed with what is happening, but not right now. You've been through so much, and you'll need time to adjust.'

She stood up, suddenly alert. I could hear footsteps running up the stairs, and then a loud thudding at the door.

Pascal tip-toed to the security viewfinder and peeked at his visitor.

'Crap,' he said, stubbing out his roll-up and wafting away the smoke. 'It's Cecile. Take Ignatius to the bedroom and make sure he says nothing.'

He began unlocking the front door while Tania ushered me to a room with a double bed and a plain chest of drawers. It didn't look like anyone had slept in there for some years. She indicated that I should wait in silence while she returned to Pascal in the other room. I put my ear to the door and listened.

Instantly I could tell that Cecile was not happy. The tone of her voice and the rapid-fire sentences indicated someone under great stress.

'Where is he? I know he's here. Get him out. Now.'

I was clearly unpopular. How could a stranger possess such a strong dislike for me?

'Cool it, Cecile,' said Pascal. 'We won't keep him here long.'

'He's exhausted. Give him a little time,' said Tania.

'We're all exhausted,' the visitor replied. 'We're all fed up with living like this. And I can't take any extra shit. Get him out of my property.'

'Taking him out right now is too risky,' said Tania. 'We need time to clean him up, explain to him what has happened. Poor Ignatius doesn't even know!'

'I've had to climb mountains,' I heard Cecile say, curiously. 'I've swum rivers and wrestled with snakes. I've climbed trees and walked barefoot over broken glass. All in the name of survival. And I've helped you guys. Time and again. Helped you keep out of the loop, free from these goddamn text orders. I know the risks and I can live with that, but Ignatius is a risk too far. This is way out of my comfort zone. I want him out of my property. I don't care where you go, just get him out of here before it's too late.'

'You think we're not out of our comfort zones, too?' shouted Pascal. 'This is the bravest thing we've ever done. Sheltering Ignatius is terrifying to us, too. I know the consequences. I'm well aware of the risk. It's running through my mind constantly. But you know why we're doing this, Cecile. You know it matters. We need this apartment. We need you to support this for a little while longer.'

At this point Cecile seemed to make a shriek of frustration. I guessed she was giving in, albeit reluctantly.

'Well let me at least see the man I'm risking my neck for,' she said, more calmly now. 'No point keeping him hidden from me.'

I heard steps approaching, and Pascal opened the door.

'Come,' he said.

Cecile appeared underwhelmed by the sight of me as I entered the living room. I wasn't exactly looking my best, but such blatant disappointment was a bit of a shock to the system, especially right after the grand build-up she had just given me.

'So you're Ignatius, huh?' she said, eyeing me up and down through dark-framed spectacles that rested on a generous nose. She was in her fifties, but there wasn't an ounce of fat on her body. My first thought was anorexia, but then I remembered her comments about climbing mountains and so on, and I realised this woman was ultra-fit, a middle-aged athlete. She wore trousers that had been ripped and repaired several times, and a jacket that was stained with grime. It was an oddly bohemian appearance for a presumably wealthy landlady. Apartments in this waterside development couldn't be cheap, even in a tatty condition.

'That's me,' I replied. 'You can call me Iggy if you prefer.'

'I'd prefer not to have anything to do with you,' she told me, then looked at Pascal and Tania before adding, 'I hope you know what you're doing. It had better be worth it. And you,' she said, looking at me again, 'had better be worth the trouble you're going to put us all to.'

She left without another word. Pascal pointed me to the bathroom and invited me to clean myself up. After a cold shower and a refreshing shave, I found clothes waiting for me in the bedroom. Black jeans, black shirt and a black sweater. Something told me they didn't want me to stand out. I rejoined them in the sitting room.

'There is much you need to be told,' said Pascal, 'but I am afraid that you may not believe us. We have been thinking about how to convince you.'

'Did you have family nearby?' asked Tania.

'*Do* you have family,' corrected Pascal.

I didn't know it then, but they were both fully aware of my family situation. I was cautious, however. I'd seen the ruthless streak at work in Tania and I still didn't know what could trigger it. The last thing I wanted to do was to bring these people into the world that my Pops inhabited. They couldn't know about Grand View-on-Hudson.

'No,' I lied. 'No family.'

Their shared look of surprise should have told me that they knew more than they were letting on.

'No matter,' said Pascal, rolling up a new cigarette. 'We'll rest here tonight. You need to eat and regain your strength. Tomorrow we'll take you to an important place. Tomorrow you will meet more of us and your questions will be answered.'

If Pascal expected me to be satisfied with that promise, he was mistaken. I was unsure that I wanted to go to an

41

unspecified place with these people. I didn't feel the need to meet more of their group. And, despite the clothes and the food, I didn't truly know that I could trust them.

I ate heartily that evening. The food was simple: potatoes, greens and chicken, but the portions were generous and it tasted good. Pascal and Tania made small talk with me, but carefully avoided discussing anything to do with my situation or what had happened to transform New York and New Jersey so quickly. I still couldn't shake from my mind the possibility of a reality television show with an astronomical budget. Part of me wondered if the important place they wanted to take me tomorrow was a studio where I would be reunited with the two policemen shot by Tania, who would turn out to have been actors, and an audience would laugh at how I'd been fooled into thinking I was a fugitive. I could handle that. Everything would be back to normal when the show finished.

That, of course, had to be wishful thinking. There was no way the woman I'd seen murdered this morning could have been acting. The drowning and resuscitation were real. The devastation to her body caused by that bullet, equally so. I was kidding myself if I thought there was any way this could end well.

At ten o'clock that evening, the power went off. The apartment fell silent and dark at once. I waited for Tania or Pascal to fumble for a flashlight and find the fuse box, but they sat serenely, saying nothing.

'Anyone have a quarter for the meter?' I quipped, attempting to instigate some explanation from them for their behaviour.

'Power is not an unlimited resource,' said Pascal. 'They will turn it back on again in the morning.'

Scheduled power outages belonged in the Third

World, not in the most developed nation on Earth, but that brief comment from Pascal put much into perspective for me. There had been no power in my apartment yesterday morning, and yet there was by the time I arrived at work later. The whole of New York had been blanketed in darkness last night. The Government must have instigated power rationing at the weekend. Perhaps there had been a meltdown at a nuclear reactor, or a terrorist attack on several power stations that had virtually plunged the nation into the Middle Ages overnight?

I knew what I had to do. As soon as I was confident that Pascal and Tania were asleep, I let myself out of the apartment and began the twenty-mile, midnight hike to Grand View-on-Hudson. I now knew that the two main towns on the route, Hoboken and Union City, would be in complete darkness. My chances of completing the journey successfully had therefore improved dramatically. I had a full stomach, I was hydrated, and I was motivated to discover the truth. I trusted no one but Pops. He would have the answers.

Chapter 6

Dawn was already breaking by the time the Tappan Zee Bridge came into view. Usually I would hear it before I saw it, but this morning the steel colossus spanned the river in lonely silence. The rainclouds of yesterday had drifted away, and today was looking to be bright and warm. I had been walking for five hours. My feet were sore – I guessed they were blistering. I had cramp in the calf muscle of one leg, and it forced me to walk with a limp, but my spirits were high. I was in Grand View-on-Hudson, already past the village church and graveyard, and I had arrived at Pops' house.

I dismissed the curiosities I had witnessed along the way. A scrapyard piled high with nothing but wheelchairs and mobility scooters. Apartment buildings seemingly empty whilst neighbouring houses with gardens were bursting with life, every square inch of land dedicated to what looked like vegetable plots. Parking lots ploughed up and put to agricultural use. There were more of the bizarre billboards I'd seen in Manhattan. As far as I could tell in the faint starlight, they were promoting those old-style cellphones. And, oddest of all, was the quantity of horse manure in Hoboken. The stuff was all over the streets. Hard to miss in the dark. My shoes were covered in the stuff.

The sight of Pops' house made the past couple of days feel like a bad dream. This was tangible reality. This was a safe, wealthy area, where the crème of New York society lived. Pops' neighbours included movie producers, dotcom millionaires, bestselling writers and a couple of A-list actors. This was familiarity. This was–

I paused my thoughts as I stood in front of the property. This was not the same house. Well, it was the same house, but it wasn't *exactly* the same. It needed painting. Pops always kept up the maintenance – he took pride in how his home looked – but the paint was peeling all over. There were unfamiliar steel bars over the windows, ventilation ducts that hadn't been there before, evidence of horticulture instead of a lawn.

A sense of panic filled me. This was wrong. Very wrong. I could cope with the concept of unexplained changes in public spaces, but now it affected my family. I ran to the door and banged hard on it, determined to wake Pops. I heard footsteps in the hallway and a clunking of metal as security bars were released. Lots of them. The door opened a chink.

'What the hell you think you're doing, banging on my door at this time of the morning?' screamed a man I had never seen before.

I was disappointed and a little scared, but not surprised. The signs had not been good. I wasn't going to give up this easily, though.

'What the hell are you doing in this house? Where's my old man?' I retorted.

'Get off my property before I call the cops,' was his reply.

Mutual aggression was getting me nowhere. I tried a more gentle approach.

'Please,' I said, 'help me out here. I don't know what's going on, but my old man has lived here for more than ten years. Inuus. Alex Inuus. Tall, grey hair, trace of a

European accent. He planted that tree over there.' I pointed to an evergreen. It was double the height I remembered.

'Come on, don't play dumb, you know perfectly well what's going on. Everyone does. And I've been in this house nine years. Previous owner died, I think. There was a lot of that going on back then. Hardly newsworthy.'

I stepped back. I felt as if I'd been punched in the stomach. 'What did you just say?'

'Inuus was your old man, was he? Sorry about that, bud. But as I say, that was a long time ago. You should be over it by now. I'm going back to bed.'

He closed the door on me. Left me standing alone, truly alone. What was I to do now? I faced a wall of grief, but I couldn't begin to climb it without more proof. I ran to the village graveyard. The pain of my blisters was absent, masked by a shot of adrenaline. I was temporarily invincible, powered by despair and desire, a locomotive charging headlong towards the truth.

I hadn't paid attention before, but the graveyard had grown. It had to be three times larger than I remembered. Mom was in there, so I knew the place. She had passed away in 2001, weeks before the world went mad. The only comfort me and Pops could draw at the time was that she hadn't lived to see 9/11. It wasn't the world she had planned for me to inherit. I looked for the solemn yew trees and well-tended plots, trying to get my bearings. What confused me were the new zones, an expansion encompassing the parking lot of the church and a neighbouring garden. Countless people had died recently. This was a tiny village, no more than a hundred homes. It seemed there were more new graves than there were houses around here.

Then I found it. The proof. The answer. The

46

nightmare. The truth.

Pops was dead. Here was his grave. Alexander George Inuus. Date of birth and date of death, chiselled in white stone. But that was when the mystery simply became deeper, because the old man's demise was recorded as more than a year in the future. What the hell was that about? Through a fog of tears I scanned the inscriptions on other gravestones. Some recorded deaths that were almost a decade in the future. How could this be? A sick practical joke? Did we all now have a pre-arranged date of death in this twisted world and our graves were already marked out, waiting for us? Or was it me that was out of synch? Was I suffering amnesia?

I tried to remember. Was I a decade older than I thought? That might explain the haggard appearances of my colleagues at work, and the rough state of my own body. If I had forgotten the passing of the last ten years, maybe there were memories locked away that might emerge with some effort? But every time I tried to stimulate the sleeping synapses I found no recollection of anything to do with my family, with political and social change, or even major personal events like birthdays or Thanksgivings. The only things I could recall – and I wasn't sure if they were even real memories or just my imagination – were doctors, pain, injections, tubes, concerned faces and darkness.

Was it possible that I had spent a decade in hospital while the world outside went crazy? Had I been in an accident? Had I been shot? I hadn't noticed any significant scars that would have suggested a violent cause for my extended sleep. Perhaps I had caught something, some disease that rendered me unconscious for years? I wasn't aware of any such thing, but then I wasn't exactly a medical expert.

I returned to Pops' grave and stood respectfully. There was a patina on the stone that suggested it had been exposed to a few years of changing seasons. There were no flowers, of course. I was the only close family member, and I'd not even been at the funeral. It pained me to think that I wasn't there for him at the end.

The morning shadows were shortening. People would be up and about soon. I had to figure out where I could go. I had to find some shelter before my options ran out.

I should have moved faster. I felt something press against my back. My options had already run out.

I turned around slowly. A man held a shovel at me. If I hadn't been in a shock and daze at my unexpected status as an orphan I would have laughed.

'Don't say a word to anyone,' said the man.

'About what?' I asked.

'The potatoes,' he whispered. 'Just get out of here and forget you saw me.'

I was tempted to make a hasty exit, but there was something about this man that I couldn't quite place. An old memory. I knew him.

'It's me. Iggy,' I said, desperately trying to recall his name. He was a local man. Friend of Pops. A novelist. Some of his books had even been made into films. Lived in a huge house with panoramic river views and a revolving shed in the garden from which he wrote, whilst aligning it always to the optimum light or view. He was older than I recalled, but then so was everyone. Then the name hit me. Dan Block. Wasn't his real name, of course. Rather a stupid pen name, actually, but he had become quite famous using that name.

'Iggy?' asked Dan. 'Young Iggy Inuus? This is a surprise and an honour!'

Ignoring his obviously false flattery, I whispered, 'Can

you help me? The cops are on my tail.'

'Come with me, then,' he replied, putting down his shovel and guiding me out of the cemetery and across the street to his mansion. The mock-Gothic columns and gargoyles gave the house a creepy feel, but it was sufficiently fake for any such feelings to be fleeting. He led me in through the front door and locked it behind him. We walked through to the kitchen and he invited me to sit on a stool.

'What happened to Pops?' I asked, dreading that the answer would confirm my worst fears.

'I'm sorry,' said Dan. 'Alex was one of the weak ones, one of the first. Seems ages ago now. Nobody told you? I'd have thought that you of all people would be kept informed.'

'Me? I don't know anything,' I replied. 'Just woke up into this nightmare. And why were you stealing potatoes?'

Dan laughed as he made me a coffee. 'Stealing? Ha! I was planting them.'

'In a cemetery?'

'Ran out of land. Had to improvise. If it's a tough winter I'll be needing all the extra crops I can get.'

'What do you mean? You're a writer. Why can't you buy food in the stores?'

He handed me the coffee. It scalded my lips, but I drank it fast. I needed it.

'Writer? Those were the days. No room in this world for art and literature, Iggy. You must know that.'

'I guess I do now.'

'Culture is a luxury that the whole world has had to put aside for a century or two. It'll come back, in its own time. It always does. But right now we all have higher priorities. Novels don't put food on the table. Haven't written a word since it happened.'

I sensed this was the moment. 'Since what happened? No one has told me,' I said, bracing myself mentally for what I was about to discover.

He looked uncomfortable, as if about to confess a heinous crime to me.

'What's the last thing you remember?' he asked.

'Doctors and stuff. I was in pain. Probably in intensive care.'

'Ah, I see. Before that. In the news, I mean.'

I listed one or two run-of-the-mill stories I recalled about a senator being forced to quit after admitting an affair and a guy who had fallen from a window-cleaning platform on a skyscraper and survived a fifty-floor drop because the wind blew him onto a canopy and then into a bush.

'No, forget the local stuff,' said Dan. 'What do you recall happening on the world stage?'

'Nothing much,' I admitted. 'There was that bird flu thing in China.'

He clicked his fingers. Now I was getting somewhere.

'Turned out it wasn't actually bird flu, but that was the starting point.'

'How could an outbreak of flu in China turn New York into a technologically backward fascist state?' I asked. The link seemed improbable. It was going to take one hell of a storyteller to convince me that this event had triggered everything I had seen these past few days, so who better to deliver this news to me than someone who was once a professional novelist?

'It's early,' said Dan. 'I need another coffee before I try to make sense of the past decade. Is there anything else you want? A refill?'

I nodded and passed him my cup. He made two more coffees and we strolled to some armchairs. He wanted me to be comfortable. I guessed this could take some time.

'Coffee is getting scarce, you know. This is old stock. Like a rare wine. Once it's gone, it's gone.'

I sipped it appreciatively as if it were a fine St Emilion and waited for Dan to continue.

'It was all very hushed up at first. That was the problem. If the Chinese had been more open about the virus, we might have been able to avoid the horrendous decision that we had to take eventually. But I'll come to that later. So, you know about the outbreak of sickness. You may remember that it started on the island of Hainan.' He must have noticed my blank look, and decided to explain where this island was. 'Hainan is the southernmost province of China. Kind of sits between China and Vietnam. Twice the size of New Jersey, with a similar population. And that's where the Chinese built a space centre: Wenchang, the place was called. State of the art launch facility. Thousands of residents were forced to move to make room for its construction. Their only consolation was a space theme park that was planned for the island, but as it turned out things went wrong before they could open it. And it'll never open now, of course.'

'Of course,' I echoed, despite having no idea why it would never open.

'But it wasn't just launches that they carried out there. It was also a receiving facility. The Chinese sent a robot to Mars, just like NASA had done so many times. But China took the lead by achieving the first ever sample return mission. Their robot found some interesting rocks and dirt and sent them back to Earth. It was the first time Martian soil had been brought to our planet. And the container went directly to the receiving facility at Hainan.'

'I remember that. Vaguely,' I said. I hadn't been too

51

interested in it at the time, and the news of the returned rocks was very sketchy due to the secrecy of the mission. Besides, rocks were rocks. I was no geologist, and frankly I couldn't think of anything more dull.

'The scientists couldn't wait to get their hands on them. No one had ever been up close to so much Martian material before,' said Dan. 'Geologists in the west were fuming with jealousy – this was the biggest event since the first moon rocks came back – but then the Chinese scientists got sick. And I mean *real* sick. It was hideous – like a mediaeval plague – and no antibiotic on Earth had any effect. The infection spread fast amongst them, their children, their friends, their families and their neighbours. The hospitals on the island were quickly overwhelmed, and soon the doctors and nurses had all succumbed, too. The authorities acted quickly. The outbreak was on an island, so it was a natural quarantine zone. Eight million people were cut off from the outside world. The Chinese navy stationed boats all around the island to prevent anyone leaving.'

'They just abandoned that many people?' I asked, incredulously.

'Not at first. They sent in medical teams and equipment to try to control it early on, but because the scientists were living on various parts of the island, it had spread to all the towns within days. Rumours spread about a new strain of bird flu, but there was no official announcement. Those not yet infected were desperate to escape, and a shoot-on-sight policy was introduced for anyone seen on the beaches, in boats or in the water. People compared it to East Berlin in the fifties. The air force delivered food parcels and medical supplies by parachute. People were dropping like flies. Boat patrols were doubled. Reports reached the mainland that the suffering on the island was unbearable. When there was little hope for the remaining inhabitants, the Government even considered what they called a humane solution. It would have been the largest mass murder ever committed, and yet it would have been the right thing to do at that stage.'

Dan could see the horrified look on my face. Although I couldn't see my own expression, there was something about it that felt familiar. Like I'd already made this face. Like I'd known about this situation before and had been appalled by it.

'How could mass murder be the right thing to do?' I asked.

'It would have put them out of their misery. Painlessly. And it would have saved the world from what was to follow. Gas the entire island from the air. Kill off the population and the disease at the same time. It was politically difficult. No leader wanted to go down in history as the next Hitler. But the photos and reports from the island convinced them that any delay in this policy would be cruel. Of the eight million thought to be living on the island before the outbreak, it was estimated that less than a million were still alive, and, of those, the vast majority were already dying an agonising death. There was no prospect of medical care, still less chance of a cure. By now, the rest of the world had a clear idea of what was happening there. No nation would say it, but all of them wanted the problem dealt with firmly. Finally, the order was given. Despite the horror, the world breathed a sigh of relief.'

'So a million people were executed by the State to stop the disease spreading?' I asked, even though a part of me felt that I already knew it. Buried deep in my mind were the embers of a memory that once burned fiercely with this ghastly knowledge. 'That's insane,' I said. Even if the facts were not entirely new to me, the shock factor was.

'How many were killed in Hiroshima and Nagasaki? Maybe a quarter million. Mostly innocent. But they were wiped out deliberately to bring an end to the war and therefore to save far greater numbers of lives. It's never an easy thing to do, but sometimes it's necessary.'

'OK,' I said. 'I get it. Shitty episode for China. Probably caused a few issues elsewhere. Whole island sealed off for ever. What then?' Whatever had caused the loss of my memory had done a thorough job. I had no clear recollection of anything else, just an opaque recognition of the shapes it created in my mind.

'Of course, the inevitable happened,' Dan continued. 'Someone got out before the gassing started. The authorities took too long. Should have done it quickly and with no warning. The knowledge of the impending executions for those affected was probably a greater cruelty than the suffering of the disease. No one knows who it was or how they escaped. Maybe they built a submarine, or managed to swim past the naval boats, but next thing we knew there was an outbreak in Hanoi.'

'Vietnam?'

'That's right. And that's when things started to get real nasty.'

'So, like, Hainan island and the death of eight million people wasn't nasty?' I asked.

'It was peanuts. When you put it into perspective, it was nothing. Listen, Iggy, the rest of what I have to tell you is gross. I'm not sure you should take this all in right away. I lived through it. Events unfolded fast, but at least we had time to sleep on each new development before learning of the next horror. I don't think it's right to dump all this news on you in one go.'

So instead of the full answer I'd been hoping for, all I got was a history lesson. It filled in the blanks in the memories I already had, but it didn't go as far as I wanted. Still, it was depressing stuff, and I knew it would only get worse. Somehow, it would lead to Pops' demise, and though part of me didn't want to know how a tragedy in China and Vietnam could have done that to him, I knew I wouldn't be able to rest until I found out the truth.

'There's someone living in Pops' house,' I said. 'And the cops chased me out of New York City. Don't think I can go home again.'

It was obvious I was fishing for somewhere to stay. He didn't need to say it. A nod of the head was enough to confirm that I would have a bed for the night.

That evening I examined Dan's library. It was an oddly shaped room, in the centre of the house. It felt like there should have been another room behind part of it, but I couldn't find any trace of it. I perused the shelves. There were dozens of copies of the novels he had written, published in all kinds of languages. I felt bad that I'd never taken the trouble to read any of them, but from their covers they looked interesting enough. Thrillers about a heroic soldier on army missions. I flicked through several of them: none of the printing dates inside had occurred within the last decade.

'So much for the eBook revolution,' I heard him say behind me. 'Just as we started to embrace the digital age we plunge back into the dark ages. Now there's not even a market for paperbacks, let alone Kindles and all those kinds of things. Shame, really. There's so much happening now it would be amazing to write about it. But what's the point?'

'Posterity?' I asked. 'Surely future generations would like to know about our world?'

'Nice thought. But there's wood to cut, vegetables to harvest, clothes to darn, leaking roofs to fix, broken chairs to mend. There's always something.'

'Can't you get someone in to do those things? You made enough from all those books to hire workers when you need them, surely?'

Dan laughed. 'And as if that weren't bad enough,' he continued, without even bothering to answer my question, presumably because it was so dumb it didn't deserve a response, 'there are those damn text messages. They drive me mad. They drive everyone mad. And they're getting worse.'

'How often do they come?'

'It's completely random,' he replied. 'Could be twice in one day. Could be twice in a year. You never know when it will come, or what it will instruct you to do. When the text arrives, though, you know the police are already watching you, waiting for you to slip up, judging if you deserve to live or die.'

'I got one,' I said. 'Sent a rude reply and threw the phone out of the window.' Dan regarded me with a mixture of fear and respect. 'Next thing I knew, the building was being raided by the cops and I was on the run.'

'I'm not surprised,' said Dan. 'I haven't heard of anyone being that foolish since this all started. It's a miracle they didn't kill you.'

'I had some help,' I confessed. 'Some woman I'd never met before dragged me off the street and hid me from the cops. Then she—'

I stopped myself. It seemed unwise and ungrateful to blabber about the fact that she had killed two police officers. Even if I thought I could trust Dan, I had to consider whether he was just playing along, or if the room was bugged, or if he might be tortured. It seemed that the less he knew about Tania and Pascal the safer they would be. I dampened down the powerful urge to talk and talk and talk about everything I'd been through. As Dan said, I should take things slowly. Take my time to adjust. It seemed I'd missed the last ten birthdays. That was weird. I was probably in shock.

I picked up a framed photo from the shelf.

'This you in your army days?' I asked, grateful to have found a reason to change the subject.

'Me? God no, that's Marty.'

'Little Marty? He was just a kid.'

'You've been away a long time, Iggy. Marty followed my footsteps into the military – well, into what's left of it. He's made me very proud.'

The power went off at ten. The house plunged into darkness. Dan was ready with candles, and showed me to my room. I slept soundly for a few hours, then lay wide awake in bed. I thought about Pops. I remembered times we'd spent together when I was a child. I tried to recall the last time I'd seen him before whatever it was that had incapacitated me, but the memory just wasn't there. I played the tragedy of Hainan over and over in my mind, coming to terms with the barbarism, the cold-heartedness that humans had needed to take on in order to end the suffering of a million souls. Someone had played God. Someone had authorised the killing of sick and healthy alike, in the knowledge that there was no hope for any of them. I tried to connect these facts to other dormant memories, to see if I could join the dots in the blank part of my mind, but no coherent picture appeared. I knew I would have to wait until Dan felt ready to impart the next tranche of knowledge to me.

Soon after sleep came, I was suffocating. I knew it was

a dream, and I remember trying to push through the barrier of consciousness. On the other side, I would awake to fresh air and safety. I clawed my way through the depths of slumber, looking for a way out. And when I found it and opened my eyes I saw an arm leading to my face and could feel a hand clasped across my mouth.

Chapter 7

I spluttered and coughed, struggling vainly against the pressure. Then I relaxed. I could still breathe through my nose. If someone were trying to suffocate me, they would have covered my nostrils too. My pupils adjusted to the dimness and I recognised the outline of Dan standing beside the bed. He held a finger up against his lips indicating the need for silence. I got it. I climbed out and listened carefully to the noises we could both hear outside the house. Sounds that were barely discernible. Dan must have stayed up all night. No one could have been woken by the padding of these cautious steps.

Dan took me by the wrist and led me to the library. He stopped at one of the bookcases I had looked at earlier. He plucked a dictionary from the shelf and pulled a small handle behind it. The bookcase swung open, revealing a small, windowless room in the heart of the house.

'I believe this is what is known as a panic room,' he whispered in my ear as he ushered me inside.

The heavy bookcase swung closed, sealing us in. He turned on a small flashlight and pointed out the various features of the room, speaking softly as he did so.

'Most people have something like this, these days,' he said. 'You never know when you might need it. Some fortify their whole house. Your old man's house has been adapted like that. You probably noticed bars on the windows and the ventilation system. It can be sealed against the outside air, in case of gas attacks like those poor bastards in Hainan had done to them. When the air inside gets stale, it has a filtration system to scrub any air that is sucked inside.'

'I didn't see any of that in your house,' I said.

'No. This place is too big to turn into a fortress. I just made this little space instead. Kind of cosy, really. If I was still writing, I'd be tempted to have it as my study. Guaranteed not to have any distractions here.'

I looked at the four walls that sat oppressively close to us. Cosy wasn't the word I would have chosen. Claustrophobic suited it better.

'Nice,' I lied.

'It's supposed to have cameras and monitors and stuff, so we can watch any intruders from here. But that needs power, and there won't be any until nine tomorrow morning. So I suggest we wait it out, check the monitor when the power grid switches on for the day, and if it looks all clear we can open it up and get some breakfast. How does that sound?'

It sounded quite frightening. 'Great,' I lied again.

'There's a fortnight's supply of food and water on the shelves. Actually, I set it up just for me, of course, so it will only last seven days with both of us. But that's fine, because I'm sure we'll be out of here in a few hours. There are books to read, but please wait until the power is on. There's a proper light bulb on the ceiling. I also have a chemical toilet behind my chair, which I very much hope you'll avoid using. Finally, I have hundreds of old batteries and a couple of flashlights. No one makes decent batteries any more, so stockpiles of the old ones are like gold dust. With that in mind, I'm turning out the light. Good night, Iggy.'

I sat back in my chair. It was soft, but it couldn't

compare to a real bed. The room was too small to be able to stretch my legs fully. I guessed the walls were no more than four feet apart.

'Aren't you worried?' I whispered. Dan had been ever so un-panicked about hiding in this panic room. I found his attitude reassuring, like the soothing and unflustered voice of a pilot preparing his passengers for a crash landing.

'Worried about strangers in the house?' he asked, sounding like a disembodied voice in the darkness.

'Well, yes. They might damage the place. Steal your potatoes. Anything.'

He laughed. I heard him stretch and relax.

'If you only knew how many times I've been in this room in the last ten years, Iggy. All will be well.'

As I closed my eyes and tried to relax, I could tell immediately that all was not well. This panic room had thick walls, but it sat on the same floorboards as the rooms that surrounded it, and it was plain that those boards were vibrating. Someone was walking around Dan's home. He gave no reaction, even as the floor shook with the arrival of a second, heavier person and unsubtle, clomping feet seemed to circle ever-closer to our hideout.

It was then that I heard my name. The voice was heavily muffled by the book-lined walls, but it was recognisable as Pascal's. A second voice shouted my name, too, and I knew it was Tania. Somehow they had managed to find me, once again.

The flashlight came on. It shone directly at my face, accusingly.

'Who are they?' asked Dan from behind the light. Despite the softness of his voice, there was an unmistakable sternness. I had declined to talk about Pascal and Tania previously, not wanting to cause any problems for them. Now I had no choice.

'Some kind of underground group,' I replied. 'They keep following me. But I don't know what they want with me.'

'Iggy!' shouted Tania. She was much closer now. Probably just the other side of the bookcase door.

'Do you know the name of their group?' whispered Dan. He seemed less worried now. As if underground groups were not something to fear.

'No,' I said. 'She's Tania and he's Pascal. They have hideouts everywhere. When the cops were after me, they took me in. I ran away and came here.'

'I think you should go to them,' said Dan.

'Why?'

'They'll be able to protect you from the police much longer than I could. If you really want to stay off the police radar, you'll need to keep moving. You'll need a wide network of supporters in different places. I can't offer you that, Iggy. Sooner or later they'll find you here and then we'll both be shot.'

'Shot?' I asked. 'Just like that? No trial?'

'Trial! Hah!' he said, turning on the flashlight and opening the secret door. 'Come on. It'll be fine.'

I followed him out to the library. Pascal and Tania were waiting patiently in the shadows.

'Iggy, why did you run?' asked Tania. 'After everything we've done for you.'

'I don't know,' I replied.

'We're on your side,' she said. 'You have to believe that. We've risked everything for you.'

'This is Dan. He's been taking good care of me,' I said.

'How did you find him?' asked Dan.

'We knew about his father,' said Pascal. 'When he

attempted to conceal the truth about his family, it was obvious where he intended to go. We went there, the new owner pointed us to the cemetery and said you were often to be seen hanging out there. Wasn't difficult.'

'We can't afford to lose you, Ignatius,' said Tania. 'You're too important.'

'But why? I'm nobody. What the hell is so important about me?'

'How much have you told him, Dan?' Pascal asked.

'Not everything,' replied Dan. 'It's too soon. He's only just found out that his father didn't make it. I told him about Hainan and the decision to gas the remainder of the population, and I think I mentioned the next outbreak in Hanoi, but we left it there. I wanted him to sleep on it before I hit him with anything else.'

'Good,' said Tania. 'In that case it's too early to let him know why he's so important.'

I was, for the moment, content in my ignorance as to what had happened after Hanoi and how I fitted into everything.

'We have a few hours before dawn,' said Pascal. 'It's too dangerous for us all to stay here. We need to make the most of the darkness to get Ignatius to the next position.'

I didn't like the sound of that. I was drained of energy after my previous night-long hike, and my blisters made me wince when I walked. I craved the opportunity to spend a few days in one place, to give my mind and body the space they needed to recover.

'They're right,' said Dan. 'No point sitting here waiting for a raid. Your best chance is to keep moving.'

It was as if I was no longer an individual. I was a valuable antique – a stolen one – shunted around from hiding place to hiding place. People had a strong incentive to shelter me. Something must be in it for them. Sure, there was a place for altruism in the world, but I'd never seen anything on this scale before. No one risked their lives and murdered cops for someone they'd never met, not unless there was serious cash to be made. But my net worth was probably zero, so where was this reward going to come from? Had I, by chance, invested a paltry sum in the next Apple or Microsoft ten years ago? Had I woken up a billionaire and everyone knew about it but me? Not likely, given the apparent state of technology and the economy. So if it wasn't my direct cash value, what could it have been? Before I put my life back in their hands, I had to know more.

'No,' I said. 'Just slow down, guys. Let's sit for a minute.'

No one protested. We followed Dan's narrow torch beam to the living room and sat down. Dan turned off his flashlight as soon as we were safely seated. He didn't even light a candle. They were probably in short supply, I guessed, and he wouldn't want to draw too much attention to the property in case anyone was passing outside. It was odd sitting in plush armchairs in something akin to a civilised environment, only in pitch dark.

'You really should go with them,' said Dan. 'Take a few minutes by all means, but you know it makes sense.'

'I know, I know,' I said. 'Will the cops really come here if I stay?'

'Word spreads fast,' said Pascal. 'Without Twitter and Facebook and e-mail and all those things you remember from your old life, people have rediscovered the ability to talk to their neighbours. Gossip spreads like wildfire. Most people are on our side, but it only takes one to try to earn a credit with the Government and you're screwed.'

'Earn a credit?' I asked.

'It gives them the right to ignore their next mobile

phone text instruction. Loyal citizens who report crimes and such things are rewarded like that. They get a single-use code they can use to reply to the text and it gets them off the hook. You've made contact in this village, and I don't know if we can trust the man in your father's house. I also don't know if we can trust other residents who might have seen you.'

'You don't know if you can even trust me,' said Dan. I knew he was joking, but I wished he wouldn't. He didn't know how brutal Tania could be.

'The subject of whether we can trust you is an interesting one,' said Tania. I listened for the click of a revolver at this point, and was relieved that she simply continued speaking. 'We have three options, in this respect. We can take a chance that you are worthy of trust,' she began. 'The second option is to take you with us, but that could lead to all kinds of complications, as I'm sure you'd appreciate. And then the third option is–'

'The third option is to shoot me,' said Dan.

I sank lower into my seat, fearing an invisible bullet might fly across the room. I needed to help dig Dan out of this hole.

'Dan has been one hundred per cent supportive of me,' I said. 'If he was going to hand me over to the authorities he would have done so by now.'

'I know,' said Pascal. 'Even though he has no official affiliation with our group, I know we can trust him and I would like to thank him for sheltering you until we arrived.'

'You're welcome,' replied Dan.

'Shall we go?' asked Tania.

'Wait up,' I said. 'I need to know one thing. Why am I important to you guys?'

'You are not important to us,' Tania whispered,

obliquely. 'We have nothing to gain personally from protecting you.'

'So why do all this?' I asked her.

'You are important not to us, but to the world.'

Chapter 8

My feet were killing me after less than a mile. Half-healed blisters burst open, raw wounds crying at me to let them rest. No idea where we were or where we were heading. Tania and Pascal wouldn't tell me our destination nor how long it would take to reach it. In case of ambush and capture, it was safer that way, they told me, and I was too downtrodden to question their wisdom. We walked along narrow roads, the twisty kind that circled the periphery of every homestead or housing development. There was less chance of interception here, but it meant we were unable to take the shortest route to wherever we were going. One time we saw a light ahead and hid for a few minutes in a ditch, which Pascal took as an opportunity to roll up another cigarette. Other than that, the journey was uneventful. Not long after dawn, we arrived at a door.

Perhaps 'door' isn't sufficiently strong a word. It was more like the entrance to a bank vault, set into a steep hillside and hidden from the view of curious eyes by thick and spikey bushes. When we pulled back the vicious undergrowth, I could see the door was circular, attached with ponderous hinges, and built from steel thick enough to withstand a direct hit from a nuclear blast. Corrosion had taken a firm grip on the metal, however, and its surfaces were brown and flaking.

'What is this place?' I asked.

'Nike launch site,' said Pascal.

'What the hell's that for? Sending sneakers into space?' It was a bad joke, but I was in a great deal of pain and it was the best I could manage.

'Nike was a type of anti-aircraft missile,' Pascal explained, patiently. 'Back in the fifties the army put a ring of bases like this around Manhattan. This is the most northerly one. Campgaw Mountain, near Franklin Lakes. It was decommissioned in '71, and was supposed to have been demolished so they could develop a riding school here. But it was expensive to rip out the bunkers that housed the missiles. One of them was hidden and left intact to save money.'

'How did you find it?' I asked.

'From this guy who used to be a doomsday prepper,' replied Pascal. 'Remember those?'

I certainly did. I'd seen dozens of television episodes documenting the preparations that extremist weirdoes had made to secure their survival in the event of natural or political disaster. It had seemed like watching a freak show at the time. They would pour the majority of their family income into the creation of secure underground fortresses and purchasing reserves of food they would never eat. I used to laugh at them and be glad that my attitude to life was not skewed and paranoid like theirs.

But that was then. From what I'd seen and learned these past few days, the approach of the preppers had been sensible. Those who made no contingency for catastrophe were the fools, and I was firmly in the foolish camp.

'This prepper,' Pascal continued, 'was looking for somewhere to build a sanctuary for himself and his daughter. He checked out all of the old missile sites in New Jersey, and found an entrance to this one, hidden in the woods. I think he was preparing against everything he could think of, from an economic meltdown to a tsunami. He filled it with food, water, weapons and tools. He wanted to have enough stored to be able to provide for his daughter for years if necessary. Of all the thousands of preppers in the States, he was one of the best. The irony was, when the big day happened, he was on a business trip in the Far East. Didn't stand a chance.'

'Shit,' I said, unable to repress a giggle. 'Idiot! What's the point of doing all this preparation if you don't stay close to it?'

'Setting up this bunker cost him millions and that meant he had to work hard to keep the money coming in. He had a business to run and sometimes he had to travel to get the deals.'

'So how come we have use of this moron's hideout now?'

'Because his daughter was able to access it in time,' replied Pascal, suppressing a smirk.

'I think you will find,' said Tania, 'that my father left me a very useful inheritance. He was no idiot.'

'Your father? Shit, I'm sorry Tania. I didn't know.' I felt myself shrink into my shoes. 'It's me that's the idiot.'

'It doesn't matter,' she said. 'You're too important for me to be angry at you. I'm very proud of what my father achieved. He gave me everything I needed to survive the awful things that happened. And what he left me has, in turn, enabled me to ensure your survival and your freedom. His paranoia may well turn out to have saved the world. Welcome to my missile bunker.'

More meaningless hyperbole. She had said stuff like that so often that I just let it wash over me. There was no way it could be anything other than inflated nonsense.

With the mighty steel barrier left ajar behind us, we walked down a set of dank concrete steps to a second door. More rusty steel, but not anywhere near as substantial as the first. Tania spun the wheel in the centre and the door swung open. I gasped for breath. The sight that opened up before me was overwhelming: a subterranean concrete chamber the size of a warehouse, lined floor to ceiling with storage shelves and boxes, machinery, construction equipment, water-purifying gear and weaponry ... racks of it, enough for a small army. On cable television, I'd seen the lairs of many doomsday preppers, but no one had created anything on this scale. Tania's late father really had poured a fortune into it.

'Most of the boxes are empty now,' she told me. 'I moved out of here years ago, just before I got—'

Pascal shook his head and she halted her sentence.

'This place was only designed to store enough for two or three years,' said Pascal. 'Like everyone else, we're now dependent on home-grown produce.'

'No tins or anything left?' I asked.

'Very little now survives since before the Annihilation,' said Tania.

'The what?'

Pascal shook his head again. I was destined to remain in the dark.

'We have plenty of medical supplies, though,' said Tania, deliberately changing tack. 'You can treat your blisters if you want.'

It was precisely what I wanted. Amongst racks of bandages, saline drips, heart monitors and pills, I located a humble bottle of disinfectant and a packet of plasters. I cleaned my sore feet. Bliss.

'Power is hydroelectric,' Tania said, offering me a steaming cup of coffee. 'Dad put in a generator in an underground stream in the mountainside. Not too many watts, but it keeps the place lit and doesn't attract attention like solar panels or wind generators would.'

I noticed a television set up in a corner, next to a couple of sofas and a plastic plant. Someone had tried to make a small section of this bunker look a little bit homely.

'Any channels still broadcasting?' I asked, pointing at the screen.

'Just one official channel,' she replied. 'Analogue signal, of course. But there is so much wavelength available that various groups have set up intermittent pirate broadcasts. They get shut down and executed pretty fast. It isn't hard to detect the source of a signal, so we've not got involved in anything like that.'

'So what's the official channel? Fox News?' I asked.

'No, but you'd struggle to notice the difference,' she sighed. 'Government propaganda. Designed to scare the populous into complicity and acceptance. Subtle as a brick.'

'At least we have old DVDs and videos,' said Pascal. 'No one makes movies any more, but enough were made during the first century of cinema to last us a lifetime. Mind you, that's assuming our players last a lifetime, since no one is making new ones to replace them when they break.'

'And you have to be prepared to embrace foreign films, low budget independent stuff and the black and white classics,' added Tania.

'No new movies in ten years?' I asked. 'So at least I didn't miss much.'

'Didn't miss much?' echoed Pascal. 'That's got to be a world record for understatement.'

He showed me to a bunk where I was to be permitted a few hours of rest. It was grubby and smelled of mould, but details like that seemed not to matter in this new world. Sleep approached so fast I feared I wouldn't wake

71

up for another ten years, but a now-familiar pressure on my ankle brought me from my dreams back to the stale bunker.

'It's time to continue your education,' she told me. 'There is much you still need to learn.'

'What time is it?' I croaked. In this sunless pit, there was no sense of day or night.

'Three,' she replied.

I worked out that I had slept for eight hours. A rare privilege indeed. I sat up and rubbed my eyes.

'Is everything OK?' I asked.

'This bunker is invisible,' she said. 'Of course everything is OK. No one knows we are here. Come and join me by the television when you're ready. I want to show you some old tapes.'

I was fresher and brighter than I'd been for days when I sat next to her on the sofa. She inserted a VHS tape into an old player and switched on the television. A documentary began to play, looking completely contemporary to me, but, I assumed, it was somewhat anachronistic and dated to Tania's eyes.

There was a sombre voiceover and some computer graphics. The narrator talked about the spread of the virus from China to Vietnam and the panic that ensued. There was footage of the horrendous suffering experienced by those who caught the illness.

'This bit of the film was shot by someone who was already dying,' said Tania. 'No one else would go close enough to a victim. Whoever shot this video would have been dead the next day.'

The colours I witnessed in that film were unnatural. They should never be part of the human skin palette. It was just how I imagined a mediaeval plague victim would look. Seeing my distress, Tania paused the tape.

'Nasty,' I said.

'That was Vietnam. Early days. But the West was already taking action. All flights to and from Vietnam were grounded. Sea ports were blockaded by an international task force. People quickly started referring to it as the Second Vietnam War. United Nations troops attempted to patrol hundreds of miles of remote Vietnamese borders. Containment is never easy, and a country like Vietnam which borders Cambodia, Laos and China, was impossible to quarantine.'

'So what happened then? Another population gassed?'

'Unfortunately not. The situation rapidly became too complex. Planes, boats and cars could be controlled, fuel supplies were cut, roads and ports closed – that bought everyone time – but even when reduced to walking speed, the spread of the disease was relentless. Each day we received reports of its arrival in another new town, and then another, and then confirmation came that it had reached Cambodia and Malaysia.'

'How long since Hainan had been wiped out?'

'Just two weeks,' she replied.

'Shit.' I knew little of the geography of the region, but I guessed an epidemic would be hard to control across so many countries.

'The world shut its doors,' she continued. 'International travel was banned just about everywhere. Even short journeys were discouraged. Anyone on vacation became a refugee. Families were divided arbitrarily. No one wanted to mix socially or for business or any reason. Movie theatres closed. Broadway closed. Supermarkets were swamped with panic buying and then abandoned. Trading stopped. Businesses collapsed. Currency exchanges halted. Inflation spiralled. And yet none of that mattered to anyone. The only concern was keeping the sickness in one corner of South East Asia.'

'How could I not know about this stuff?'

'You were already in a coma,' Tania replied. 'In many ways you were lucky to have missed it. No one has pleasant memories of that period.'

'How much do you guys know about why I was knocked out for so long?'

'Well, pretty much everything, of course. Don't you know yourself?'

'No. Just vague dreams about being hooked up to stuff and people crying and me being in a whole shitload of pain.'

'But you don't know what was wrong with you?'

'No,' I replied. 'Hit on the head, probably. Car crash. Bad fall down some stairs. That kind of thing.'

'That explains why you have no idea why you are so important,' Tania said.

'If I matter so much, why haven't you told me what this is about?'

'You matter for many reasons,' she said. 'The first is that you are a survivor. Possibly the only survivor.'

'What? Plane crash? Terrorist attack?'

'No. You survived the Hainan plague.'

'Well, sure. We all did. That's why we're still here.'

'No. What I mean is, you caught it and it didn't kill you. Very nearly, but somehow you had a unique set of antibodies. You had what was needed to hang in there. It took you ten years in intensive care, but you made it. We don't know of anyone else who had this thing and lived. I think that makes you pretty special.'

'But how could I have caught it? I've never been anywhere in Asia, let alone China or Vietnam.'

'It doesn't matter now,' she said. 'You came through, and that really was something. And even while you were

74

out of it, you probably don't realise, you've achieved something amazing in the last ten years.'

That seemed unlikely. I pushed for more information, not expecting anything worthwhile.

'What could I possibly have achieved whilst in a coma?'

'Company!' shouted Pascal, from the other end of the bunker.

'Shit. Lockdown,' returned Tania, springing to action. She threw some hefty-looking switches on a control panel, causing the lights to dim and the faint hum of the airflow system to cease. She then manually closed a couple of ventilation flaps. Pascal was in the tunnel that led to the secure entrance. 'Go with Pascal,' she told me. 'Help him get the door locked.'

'Why didn't you lock it when we came in?' I asked.

'It's rusty. It jams. Makes it hard to open again if there's only two of us in here. We only close it in emergencies. Don't want to get sealed in for good.'

'I thought places like this always had another exit?'

'Yes, but it's not as well hidden. There are people living up there. We've never used it. Once we do, we'll have to abandon this place for ever.'

'Shit,' I mumbled, sprinting to help Pascal in his task. I found him pushing the thick door into its housing, and put my shoulder up against it to help. It looked like it was ninety per cent into its frame, but corrosion and the distortion of time made it impossible to close the final inch. There was no way to lock it.

'Forget it,' said Pascal. 'We can secure the inner door.'

The secondary door wasn't thick enough to survive a bomb blast, but it was still a substantial barricade against unwanted visitors, and I got the feeling that *all* visitors were unwanted. Steel closed against steel, easily this time, and we bolted it securely from within. If the location of this hideout had been compromised and the main door was breached, it would take a blowtorch or explosives to break through to the main chamber. Pascal returned to the security monitor and watched the input from three cameras located at ground level. I looked over his shoulder and could see no one on the screens.

'Who did you see?' I asked him.

'Dunno,' he replied. 'Looked like cops, but it was too blurry to see. Probably ten of them. They've never snooped around here before.'

Five indistinct figures flashed across the screen. A couple more followed. When the three of us held our breath in the bunker, I swear I could hear our heartbeats pounding out a rhythm of fear.

A minute passed. No more human shapes appeared on the monitors. I could hear Pascal breathing more steadily. It seemed the danger had receded.

'Close call,' I said.

'Hopefully that's all it was,' whispered Tania.

'We'll lay low for the rest of the day,' said Pascal. 'Can't take any chances showing our faces up there until after dark. There are some books if you want to read. Tania will show you where they are.'

'Can we talk some more about the plague?' I asked.

Tania looked at Pascal. He nodded.

'Sure,' she replied. 'Why not?'

'You said I'd achieved something during my coma. What did you mean?'

This time Pascal remained blank when she looked at him, but there was a tone of awkwardness in her answer that hinted at evasion.

'I meant on a cellular level,' she said. 'Your cells achieved some amazing stuff. All to do with survival.'

'I still don't see why I had that plague in the first place without going to the affected countries?'

'Do you remember your history lessons?' she asked.

I shook my head. I barely remembered my own life story, let alone that of the planet.

'The Black Death was really two kinds of plague: bubonic and pneumonic,' she reminded me. 'The first was carried by fleas on rats, and the second was transmitted person-to-person. Living conditions in the fourteenth century were primitive. People and animals lived in close proximity. Rats and fleas were part of the fabric of life.'

'Nice,' I replied.

'Well this modern plague had a twin-pronged attack, too. A perfect storm. Without evolved immunity or sufficient time to develop a cure, we were helpless.'

She stopped and looked at the security monitors. The unwanted visitors were back.

Pascal grabbed an armful of terrifying weapons and divided them between us. Tania held a sub-machine gun in confident hands and I held something similar in a nervous grip.

Our sights were aimed at the door.

The white flash preceded the noise and the pressure wave. I was gone.

PART TWO

Chapter 9

'Is he conscious yet?'

I opened one eye. I lacked the strength to move both eyelids at once. Parts of my body started to connect to my brain, delivering messages of pain and discomfort. Two women stood beside me.

'Looks like he opened an eye,' said one of them. 'Did you see it?'

'Hey there, Ignatius,' said the first woman. 'Can you hear me?'

I could hear her voice perfectly, but could find no method of communicating my awareness. My open eye slid closed as if pulled down by immense gravity, and there it remained.

'Probably shouldn't touch him now,' said the other voice. 'Might confuse him.'

'I'll miss him,' said the first woman. 'When you know someone so intimately, it's hard to let go.'

'What you've been doing hardly constitutes a relationship.'

'It's been better than most I've had.'

There were giggles. I heard them leave, closing the door behind them.

I opened both eyes. I was alone in a hospital room. Various machines were connected to me. Some were switched off. A dull light bled in through a gap in the blind. Couldn't tell if it was filtered sunlight or a street lamp. I tried to move but my muscles felt as if they had forgotten how to react to my desires. I thought of Pascal and Tania. Had they survived the blast in the bunker too? Were they bandaged and recovering in adjacent rooms? From what I knew of the law enforcement situation, if they'd survived the initial attack I doubted they would have received any care or mercy from the intruders.

But I had survived. Now I had to question whether I would regret it. I had already learned that survival was not automatically a ticket to happiness.

Rapid footsteps preceded the arrival of a young doctor. He burst into the room, a whirlwind of energy and purpose. With the slick confidence of someone who had done these things a thousand times, he disconnected me from each of the machines, patched up the uncomfortable holes left behind in my skin, and performed a rapid check of my physical health.

'Awake?' he asked me, checking my pulse the old-fashioned way and looking over his shoulder cautiously, as if not wanting to be seen with me.

'Barely,' I whispered. It hurt to talk. The muscles in my throat seemed to have forgotten what to do.

'Good. Now bear with me. There's not much time.'

'Where am I?' I croaked, a little more audibly this time.

He said nothing and prepared a syringe, which he then slid into a vein in my arm. Within seconds I felt my heart rate accelerate. Energy was surging through my body. My eyes were now firmly pinned open. I twitched and wriggled in the bed.

'That should bring you back to the land of the living,' said the doctor.

'What was that?' I asked, almost at a normal volume.

'A little cocktail of my own invention. Viagra,

caffeine, adrenaline and guaraná. Works miracles, but only for a short time. We have to move fast. Come on.'

He put his arms around my back and tried to help me sit up. I was trapped in a body that wanted to move but had remarkably little capability.

'I was knocked out by an explosion yesterday,' I told him. 'I don't think I should be moving yet.'

'It's important. Trust me,' he replied, swinging my legs off the side of the bed so that I was now sitting properly. He slid a pair of loose-fitting trousers on to me, then forced my feet into shoes that were at least a size too small.

I could see his face more clearly now. He was of Chinese origin, with a handsome skin tone and dark, purposeful eyes. His small stature made him seem younger than the greying sides of his otherwise jet-black hair would suggest. He wore a white doctor's uniform, with an ID badge clipped tidily to his breast pocket. I squinted, but struggled to focus sufficiently to be able to read his name.

'Who are you?' I asked.

'Umberto Tang. I'm your doctor. Can you stand up?'

I was flooded with endorphins and energy. I felt that I could dance, maybe even fly. Standing up would be a piece of cake. I tried to push myself up onto my legs and fell instantly into Tang's waiting arms.

'OK, we'll try again,' he said, planting me back on the bed whilst looking over his shoulder at the door. I was buzzing so much inside I didn't question the need to rush my elevation from the bed. It just felt so good to attempt movement of any kind, no matter how inept at it I appeared to be.

I concentrated hard on controlling my leg muscles. Tang took hold of my arms and steadied me. The feeling of standing upright was dizzying, but I was euphoric.

'I can do it!' I cried.

'Shush,' he whispered, a sudden look of fear flashing across his face. 'It's important that we do this quietly. Now try a few steps.'

He held me by the waist while I staggered drunkenly around the room, trying to avoid the tubes and cables that he had dropped to the floor. I wondered if that was a hygiene issue, and was about to question his apparently sloppy ways with high-tech equipment when he said something that grabbed my attention fully.

'It's going to be hard to walk,' he began, 'because the muscles have partially atrophied after a year spent in bed. You've received an intensive programme of thorough daily massages and electronic vibration toning and–'

'What did you just say?' I interrupted.

'I'm one of the team that's been taking care of you this past year.'

'Year?' I echoed with a sigh, feeling myself plummeting from the pinnacle of ecstasy on which his drugs had placed me.

'Well, eleven months and a couple of weeks, I think. Close enough to a year. So keep moving. We don't have long.'

I couldn't believe what I was hearing. I had been robbed of yet another year of my life. Denied the experiences, the learning, the relationships and the personal growth that ought to have been mine. Pops had been dead over a decade and yet it still seemed like only weeks ago that I was with him. It was too much for me to put into complex sentences. I expressed the sum of my emotions in just two words: 'Not again.'

'Never mind that, now. Can you stand without my help?' He released me and watched me wobble. 'Sit on the bed and rest a moment, then we'll try again.'

Grateful, I sat down, panting as if I'd climbed a steep hill, trying to come to terms with the disappearance of another chunk of my limited time on Earth. Tang opened the door and peeked out into the corridor. He slammed it shut and dragged a chair against it.

'No time,' he said, sounding panicked. 'We'll have to go as you are. Stand up. Quick!'

'Go where?' I asked.

'I'll tell you when we're safe. Right now, you're in danger. Listen, I'm going to help you, but you have to give it everything you've got, because finding the strength isn't going to be easy for you.'

I pushed myself into a standing position again, pleased to note that it was less of a challenge this time. Tang guided me to the side of the room, then dragged the bed to a position where it aided the chair in blocking the door. I glanced at the window: were we about to escape through that? I had no idea how many floors up from the ground we were. I could see no other exit from this room.

Tang ripped the blind clean off the wall and pushed the window wide open. I blinked at the bright light that poured in. I now knew for sure that it was daytime. I squinted at the view, and confirmed my fears: we were not at ground level. I wasn't sure how high we were, but to be looking down at the tops of the trees was not something that filled me with enthusiasm for his plan.

'Wait,' I said, resisting his attempt to push me to the window. 'What is this? Why am I in danger?'

'If I don't get you out of here in the next sixty seconds you will be on the fast track to death.'

'How do I know you're not just some nut?'

'You don't,' he replied with breathless frustration, 'and that's because I *am* a nut. Saving your ass will cost

85

me my career. Might even cost me my life. I'm crazy to do this, but someone needs to make a stand for you and no one else was prepared to lift a finger to help you.'

My resistance waned and I let him guide me to the open window. I stuck my head outside and could now see a window cleaner's platform suspended there, so conveniently situated that Tang must have been planning this for some time. He climbed out first, then helped me through the window and onto the platform. I clung tight to the handrail as he lowered us to ground level, then held his hand as he led me to the cover of some nearby trees and hedges surrounding what used to be a parking lot. A piercing ache began to spread through my unprepared muscles.

'Everything's starting to hurt,' I complained. 'Feels like those drugs you gave me are wearing off.'

'It's normal. The effects are temporary.'

'Any chance of a booster?'

'No. If I give you the same again, your aorta will burst.'

Tang looked back at the hospital building. From this far away, I couldn't pick out from which window we had just made our escape. He appeared satisfied that his plan had met with success.

'What now?' I asked.

'Can you still walk?'

I stood up and tried some steps. The muscle pain was excruciating, worse than the cramps I used to get towards the end of the New York marathon. But I could take it. When you can drag your cramping legs six miles to the finish line of the marathon in Central Park, a few steps was nothing. At least, I hoped it would be just a few steps.

'Follow me,' he whispered, leading the way along the line of a hedge towards a small hut at the periphery of the hospital grounds. It looked like a store room for the groundskeeper, somewhere to keep his garden tools and a quiet retreat from the world. Tang opened the tattered wooden door and showed me inside. A makeshift seat had been created out of bags of fertiliser, and a bottle of water had been placed next to it. 'Sit there and drink the water. Hydration will help ease the muscle pain. This is as far as we go today. I'm aware of your limitations, and I don't plan to stress your body too much in its current state.'

'Will they find us here?' I asked, panting and gurgling down the mineral water, and wondering who 'they' were.

'No. They'll be looking for you in the hospital and main outbuildings first. This is the last place they'll come. We'll be gone by then.'

'What's a day matter when I've just lost a whole year?' I groaned.

'But you've not been idle. At least, we've kept you productive, in a manner of speaking.'

'First I miss a whole decade, then another year zips past without me knowing. Why is this happening?'

'It was all for the best, believe me,' said Tang.

'How badly was I injured?'

'In the blast? Hardly at all. More of a theatrical flash, an illusion. Just enough to knock you off your feet and give you a touch of concussion. We induced the coma to get you back on the programme.'

I had no idea what he was talking about, and lacked the will to ask for clarity.

'Tania? Pascal?' I asked, instead. 'What happened to them?'

'You don't need to worry about them. Listen, there are some things I need to explain to you. I know you're feeling weak, so I'm going to take my time. There's no hurry, now.'

I wriggled. My circulation was declining, and I felt numbness on my back. Movement helped restore blood to thirsty extremities, but it was my head that needed it the most. For some reason I was unable to process everything the doctor was saying. I was an animal in a vivisectionist's laboratory – helpless and confused, experimented and abused for reasons I couldn't understand.

'Is everything still crazy?' I asked.

'What do you mean?' the doctor replied.

'Out there. Those old cellphones and stupid text messages. Everyone living like the Waltons.'

'That didn't affect you. You had a privileged position here. The opportunity to serve humanity and avoid the horrendous shit that's going on for almost everyone else.'

'Almost?'

'The vast majority.'

'So some people get to live normally?' I asked. 'Who are they? The cops who shoot those who fail to complete their texted instructions?'

'No, no. Imagine having to do that. Awful job. Besides, the cops get tested themselves.'

'So who doesn't have to do it?'

He was silent on this subject, shaking his head gently. I tried another angle.

'But why are people tested?'

'We nearly lost it all,' said the doctor. 'We grew weak. In a way, you could say we stopped evolving.'

I thought humans had stopped evolving hundreds of thousands of years ago. Monkeys came down from the trees, starting walking on two legs and hitting each other with clubs, and modern man was born. Job done. Or something like that. I told him so.

'No, I am afraid not. We may not have changed much

on the outside in the past few thousand years,' he told me, 'but the human machine had been tweaked and oiled and kept in tip-top condition during that time by the hand of nature.'

'The hand of nature?'

'In brutal terms, I mean infant mortality,' he said, almost with a guilty whisper. 'Nature weeds out the weak before they are old enough to pass on their genes. At least, that's how it worked before we developed modern medicine. Once we had the ability to permit nearly all children the chance to make it to adulthood, we interfered with natural selection. I'm only talking about the past five or six generations, but it's been significant enough to dilute the strength of the species.'

I didn't like the tone of his argument, and quickly gathered the strength to say so.

'That sounds like Nazi eugenics to me,' I told him. 'I don't buy that kind of fascist crap. Of course we should save every child if we can. That's what makes us human.'

The doctor nodded his head. Turned out he wasn't about to enter into an argument with his patient. 'You're totally correct,' he said. 'Correct from a moral standpoint, that is. When you look at it from a medical perspective, and when you take a more global view of things, however, the logic of eugenics is sadly irrefutable. It sounds awful to say it, but those Nazis were on to something. Maybe their motives were flawed, but the medicine was heading the right way.'

'How can you possibly think that?' I asked, aghast at the attitude of a seemingly intelligent man.

'Take antibiotics,' he continued, in what seemed an evasive side-step. 'Antibiotics have saved millions in the last century, but their effectiveness will soon be zero. Infections develop resistance to our drugs. We have merely postponed deaths by their use. Antibiotics bought us time, saved one generation at the expense of the next. It was a Faustian pact. It was one of the many ways in which we were propping up a substandard species.'

'Was?' I asked, not wanting to hear the answer.

'Medicine is very different now,' was all he would say on the matter, before he continued on his evolution theme. 'When I said evolution had stalled, it's actually worse than that. The erosion of the strength of our species is effectively a process of reverse evolution. We were going backwards for generations. In our weakened state, the Hainan plague almost finished us off. That is why we had to do what we did. No one likes it. No one wanted this situation, but no one came up with a viable alternative, so this is what we have.'

'You mean the text messages are designed to weed out the weaker members of society?' I asked, although I'd kind of worked that out by now.

'It's part of it, yes,' he replied. 'Part of the process of Accelerated Evolution, as it became known. The frail, the sick and the disabled all fell victim to the new policy in the first few months. In the context of what we did globally, this was relatively insignificant.'

'You mean killing all those innocents, the million people gassed on Hainan island?' I asked.

'No, I don't mean that. I mean the disease control measures that were instigated afterwards. I mean the decision that the West took. You know the one I mean.'

'I don't know what you mean,' I replied.

'You mean no one told you what happened during your first coma?'

He seemed astounded, thrown off course. When I confirmed my ignorance, he paced around the hut, unsure how to proceed.

'Look,' he said, 'it's not my place to fill you in on this. I think it might be better coming from a trained psychologist. I was prepared to tell you about your direct role in the healing of the species. When all this madness has died down, I'll see to it that I find someone to tell you everything in an appropriate manner. Don't want to cause any unnecessary stress by blabbing about it the wrong way.'

His evasion matched the unwillingness of Tania, Pascal and Dan to reveal everything to me. That only heightened my anxiety at what would eventually be revealed.

'I need to know,' I said. 'Everyone I've spoken to has avoided this, whatever it is. Why can't someone just tell me? I've already lost everything that mattered in my life. It can't get any worse.'

'I'll make sure you're told at an appropriate time,' he replied. 'Now is most certainly not appropriate. Anyway, since you already know about the text messages I'll stick to that part of the story. Accelerated Evolution. The process of preparing the population for the next wave of plague infection. We had to get everyone ready. Those of us who survived the initial pruning of the numbers had to stay alert. We had to get fit. We had to respect our bodies. We had to take care of ourselves and eat nutritiously. No one was going to help us if we lacked the strength to carry out our text message challenges.'

'Accelerated evolution? Isn't that just another way of saying eugenics?' I asked.

'It was just the first step. Obesity disappeared within a year. Diabetes became rare. People quit smoking. Rates of heart attacks and cancers fell. The population was smaller, but it became stronger very quickly. The text message challenges were a blunt instrument, but they sure were effective. Inevitably, some people went underground and tried to keep off the radar and avoid the texts, but the majority went along with it, enough to make it a success.'

'But I saw an innocent woman get killed last week … I mean last year. It was horrific. How does that kind of institutionalised murder help the planet?'

'It isn't the planet we are trying to help. It is the people who occupy it. The bottom line is, there is every likelihood of another plague in the near future. Possibly a variation, a mutation, of the original one. Only a fit population can have any chance of surviving it. Healthy individuals succumb less, and therefore spread the disease less. It has less chance of gaining a foothold. So it is for that eventuality that the world is preparing.'

'And what is my role in this?' I asked.

'Well, that's why I've come to see you. Are you aware that you survived the plague?'

'Tania told me. But I've never been to China or Vietnam. How did I get it?'

'You didn't need to go to those places,' the doctor told me. 'The initial attempts at isolation and quarantine failed miserably. Supplies of oil were blocked to prevent people from driving or flying or boating out of the affected areas. Even with the region reduced to travelling by foot, the plague still spread, just as it had in the Middle Ages.'

'But I never even visited Asia,' I protested. 'Not anywhere. At least, not that I remember.'

'To be honest, we're not a hundred per cent certain how you contracted the disease, but our best guess is that you ordered a package online. It was shipped to you direct from China, and was already in transit by the time the first quarantine area was set up. The plague is transmissible by spores, in a similar way to anthrax. Do you remember buying anything from China?'

I tried to recall receiving parcels in my apartment block. I used to order online all the time. Often I found it easier to buy cooking ingredients on the internet than to bother to find the right store. Herbs and spices were ideal for online delivery. When I was planning to cook a Chinese meal for my friends I would plan weeks in advance and order most of what I needed from the comfort of my office. I tried to recall the last item I had ordered.

'XO,' I said.

'The Chinese sauce?'

'It's a specialty of southern China,' I said. 'It could have come direct from Hainan.'

'That's your source of infection, then, if you'll forgive the pun.' He looked pleased with himself for that one. I was not amused, however. 'Spores could have been inside the bottle or in the packaging materials. There were only two other cases of transmission by this method, luckily none in the US.'

'If I had the plague, and it was so infectious, how come I didn't spread it to the rest of New York?'

'Lucky break, on many levels. Various factors came together. Your symptoms were spotted incredibly early. Records show it was your dentist, in fact. Routine check-up, but at a time when the world was becoming paranoid and all medical professionals were looking out for signs of the plague. As a precaution, you were placed in an isolation unit in hospital immediately, as was the dentist and everyone who had been in contact with you in the previous twenty-four hours. It was all hushed up, of course. Didn't want to start a panic and a stampede out of New York. The National Guard were already in position, ready to quarantine the city and block all routes in and out as soon as we gave the word.'

'All that because I went to see the dentist?'

'If anyone had caught the disease off you, we would have had no choice but to initiate the city-wide quarantine. But the dentist, his assistant, his receptionist, the other patients and your co-workers showed no signs of having caught it. The National Guard stood down. The focus was now on you. We expected you to die within days, but you hung on. Your symptoms were muted, compared to what we had seen of the victims in Asia. We concluded that something unique in your DNA suppressed the virulence of the disease, reduced its transmissibility, and supplied your immune system with the tools it needed to win this battle.'

The idea that my DNA was special made no sense. I was part Italian, part Greek, and probably a few other parts in the mix, too. Not a unique combination, I was sure of that. I thought about that damn bottle of sauce. I couldn't get it out of my mind.

'Who would have thought a bottle of sauce could cost me ten, no, eleven years of my life?' I asked.

'You make it sound like a bad thing. Actually, it's good. It's saved you.'

'How has it saved me?'

'You had a decade of freedom from the text messages. You might have failed any one of them and been summarily executed. And more significantly, it meant we were able to embark on the project that I need to talk to you about now.'

'Project?' I asked, raising my eyebrows.

'We call it the Seeding Project. It's very simple. Once we suspected there was something special in your DNA, we sequenced it. We mapped it entirely. It took hundreds of doctors several months, but we found it.'

'Found what?'

'We identified the gene in your DNA that enabled you to develop the necessary antibodies to counter the effects of the plague. Turned out to be a mutation. You didn't inherit it, and no one else had it. You are evolution in progress. You have evolved. Just one gene, lying there, doing nothing until the time came to defend you. It took you years to fight it off, but you got there.'

'I know. Ten years.'

'No, nothing like that. Only three or four, I think. After that you were simply kept in an induced coma to enable the Seeding Project to go ahead. Right, I haven't explained about the project, yet, have I? It's rather a sensitive matter. I've been imagining this moment for a long time, wondering how you would react. There's no known precedent for anything like this, but then, the world has never been in such a mess before. So I'm going to come straight out and tell you, and all I ask is that you remain as calm as possible and think a while before you react. Whatever you do, don't run outside and get yourself caught.'

What was this man building up to? I was on edge. My heart was pounding again. I feared for my aorta. I breathed deeply. I wished he would just get it over with.

'While you were in an induced coma,' he told me, 'you became a father.'

Chapter 10

I did exactly as I had been instructed. I remained calm and let the news sink in. It didn't seem so bad. It was a shock, of course, and it had to have been a violation, but on some level, I think I was pleased. It wasn't the first time. I had been a father before, albeit briefly. In my late twenties, I'd got a girl pregnant. I was devastated, all the more so when she told me she wanted to have the baby. We weren't even a couple, but I hung around during the pregnancy out of a sense of duty, helping out where possible, dreading the day of the arrival. I was even there at the birth, pretending to be supportive whilst thinking my life was about to change for the worse. I didn't think I was ready for fatherhood, wasn't prepared to give up my freedoms and selfish lifestyle.

She was stillborn. Something had gone tragically wrong during labour. I should have been relieved, should have been delighted at this unexpected exit from the road of responsibility. But when the resuscitation attempts were called off, the midwife insisted we each hold her for a few minutes. She looked like she was sleeping. As I cradled the body I could see her face, serene and perfect. Her mouth had never had the chance to cry. Her eyes had never had the chance to see. She was just this tiny person, denied all the experiences that I took for granted. I hadn't had the opportunity to get to know her, and I hadn't wanted her to be part of my life. And now she would never grow up. In that moment, I sensed the enormity of her lost life. I felt the unfairness that she should be so close to life, and yet be so far. I was instantly overwhelmed by grief. I wanted her life more than anything I'd ever desired before.

It surprised me how long I mourned that baby. I wasn't sure that I could go through anything like that again, and was careful in relationships not to take chances with birth control. And now, without my knowledge, it had happened.

'Boy or girl?' I asked, wiping a small tear from my eye.

'Actually, you have both,' replied the doctor, with a hesitation in his voice that suggested he was still hiding something from me. The concept of fathering a boy and a girl swirled around my head. I liked it. I wanted to get to know them. I wanted to know their names and their ages.

'Can I go see them?' I asked. 'I mean, once we're safely away from the hospital.'

He shook his head.

'Can I at least know their names?'

Again, he shook his head. I could tell he was building up to another confession.

'There are more than two,' he told me. 'It would not be practicable to visit them.'

I let that sink in. Another revelation. I could see why he was taking his time.

'How many?' I asked.

'Before I give you numbers, I want to explain why we have initiated this programme. The world has changed since before you went into your first coma; it's not the place you remember. Society's values and priorities have had to change. We came so close to being wiped out, Ignatius. You have to remember that. An experience like that cannot be ignored. Its impact trickles down to future generations. We still say 'bless you' when someone sneezes, because that's what everyone started saying when the mediaeval plagues erupted, and the fear of those events returning has kept that superstitious habit alive for centuries. Those early plagues changed us. So you must see the Seeding Project in those terms. Only instead of superstition, we have science. Saying 'bless you' won't arrest the onset of infection, but improving the genetic make-up of future generations will provide the protection that our ancestors thought they would get from a blessing. That is why we have been using your sperm. That is why we have created babies using in-vitro fertilisation techniques.'

'How many?' I repeated.

He looked at the floor, as if about to confess to multiple crimes. 'The first round was ten,' he said. 'We wanted to test the theory, see how many offspring were born with the gene. The majority had it.'

'Ten? You serious? I have ten kids?'

'We scaled it up for the second round. Two hundred pregnancies were created. After that we went global. Ten thousand babies, give or take, in the third round.'

By now I was speechless. As if deliberately trying to flummox me, he kept going.

'We kept scaling it up, in line with every country that was prepared to bring in the new laws on procreation.'

'What laws?'

'The scientific case was strong enough to persuade many nations that your DNA should be present in a significant proportion of births. It varies from country to country, but here in the States it's been set at twenty per cent. European countries set the level at between ten and thirty per cent. Less in places where you don't fit the racial profile so well. Canada went for forty per cent.'

I was being bombarded with meaningless statistics. I only wanted to know how many children I had. Tang was fixated on explaining the new law to me.

'Genetic diversity remains important,' he continued. 'We can't have you fathering every child on the planet. That would result in problems from inbreeding. Essentially everyone would become half-brothers and half-sisters, and there would be no way to avoid incest. So we had to limit the percentage in each country and spread them geographically. Governments decreed that all IVF cycles should use your sperm, and couples were rewarded either financially or in other ways if they volunteered to breed with your assistance. In cases where that wasn't enough to meet the targets, random selections were made and couples were forced to have your babies. By the time you woke from your first coma, you had probably sired more than a million children. In the eleven months of your second coma, we at least doubled that figure. That's a lot of birthdays to remember,' he said, attempting to lighten the mood and looking relieved that he had finally given his confession.

I stared at the roof, numb to the core. I didn't know what I was supposed to feel. I wanted to be angry at the imposition of fatherhood upon me without my consent. I wanted to rage at the audacity of this crime. Instead, I welled up inside. A profound sensation of love for mankind took hold of my mind. I could love everyone. I had a stake in the whole planet.

The cynical side of me returned. Was this a wind-up? Was I a victim of the outrageous imagination of a cruel hoaxer? The hospital was real. This man, Tang, looked and sounded like a doctor. And I knew the plague was a real event.

'Let it sink in,' said Tang. 'I know it's a lot to accept. On the positive side, you could be single-handedly responsible for saving humanity. Next time a plague scythes its way through the population, those with your genes will carry us through.'

'If I'm so valuable to society, why am I in danger?'

'All value creates danger,' the doctor replied, cryptically. 'You are the most sought after commodity on the planet. That kind of value engenders greed and corruption. And the only one who would suffer in that circumstance is you. That's why I had to save you.'

'None of what you just said makes any sense,' I told him.

He sat down on the floor beside my makeshift chair and took a long breath.

'Ignatius, did you ever stop to wonder why you woke up in your apartment after your first coma? With no warning, or explanation or preparation? Didn't that strike you as odd?'

'Sure it did. That whole morning was bizarre.'

'It must have been pretty unsettling for you. Did you consider that it tested you to the extreme?'

'You could say it was a tough time,' I replied. 'Hard to imagine anything tougher.'

'And would you believe me when I say that the reason for putting you into that situation with no assistance was an economic one, driven by the desire for profit?'

'Probably not. How could anyone have made money out of me going to work and getting chased by the cops and floating down the Hudson?'

The American government is not dumb. It knows an opportunity for profit when it sees it. Your sperm was not donated for free to overseas fertility clinics. It was sold, the price went crazy, and then the managers at the hospital

100

thought up a way to increase your prices still further. You see, it was not in dispute that you carried the gene necessary to have a chance of surviving the next plague, but no one knew about your general strength and quick-wittedness. Those attributes were just as important in the new world order. So a group of doctors devised a plan to throw you back into life with no warning, straight in at the deep end.'

'So it was you guys who set up the apartment for me after it lay empty for ten years?'

'It was not an easy assignment, but I think the results were satisfactory.'

'Satisfactory? My office was raided and set on fire. Cops chased me out of New York City. And Tania—'

I stopped myself there, ever wary of blabbing about Tania's crimes to a stranger.

'Tania shot those cops? Is that what you're about to say?'

So he knew. There was no point in hiding anything now. 'Yes. I guess so.'

'Would it surprise you to learn that she did no such thing?'

'Huh?'

'That whole sequence of events was set up by us. Tania and the police officers were all working for us. It was a scene that we devised to make you look strong and dependable. It's what the overseas buyers were hoping to see.'

'Overseas buyers?' I asked.

'Of your sperm. We set up everything to increase your desirability to our clients. It worked. The price tripled, and still we couldn't produce enough to meet demand. But we've noticed a bit of a decline, lately. It's not good to keep you indoors and immobile. The quality of the sperm

101

would be better if you lived a more normal life, got some sunshine, ate proper food. That was one of the reasons for waking you up.'

'But when Tania found me in New Jersey, was that a setup too? Is the underground movement not even real?'

'Oh, there is an underground all right, but they're not the sort of people you'd want to hang out with,' he explained. 'Tania and Pascal were charged with looking after you, making sure you came out of your adventures smiling, strong, healthy and valuable.'

'So they weren't arrested in the bunker? They're OK?' I asked.

'Haven't seen those two since the wrap party. I know it's only yesterday to you, but to me it's a long time ago. If they've looked after themselves, they'll be fine.'

I heard a rustling noise outside. Instinctively I sank lower into my odorous seat.

'What's that?' I asked.

Tang signalled for me to be silent. He crept on all fours across the floor and listened at the door. The sounds of footsteps outside were joined by voices.

'Shit,' he whispered. 'Looks like they're searching the grounds sooner than I expected.'

I held my breath, trying to suppress the noises made by my hyperactive lungs. I was still attempting such extremes of quietness when the door swung open with a force that knocked Tang onto his back. Two of the hospital's uniformed security guards ran into the hut: one dived on top of Tang while the other held me gently in place. I didn't resist. The energy cocktail inside me was diluted, its potency fading.

Tang was a fighter, however. In a blur of what appeared to be martial arts moves, he righted himself, sprang to his feet, parried and jabbed incessantly and forced his opponent to retreat towards the door. Seeing this, the other guard released me from his respectful grip and went to assist his colleague.

'Run for it!' shouted Tang as he took them both on.

I stood up and stepped away from them, closer to the door.

'Don't listen to him,' responded the guard who had just let me go. 'He's trying to sell you to the Chinese. Just wait where you are. You're lucky we found you in time.'

'They're lying!' countered Tang as he continued to fend off four arms with his two. 'Don't let them screw with your mind, Ignatius. It's corrupt management at the hospital that's selling you to the Chinese. I'm trying to save you.'

Tang's martial arts moves kept him busy, but were ultimately futile against these bulky guys. When Tang fell, both guards jumped onto him and kept their weight there. He was going nowhere.

'Run, Ignatius!' he shouted through a mouth distorted by being pushed into the floor. 'Find the strength inside of you and get the hell away from here.'

'No, Mr Inuus,' said my guard as I inched closer to freedom, 'we're here to protect you. Stay where you are.'

The guard sounded frustrated. He couldn't prevent me from moving away without lifting himself from Tang's back, which would give the doctor the leverage he would need to slither out of their grip. I didn't have a clue what to think or where to go. Were the guards deliberately confusing me, or was that what Tang had been doing all along?

'What is going on?' I cried, knowing a satisfactory answer could not be forthcoming so long as the guards and the doctor continued to accuse each other. 'I don't know you people. How can I trust any of you?'

'You gotta trust me, Ignatius,' mumbled Tang, his face now thoroughly embedded in the dust.

I paused and thought about it rapidly. My mind processed contradictory information and tried to resolve that which was irreconcilable. Logically, if Tang wanted to sell me overseas, he wouldn't encourage me to flee without him. I was of no value to him if I vanished. He had to be trustworthy on that basis. The security guards had to be bluffing.

A few subtle breaths recharged my blood. With no idea where I was, where I could go or how I would get there anyway, I charged outside towards an uncertain destiny. The odds were stacked against me, but I was kind of used to that. My status in life as a lone outcast was becoming irritatingly familiar.

Twenty yards from the hut were bushes and borders that marked the boundary of the hospital. I sought cover in the nearest one, and managed to get there before either of the guards emerged. Hiding and cunning were all I had. Outrunning anyone else would be impossible. Seconds later I saw, through the foliage, the legs of one of the guards. He was running fast, attempting to search for me in places much farther than I was able to reach, naïvely assuming me to be fitter than I was. When he was out of sight I stumbled to the next point of shelter, deaf to the screaming of my leg muscles, focused on nothing more than the need to find a place to hide for the next few minutes.

My refuge was to be a footbridge, a former safe pedestrian passage over a now defunct highway. Long weeds choked its base and made the cramped space beneath its lower steps a secluded haven. I fought my way through the grasses and curled up against a concrete foundation block.

I wondered if I would have agreed to this bizarre Seeding Project if I had been given the choice? The shallow, testosterone-fuelled part of my mind would have accepted the role unquestioningly if the hospital had supplied me with a buxom nurse to assist with the production of each sample. What kind of hetero guy wouldn't want a job like that? I wondered if that was the method they had used during my coma. Probably safer than something invasive like a syringe. But to take my sperm again and again, to spread it across the globe and use it to impregnate millions of women without my knowledge, that was a thought that I found highly unsettling.

My hideout didn't give me a view of the hut or the hospital. I wondered what had happened to Tang. I parted the weeds and stared back at the grounds of the hospital. Tang had broken free and was sprinting across the lawn. I suppressed a desire to reveal my location to him. My sense of isolation gave me a craving to shout at him, to stand and wave my arms. I didn't trust him, but my distrust of him was less than it was for anyone else in the vicinity. Damn I was lonely. I had no realistic escape prospects. I had to move out of the shadow of that bridge sooner or later, and someone would spot me and reel me in. Tang's prospects were not bright: with me in tow, they would be even less so. But he must have had some way of smuggling me out of the grounds. His plan wouldn't have finished in the hut. My best hopes lay in sticking with him.

I gave in to my emotions and screamed at him. He altered course and ran towards me, yanking me out from the weeds by the arm and holding me steady as we tottered down a short embankment to the abandoned road, both security guards gaining on us with every step.

'You ride?' Tang panted, pointing at a horse tied to a rusting road sign. Whether it was a fine stallion or an old nag fit only for the knacker's yard, I had no idea.

I shook my head. Horses terrified me. I'd been pony-trekking in my teens, and the horse had decided that I was so inept a rider that it would do its own thing, regardless of my attempts to persuade it otherwise. On seeing a fallen tree trunk across the path it had accelerated to a gallop and jumped the trunk while I held on for my life. When that incident failed to unseat me, the same horse then took it upon itself to walk underneath a branch that was exactly the height of its back, which left no room for me, of course. I was squashed between the horse and the branch and slowly rotated until I was upside-down and ready to fall off. I hadn't gone near a horse since that day.

Tang climbed aboard first and displayed incredible lifting power as he dragged me up behind him. The beast seemed comfortable enough with the two of us on its back.

'Hold tight,' he shouted over his shoulder. The command was superfluous, since I was squeezing him as tight as my tired arms would allow. As we cantered along the highway, the security guards skidded to a halt and abandoned the chase. When the road twisted out of sight of the hospital Tang veered up onto the bank and abandoned the cracked and partly overgrown road surface, heading directly into a wooded copse.

The environment was unfamiliar to me. It didn't resemble any part of New York or New Jersey that I'd ever visited before. Ten minutes and we were out of the woods and onto another old road. To our right was a river. I couldn't place it. Nothing seemed to fit the memories I had of the New York area.

Then I saw something and I knew. It peeked above the rooflines of the hotels and office buildings to my left. An obelisk. The Washington Monument. I had woken up not just in another year, but in another city.

'Where are you taking me?' I shouted over the thump of hooves.

'Far from here. You're not safe in Washington.'

'Does the President know about me?'

'President? That takes me back. No, Ignatius, there's no President any longer. We don't have the same kind of democracy that you probably remember.'

'What is there? A Prime Minister? Polit Bureau? A dictator?'

'To be honest, I'm not quite sure. Real power lies in the hands of those who control the issuing of text message challenges. They're the ones suppressing the population. And we don't think they're doing it from here any more. There isn't much else that we know of. It's all shady and behind the scenes and if anyone gets close to the truth you never hear from them again.'

I shuddered at the thought, even though the savage reality of the new political system had been plainly demonstrated to me already.

'So we don't vote?' I asked, somewhat incredulous.

'Not since the laws of nature — law of the jungle, whatever you call it – came into force. Power resides with those strong enough to hold it, or take it, or steal it.'

'Are you taking it?' I asked, cryptically.

He ignored me and spurred the horse on towards our destination. We crossed the Potomac River, keeping to a leafy strip of land on the other side that provided some degree of cover as we headed roughly south. Then I saw the sign that unnerved me. Ronald Reagan Washington National Airport. Had I made a spectacularly bad decision to trust this doctor? Was he about to deliver me to a waiting Chinese airplane and collect a sack full of money for his troubles? I decided to broach the subject from a tangent.

'We going to the airport?'

'Uhuh,' he replied, keeping the horse pointing in the right direction.

'I thought there were no more planes flying around?'

'No scheduled flights, no, but some individuals and governments have hidden stashes of aviation fuel, and when they can find a plane that's still serviceable you sometimes see them flying. It's rare.'

'So what are we doing here?' I asked.

'I have to get you as far away from Washington as possible. You're not safe here. My contacts have procured a rather special airplane for you.'

We threaded our way through a gap in the perimeter fence and cantered onto the end of the runway. It was cracked and sprouting weeds, suffering the same neglect as most of the roads I had seen, but it didn't look so bad that it was unusable. A white object shimmered at the far end. We had a long way to trot. My arms and my backside were sore. I clung on, trying to make sense of the white thing a mile down the runway and wondering if I was being a fool to go so willingly with this doctor. The haze cleared. There were wings. Wafer thin, high off the ground. The nose drooped oddly, its razor-sharp pinnacle aimed at the tarmac beneath it. It couldn't be. I squinted. The shape was unmistakable.

Concorde.

'You're going to help me escape on a Concorde?' I screamed, forgetting the pain and overwhelmed with boyish enthusiasm. Whether I trusted him or not, this doctor certainly had style. The aircraft was tinged with green here and there, as if it had been left standing for many years and hadn't received a full makeover before being reintroduced to service. The original British Airways livery had been over-painted in a clumsy fashion, displaying a flag that I didn't recognise. I could now hear the auxiliary power unit whining loudly at the rear of the plane. This long-retired beast had been revived and was ready to take to the skies once more, and my childhood ambition to fly in a Concorde was about to be realised.

Tang slowed the horse as we grew near to the supersonic jet, and turned to face me.

'They had to cannibalise three other Concordes to get this one in a fit state to fly,' he explained. 'Without more spare parts she won't have many flights left, and besides there won't be enough aviation fuel in storage anywhere.'

'But why Concorde?' I asked. 'Doesn't this bird drink more juice than any other jet?'

'It's not a matter of economics any longer,' Tang replied. 'The ability to out-run a military jet is a more pressing factor.'

'And is there still an air force?'

'Barely. But we have to be careful. How are you feeling? Those stimulants worn off?'

'Everything hurts like hell. Feel completely exhausted.'

He stopped the horse and climbed down. 'Come on down. I'll help you,' he said.

I fell into his arms, shattered and relieved to be on firm ground. 'Thank you,' I groaned.

He started rummaging inside his pockets and produced a syringe. 'I can't give you the same dosage this time, but I have a diluted version of my stimulant cocktail. Should be enough to take away those muscle pains, wake you up and keep you mobile.'

I nodded acquiescence. In my condition, I welcomed

anything that could make me feel better. He squeezed the contents of the needle into my forearm and I waited for the jolt of vivacity to strike me.

My peripheral vision was the first to go. It blurred and swirled, and as the edges closed in on my world I entered a deep sleep into which no dreams penetrated.

Chapter 11

I felt the turbulence before my eyes opened. It felt like driving over potholes in an unforgiving SUV, and the belt across my lap snapped tight repeatedly as the jolting superstructure of the airliner flicked up and down, rendering me weightless and then doubly heavy a moment later.

The seat next to me was vacant. I looked around and saw Doctor Tang seated several rows ahead of me, chatting and laughing with others. There was a pervasive smell of mildew, and I sensed that this was not the kind of flight that would offer a stewardess service. Outside the window was a blinding brightness, and as my pupils adjusted to the unfiltered light of the upper atmosphere I could see the curvature of the Earth and flashes of ocean beneath the clouds.

So we were flying over the sea. That wasn't good. Unless Tang planned to take me to a hideout in Hawaii, chances were that my destination did not lie within the United States. The doctor had betrayed me. There was no other explanation. I had been sold. I was a piece of meat, a commodity, a slave. It was highly likely that I would never see my home country again. I was bound for a different culture, a different language and lifestyle, a whole new beginning. I didn't see that I had any way to influence my destiny. I was going to have to reignite my passion for Chinese food and make the best of the latest crap that life had thrown in my face.

Or was I being unfair? Was I being unduly suspicious of this doctor? Perhaps he had sedated me by mistake? Or had done so deliberately in order to provide temporary relief to my suffering? Maybe there was a legitimate reason for flying over water? I knew that Concorde, in its heyday, had been forced to stick to maritime routes due to the damage and disturbance caused by its sonic boom. Such considerations hardly seemed relevant in today's harsh society, but I couldn't rule it out without speaking to Tang.

'Tang,' I called, trying to generate enough volume to over-ride the white noise of the aircraft and its ventilation systems. He paused his dialogue with his companions and looked back at me. 'Where are we going?' I asked, hoping against hope for an answer that would reassure me as to his intentions.

'Ah, that wore off fast,' he replied. 'You're tougher to knock out than I thought.' At that, he returned to his discussions and ignored me.

He hadn't answered my question, but I knew all I needed to know. When I tried to lift an arm to scratch my face, the situation was confirmed beyond doubt. I was tied to my seat. I was bound for a new life in China. Even if I hadn't been restrained, there was nothing I could do about it. It wasn't as if I could parachute down to earth or take control of the plane. There were five or six men seated around Tang, all eagerly participating in whatever discussion they were having. I was helpless, lashed to the cramped cabin of this elderly airliner.

I strained my neck to see behind me. A hundred seats, all empty. My dream of supersonic flight had been nothing like this lonely reality. The digital displays at the front of the cabin read Mach 2.0 at an altitude of 54,000 feet. We were flying faster and higher than most combat jets could manage. Tang had said that the United States still possessed the remnants of an air force, but even if that were true, there was nothing they could do to save me now.

With my eyes closed, trying to recharge my batteries before we landed, the first I knew that things were going to get far worse was the heavy footsteps that stamped down the central aisle, accompanied by a voice that I recognised.

'Iggy, stay put!' shouted Pascal. It wasn't as if I had any choice in the matter. He strode confidently past me, brandishing a semi-automatic gun, and placed himself at the front of the cabin from where his stunned captives could see him clearly. None of them appeared to be armed. This was their plane. They hadn't expected company. A woman's voice behind me caused them to turn around. Now I could see their faces for the first time. All appeared to be Chinese. I looked back at the female voice, too, noting with rather an excessive degree of excitement that Tania was standing in the aisle, holding an identical weapon to Pascal's.

'Tania,' I whispered, unable to restrain my enthusiasm for her presence on this flight.

'Not now,' she replied. 'Shush.'

As I leaned backwards to smile at her, I heard a staccato thudding noise. The cabin windows splatted with blood. I turned forwards again to see that Pascal had coldly and efficiently murdered everyone, including Doctor Tang.

Well, perhaps not entirely efficiently. I felt my ears pop. A sudden and extreme pressure change overwhelmed the cabin, accompanied by a hiss of escaping air. I tried swallowing, but the drop in pressure was too much for me. Wild headaches pulsed through my skull. I saw Pascal cover his ears, and Tania did likewise, whilst fixing her gaze upon Pascal with a withering look. His bullets had penetrated the skin of the aircraft. We were in trouble.

The turbulence had ended, but the rapid descent of the Concorde threw me hard against my lap belt once more. The digital cabin display showed the altitude dropping fast. 50,000 feet. 46,000 feet. 42,000 feet. Presumably the pilots were aware of the loss in cabin pressure and were instigating a dive to equalise pressure with the air outside, but they had a long way to go. We were still higher than the summit of Mount Everest, and there would not be enough oxygen to breathe if the relative vacuum outside the Concorde sucked all the air from the cabin before we had a chance to reach a safe altitude.

Tania ran towards me and put her hand on my shoulder. 'You all right?' she asked.

'I think so,' I replied. 'That Chinese doctor knocked me out. I think he was trying to sell me.'

'I know,' she said. 'We have our contacts. We were ready for this.'

'Where were you hiding?' I asked.

'The rear luggage compartment. There's no bags on this flight, so we hid in the rear compartment behind the galley, and cut our way through the bulkhead behind the trolleys.'

Pascal was banging on the cockpit door. There was no answer, as I knew there wouldn't be following the changes in pilots' practices that were instigated after 9/11. No pilot would now open their door, mid-flight, no matter what the emergency. Pascal was wasting his time. But I knew that if we landed in China, Pascal and Tania would be executed immediately.

Still the air in the cabin was draining faster than the pilots' ability to descend. 36,000 feet, read the sign, and my throat was dry and gasping.

'We need oxygen!' Tania screamed. 'Where are the masks?'

I looked at the lockers above me and expected plastic oxygen masks to drop, like they always showed in the safety briefings. But not this time. Getting this plane airworthy clearly didn't mean much beyond the basic mechanics needed for flight. Passenger safety systems had not been a priority for whoever had nurtured this plane out of its retirement.

Pascal opened lockers in desperation. He was coughing, staggering as if drunk, clumsily searching for the bottle of oxygen that he knew to be somewhere on board. Next to a stewardess's seat he found one, took a slug of gas from the face mask to reinvigorate himself, then passed it to Tania and then to me. We all took turns to breathe deeply, watching the altitude numbers decrease, helplessly wondering what fate had lined up for us.

Outside the window there was no more ocean. Through gaps in the grey, pregnant clouds I spotted land. Which land, I had no idea.

20,000 feet. We were now subsonic. I stayed focused on the fleeting flashes of land, wondering in which country I was about to die, and whether there was anyone there who would care.

12,000 feet. The rate of depressurisation slowed and then halted. We had lost all cabin air and pressure had now equalised with the air outside. I felt like I had gone ten rounds with Mike Tyson. My inner ears were howling, like they were suffering a massive attack of tinnitus. Each breath of oxygen from the tank helped to alleviate the symptoms, but there was no avoiding the discomfort that the leaking air had caused. I silently cursed Pascal's killing techniques while he cut the bonds that had me strapped to my seat.

The change in scenery caught Tania's attention. She looked with curious eyes at the greenery beneath us.

'Europe already?' she asked.

Pascal took a burst of oxygen before nodding his agreement.

'Wouldn't it be faster to fly over the Pacific to get to China?' I asked.

'We're about to crash and all you think about is route optimisation?' he said. 'Yes, Europe long way. Yes, Pacific faster,' he continued, addressing me like an idiot. 'Fuel stash in Munich. Not available in–'

'I got it,' I said, interrupting.

'We're not going to crash,' insisted Tania. 'Despite Pascal's reckless use of firearms, we've been descending in a controlled way. The pilots have full control. They won't fly any higher than this, and they'll either continue to the fuel store in Germany or look for somewhere to land.'

'They won't make Germany,' Pascal said.

'Why not?' I asked.

'When Concorde flies at this altitude it uses twice as much fuel. Too much drag. Our range will be cut short. We'll be landing well before Germany. My guess is we're coming down in France.'

'Shit,' said Tania.

'Why? What's wrong with France?'

'You don't want to be a stranger in France,' she replied, with a sigh.

The altimeter indicated that we were, indeed, holding a steady height. None of us was able to get a precise fix on our location from the visual clues available to us. I took

116

advantage of the moment of relative calm and my new-found freedom to visit the bathroom at the rear of the cabin. The one at the front was closer, but I had no desire to squeeze past those bodies that littered the route.

Inside the toilet cubicle I welled up with emotion. I wondered if I would ever harden to senseless slaughter, and I hoped that I wouldn't, for to lose the ability to be shocked at the ending of a human life was to lose one's own humanity.

The flight became bumpy once more. I guessed we had hit another patch of turbulence. The grab rails in the cubicle held me securely as the plane pitched and bucked uncomfortably. I considered making a rapid return to a seat and strapping myself in, but the plane suddenly entered a banked dive that gave me no option other than to stay put and hold tight. The G-force was almost more than I could resist. We banked left, then right, all the time falling swiftly from the sky. I heard the whine of the motors that lowered the landing gear. I sensed the nose pitching up to increase lift at low speeds. Somehow I didn't expect this to be a smooth landing. I braced for impact, wondering how long I needed to wait for the end.

I wasn't kept waiting for long.

Chapter 12

The wheels slammed hard into the ground with a squeal of rubber that was seamlessly subsumed into a cacophony of structural failure, of aluminium girders and panels stressing, snapping and exploding. My cubicle remained intact throughout those terrifying sounds, until finally the walls folded in on me and I was catapulted into an eerily silent daylight.

My nose was embedded in damp grass. It smelled sweet, but there was something else in the air. Wisps of smoke touched me and swam away, hinting at something, teasing me. I moved my neck and looked upwards. Black smoke drilled into the clear sky. The wreckage was burning.

I rolled sideways and sat up. My limbs were still attached. I was lucid and functioning, bruised, muddied and shocked – it could have been far worse. The ground on which I had landed was soggy, waterlogged. If I had been unconscious and face-down I might have drowned in an inch of water.

I could hear a woman screaming. I staggered to my feet and looked around. About a hundred feet away, Tania was dragging a body and yelling at it.

'Don't you fucking die on me, Pascal!' she shouted, pulling him clear of the smouldering fragments of aircraft before attempting to restart his heart. I joined her to see if I could help. It was clear from the expression frozen into

Pascal's eyes and from the colour of his lips that he was gone. Tania thudded his chest and blew loving air into his lungs until she had no more to give. She fell into my arms, sobbing at the callous cruelty of a universe that saves a person in one seat whilst terminating the life of someone sitting no more than two feet away.

With a piece of metal from the wreckage she began digging a hole.

'What are you doing?'

'I have to bury him,' she replied.

'We can't take a chance out in the open,' I told her. 'It'll take too long to dig a grave. People will have seen this plane come down. They'll be here before long and we don't know if they're going to be friendly.'

She threw the metal fragment down. With my arm around her waist, just as she had done to me when I had first evaded the police with her help in New York, I walked Tania away from the crash site, away from her lover, and away from the life she had known. She brought nothing of her old life with her. Just like me, she was born again into a strange world.

We climbed a stony hillside and sat beneath a ponderous evergreen tree, surveying the scene below us. There was no runway, no airport. The pilots had attempted to land on a reasonably flat meadow. Either they'd had even less fuel than we had thought, or Pascal's bullets had severed a hydraulic line which caused them eventually to lose control. Landing a plane that large and complex on grass was risky enough, but the soft ground would have caused the wheels to dig in and snap off. They never stood a chance.

'Do you think the pilots made it?' I asked.

She looked down the hillside at the steaming tangle of metal and shook her head. Already I could see figures approaching the site from the far side. Curious locals, it seemed to me, darting amongst the sections of fuselage, intent on snatching anything of value rather than attempting any kind of rescue.

I hated what had become of my world.

'We should go, before anyone spots us,' whispered Tania. She wiped the tears from her face and stood up. I took her hand and walked to the other side of the hill. When we were out of sight of the remains of the Concorde, we paused and looked at the new vista before us. 'I used to come to France in my youth,' she said. 'Camping holidays. And later as an au pair. Used to be able to speak the language. Bit rusty now. But it sure was a beautiful country.'

'Was?'

'Well, still is,' she replied. 'But no one in their right mind comes here now.'

'Has it become as bad as the States?' I wanted to know.

'In many ways, worse. The population is decimated and fragmented. Always seemed underpopulated, even at the turn of the century, but I think it's much worse now.'

'I mean the legal system.'

'There is no legal system here. That's what I heard. Local councils, or mayors, or mini-dictators control their own patch. Whoever was strongest in a town just took it over. They have their own fighting forces, trade systems, and rules. Central government lost its power. Now it's like the old mediaeval kingdoms are back.'

'Do they have those text messages and snipers to cull you if you fail?'

'They tried it, while there was still a semblance of centralised power, but it only lasted a year. That was when it was the most effective, anyway. After the regions and towns started breaking away, some of the more sophisticated of them opted for the more positive approach of selective breeding.'

'Is that a euphemism for what I think it is?' I asked.

'Yes, I am referring to your paternal services. France was a major customer.'

'So all that stuff Tang was telling me about my genes having a unique plague-resistance is true?'

'Sure is. You're a god-send and a menace. You're the cause of more trouble than you can possibly imagine and yet you might well prove to be the best thing that's ever happened to this planet. And I owe you a great deal.'

I sensed an attempt at a smile forming on her face beneath the dirt and the blood and the tears. I had no idea why she thought she owed me anything, when all I'd ever done was create havoc. I decided now was not the time to press the matter.

'We should keep moving,' I told her. 'I don't know how far I can get, but there's nothing for us here. We need to find shelter and water.'

She nodded. We walked down into the next valley, searching for a hamlet or a village that might offer a secluded barn or an abandoned house.

'Before we crashed, did you spot anything that might tell us which part of France we're in? Mountain ranges like the Pyrenees, perhaps?' I asked her.

'Iggy, we were kind of busy hijacking that jet and killing those assholes who wanted to abduct and sell you. It was a little too stressful for sightseeing.'

'I'm sorry,' I said. 'Just trying to work out some kind of plan.'

'You've already worked it out. Shelter and water. No need to think of anything else today. We've both been through enough. What do you think that is, over to the right?'

I looked where she was pointing. Parts of a building were visible, ancient-looking stone walls, nestled into a hillside, almost obscured by trees from our position. We altered course and made directly for it, hoping it would turn out to be more than just a mediaeval ruin. Occasionally it disappeared from our perspective altogether, but as we walked the final hundred yards the full magnificence of this structure became apparent. It was a chateau. Mediaeval, yes. Ruined, yes, but it looked as if parts of it had been restored or at least maintained in a habitable condition. Of its four turrets, three still had roofs in place, and only one was partially collapsed. Ominous cracks ran diagonally across the walls, oak lintels bowed with age and relentless pressure. Limestone bricks were missing in places, but there was double glazing in some of the windows. Sections of wall had been re-pointed. This was no palace, merely an ambitious renovation project that someone had started in the expectation of creating an impressive and characterful home out of what had once been a draughty and crumbling statement of mediaeval power. Excited and nervous in equal measure, we skulked closer to the iron gates that marked the entrance to its lands. Vines and ivy had grown rampantly over the stonework, creating an environment of great charm and grace, but also suggesting at least a couple of years of neglect or possibly even outright abandonment.

The gates were unlocked. I swung one of them open, cringing at the ear-piercing shriek of unoiled metal upon metal. I looked at Tania for encouragement, and she nodded that we should continue. I closed the gate behind us and led her to the rear of the property, looking for a window or service door that might permit a less secured, and less obvious, access for us.

Tania spotted the window to the basement before I did. It was only open an inch, but it was sufficient to get a grip and pull it fully up, allowing us space to slide in. I had a sense of déjà vu; somehow I had made a habit of climbing into abandoned cellars with this woman, only this time there was no squalor, no bad smells, and no need to hide from cops in pursuit. On the contrary, amid the vaulted arches of this cellar were brick recesses into which wine bottles were stored. Hundreds of them.

'Would madam like to see the wine list?' I asked, taking a couple of dusty bottles of red wine and offering them to Tania. She needed a drink badly, I could tell. 'Come on. Let's find the kitchen, get these things opened and get smashed.'

She nodded approval of my plan. She needed this. She deserved an evening with nothing to do but blot out the pain. And I needed a drink. I hadn't touched a drop in twelve months. As for the previous decade, the less said, the better. We followed the brick staircase up to the ground floor and opened a rustic door into a farmhouse-style kitchen. I was so intent upon finding a corkscrew to open the bottles in my hand that I didn't immediately register the presence of a decaying corpse upon the flagstone floor.

Mostly bones, in fact, intermingled with scraps of skin and torn clothing. Rat droppings were everywhere. The rodents had feasted well.

Tania turned away. She had seen enough death today. I pulled her gently by the hand into the hallway and through to a high-ceilinged drawing room furnished with antique sofas, coffee tables, paintings, and a stone fireplace large enough to hold a party in. The flagstone floor seemed well-worn and cold, but was softened by a threadbare rug. Checking first for signs of droppings, I helped her take a seat, held my breath, and returned to the kitchen. I was resolute that the scene of horror would not prevent me from finding a bottle opener and a couple of wine glasses. A minute later I returned to Tania with the items, and closed the door to shut out the stark reality that lay just a few feet away from us.

Tania examined the wine bottle after I had poured her an undignified amount.

'Languedoc,' she said. 'Do you think that's where we are?'

I looked at the other bottle. It was from the same region.

'Could be. There must be better ways to find out, though. Whoever used to live here would have had an address book, business cards, utility bills. I'll search around later. Right now it's enough to sit here and drink a toast. To Pascal.'

'To Pascal,' she echoed, adding, 'the stupid bastard. Why did he have to shoot through the fuselage?'

I'd been thinking the same thing, and I already had an answer. 'To save us,' I said.

'You really think so?'

'I think he span the wheel of fortune deliberately, knowing that it could backfire, but confident that it was the only way.'

'It's not what we planned,' said Tania. 'We were going to get the pilots to turn back.'

'And how were you going to do that through a locked and bullet-proof cockpit door?' I asked.

'Look, there wasn't much time to plan this rescue. We only heard about the flight at the last minute. We had to do something. There was no one else prepared to risk their neck for you. It wasn't a perfect plan, obviously. And if we'd ended up landing in China, or whatever is left of it, we would have stood no chance.'

'I'm sorry,' I said. 'I appreciate your bravery. Both of you.'

We downed the wine as if it were water. Intoxication came quickly to me. I had the resistance of a child. The alcohol kept me warm, but I could sense the temperature falling as darkness engulfed the hillside. Cold night air found its way to us down the vast chimney. A basket of logs, a bundle of kindling and a box of matches sat next to the fireplace, set carefully by the deceased owner for a fire that he or she would never get to enjoy. I piled the kindling and some logs in the hearth, enjoying the novelty of a brick and stone inglenook that was large enough for me to stand up in behind the mantel. From Tania's position she would only have seen my legs. The fire took at the first attempt. The flames would have little hope of combatting the cold stone walls that acted like a refrigerator, but the visual effect was comforting. I stood rubbing my hands in front of the crackling logs for a minute before returning to my chair.

'I miss my kids,' Tania said, somewhat out of the blue, as she stared into the flames.

'You have kids?' I said, mildly impressed that she had retained such a lithe figure despite motherhood.

'A boy and a girl. They were taken from me.'

'I'm so sorry,' I said. 'What are their names?'

'Bert and Scarlet. Twins. They would be three years old now.'

'Why were they taken away from you? Because you were part of the underground?'

'No, just standard procedure.'

'Can you contact them?' I asked, not really understanding what she meant by 'standard procedure'.

'No,' she sighed. 'Never.'

'Not even to let them know that their father has died?'

'Why would I need to do that?'

'Because of what happened today,' I said. 'Because of what happened to Pascal.'

'Pascal? Oh no, I think you have the wrong end of the stick,' she said. 'Pascal wasn't their father. We weren't even together when I had the twins.'

That seemed to be the end of the conversation, but several minutes and another glass of wine later she asked me an odd question.

'Iggy, did you ever wonder what motivated me to risk so much to save you?'

'Kind of.' I didn't like to say that I simply thought she must have been crazy to go to such extremes on my behalf. It would have sounded ungrateful.

'We are more profoundly linked than you realise, Iggy. I can't afford to let any harm come to you. And I'm pleased that our mission was successful, even though it cost Pascal his life.'

'You're pleased?'

'I'm delighted not to have to find my kids one day and admit to them that their father is dead.'

I was confused. She was making less and less sense. 'I thought you said Pascal wasn't their father?'

'He wasn't,' she said. 'You are.'

Chapter 13

Two million children, give or take a few hundred thousand, and it had meant surprisingly little to me. There was the initial shock, of course, but the rapidly unfolding events that had hurtled me on a one-way ticket to Europe had provided a complete distraction from the revelations of my prodigious paternity. Even now, as I sat by the fire contemplating the things Doctor Tang had told me, I still regarded them as intellectual concepts, mathematical abstractions, not cold facts. I also could not ignore the fact that Tang's subsequent actions had proven him to be less than trustworthy. If he had lied about his reason for evacuating me from the hospital, could he have lied about everything else? I had to accept the probability that he was correct about the reason for my induced comas, however. If I had not been repeatedly harvested for my sperm in order to strengthen the next generation of the human race, none of the ensuing events could possibly make any sense.

Given that I could feel no emotional attachment to my millions of offspring, why was it that when I looked into Tania's misty eyes I felt such a connection with her twins, *our* twins? Why did my stomach turn itself in knots when I thought about them? Bert and Scarlet. They had names. That made them real. I tried to picture how a montage of my face and Tania's might look, but mentally projecting our fusion on a young boy and then a young girl's face just didn't work out. I wasn't sure I would even be able to recognise them if I ever met them.

'Why is it standard procedure to take your children away?' I asked her.

'Parenting is too big a responsibility to leave to the parents,' she replied. 'The State decided it could do a better job, en masse. Been that way for years. One of their arguments is that with such a strong likelihood of a parent failing a random text message challenge at any moment, it made sense to bring the children up without them to start with. They call it boarding school, only it starts after just two months and continues until adulthood.'

'Why two months?'

'Breast is best,' she replied, with an attempt at a smile. 'Then it's off to the government schools for years of training, indoctrination, survival education and, rumour has it, child labour.'

'And that's with all children?' I asked.

'No, no. They wouldn't bother with that for all kids. It's only for yours.'

'You mean, all my kids in America are growing up without their mothers?'

She nodded.

I was furious. This political system was growing more detestable by the minute. But what I couldn't work out was why Tania would opt to have babies using my sperm if she knew this was what would happen to them.

'Why put yourself through this?' I asked.

'I had no choice,' she said. 'If you're selected at random to have IVF with you as the father, there is nothing you can do about it. But in a way I was glad. I didn't really want to bring children into this awful world, but if I had to, I wanted them to be yours.'

I thought that was sweet and affectionate, until I

remembered that she hadn't met me back then. She was referring to my genes, which would equip her twins with the resistance they would need to survive any future epidemics.

'So you weren't part of the underground movement then?' I asked.

'No. If I had been, they wouldn't have been able to pick me and make me have your babies. I had a job. An apartment. A social life. I was just a regular New Yorker.'

'I thought you were hiding in your old man's bunker?'

'At first, sure. When the shit hit the fan all over the world, I was down there, sitting it out, waiting for things to improve. When the food ran out, I rejoined what was left of society for a while.'

'What did you do before the plague?' I asked her.

'I was a dancer.'

'A dancer?'

'On Broadway. When I came out of the bunker and found the theatres closed I worked in a diner for a while, then when there wasn't enough spare food for restaurants and so on I got a job at the hospital where they were keeping you.'

'What did you do there?'

'Nothing medical, obviously. Even if I had been a doctor or a nurse, there wouldn't have been much for me to do. Society stopped taking care of the sick. Unless you were assessed as having a strong likelihood of a fast and sustainable recovery, no care would be provided. So I worked in the kitchens, preparing meals for the very few fortunate ones who weren't euthanized.'

'So why wasn't I killed off?'

'Because they spotted your potential at an early stage. Your progress through the disease was slower and less severe than normal. The safe option would have been to end your suffering and remove the risk you posed to other New Yorkers, but one doctor was convinced you were worthy of study. The disease was allowed to run its course.'

'I took years to recover, didn't I?'

'Looks like he made the right call, though.'

'Who was he?'

'I thought you knew? The doctor who saved you was Doctor Tang.'

I felt a lump in my throat. 'But Tang is the one who betrayed me,' I protested.

'Pascal had a theory about that,' she explained. 'He thinks Tang lobbied to save you in the first place, in order that he would eventually smuggle you across to China to help them rebuild their population.'

'And was Pascal working with you at the hospital?'

'No, Iggy. I didn't meet him until after my babies were taken away. That was when I started to think of ways to change things. Without democracy it's not easy, but history shows that it can be done. I hung out with groups of intellectuals: radicals, poets, musicians. None of them offered any serious solutions until I met Pascal. He was a man of action, not words. I fell for his charms instantly.'

'I'm so sorry. You must really miss him.'

'Turned out to be an asshole, Iggy. He was a man, after all. I never actually had him on an exclusive basis, if you know what I mean. I just figured I'd go along with things as they were, since all the old rules and conventions had gone out of the window after the plague. He wasn't perfect, but then neither was life, and I couldn't have everything, could I? We had our moments, sure, but I know he had plenty of other moments when I wasn't around. And now he's gone for ever, and none of it means anything now. He was a part of my life which has now passed, just like so many other parts. Parents, pets, children, lovers: they come, they go, and at the end of the day, all you can count on to be there for you is you.'

I considered reassuring her that I would always be there for her, but such a promise seemed empty and hopeless given my track record, and I still didn't feel I knew her well enough, despite our shared experiences of life and death, to be so presumptuous as to consider us friends. But I wanted badly to be her friend. She was all I had. I thought of a way to reinforce our connections.

'Is there really nothing we can do to get our kids back?' I asked her, tentatively stepping over the line by expressing our status as parents to the same children. I watched her expression to see if she recoiled from my proposed intrusion into her kids' lives, but her eyes gave away no discomfort or resentment at my use of the phrase.

'No one has ever done it,' she replied. 'It would be kidnap, punishable in the usual way. Not worth risking it. Better to take care of ourselves and try to be there for them when they eventually get sent out into the world. It might take us that many years to make it back to the States anyway.'

'Let's dream a little, Tania. You're someone who makes things happen. I've seen you achieve the impossible time and again. You're smart. You're bold. You've got the initiative to think on your feet. So let's imagine we can get back home quickly. Don't think about the practicalities, yet. Just assume it can be done. Taking our kids out of their State boarding school isn't an option because the law doesn't allow it. So what should we be trying to do?'

'Change the law,' she sighed, slowly exhaling every last drop of spent air from her lungs as if to underline her belief that such a change was impossible to implement.

131

'Not just that law,' I responded, bouncing forward in my seat and finding myself animated by idealist energy. 'Repeal the law of the jungle. End survival of the fittest. Bring back humanity. Stop those text messages. Heal the sick. Take care of the old. So what if there might be another plague in ten or twenty years? We might be pulverised by an asteroid in thirty. Or swallowed by a black hole in forty. Just because human life could end, doesn't mean we have to sacrifice our souls to try to buy some time. It isn't worth it. Living like this isn't living. What we have in America right now is Orwell on steroids. Those text messages are like having a god who punishes in real time instead of leaving it until you're dead anyway.'

'Those text messages were originally devised by scientists,' said Tania. 'They ran computer models to determine the most effective tests to weed out the less fit members of society. It was cold and inhuman, but at least it had a purpose. Ten years on and those scientists are gone. Whoever is behind the texts now are just sadists. They try not to make the tasks impossible, because that wouldn't be sporting, but they are always aiming for a fifty-fifty balance of probability between success and failure. Some of us reckon it's a huge gambling racket. They bet on who will live and who will die. As you say, they are gods, and they play with us for their sport.'

'They are people,' I said. 'They shit. They drink. They sleep and they die. If we can only find out where they are, I'm sure we can do something. If they can't be persuaded, they can be forced. Just wish I could get my head around what makes people turn so callous to the lives of others so quickly.'

'The Annihilation,' Tania said, sounding surprised. 'What else?' she asked, standing up. 'Gotta pee.'

She left the room in search of a bathroom while I pondered her use of the word 'annihilation'. I'd heard her use that word before. She had mentioned it a year earlier, but hadn't explained to me what it was. Now she seemed to assume that I knew. Somehow I was aware that it referred to more than the slaughter of a million people on Hainan Island in China, and part of me was reluctant to uncover the horrendous truth about the actual meaning of the word in this modern world. It seemed she was taking an excessively long time in finding a bathroom. I suspected that maybe the sanitation wasn't working and she had gone out to the garden instead. I hoped she hadn't come across any more bodies on her journey.

'Interesting house,' she commented, surprising me by returning through a different door to the one by which we had entered. In fact, I had no idea that a door even existed in that wall. It was flush with the wood panelling, disguised to blend in. When she closed it behind her, I could scarcely see the join.

I was more interested in reviving the conversation where she had left off, however.

'You were talking about annihilation,' I reminded her.

She could tell from the tone of my voice that I didn't understand what that word meant. I had to learn the truth eventually. She decided the moment was now.

'When people refer to the Annihilation,' she told me, 'it's similar to the way people used to refer to the Holocaust. It's odd that one word can sanitise and summarise so much, but it helps us as humans to cope with it and move on. I think some news channel or other coined the phrase to start with. They always like to give something a simple name, like 9/11 or Watergate.'

'Right,' I said, nodding. 'I get that. But just who was it that had to be annihilated? The Vietnamese? Burmese?

133

The islands of the Philippines?'

She took a deep breath before continuing. I tensed up, sensing my guesses were way off course.

'Look, Iggy, this was bad. Really heavy shit. Because despite all the precautions, travel restrictions, military-enforced lines of isolation that encompassed entire countries and regions, the plague kept spreading. Countries fell one after another, just like Americans used to think they would under the spread of Communism – the domino effect, and all that kind of crap. Only this domino effect was real, and it was heading our way. With no known defence against this plague, people starting talking about sending healthy people into space to wait it out, or into undersea colonies, or down the bottom of mine shafts. Any of those things might have saved a few dozen or even a few hundred, enough to start again, if they had a bit of luck on their side in the aftermath. But that meant the vast majority of the population would have to sit back and wait to catch the plague and die. It was coming for them, a few miles closer every day. This was not an acceptable situation, obviously. Leaders of those countries as yet clean of the disease held urgent talks in secret. Despicable deals were done at these meetings. Stomach churning plans were drawn up. If the plague did not stop itself, this shadowy conclave of leaders would take things into their own hands. They would initiate the Annihilation.'

Tania stopped and held out her wine glass. It was empty. I opened a second bottle and poured her another full serving, all the time thinking about the incredible world events that had passed me by as I lay fighting for my life in hospital.

'As if the Annihilation wasn't bad enough,' she continued, 'we later learned that it wasn't a spur of the

134

moment plan. It had actually been drawn up years before as a contingency against an unstoppable epidemic of any kind of disease. The investment in bio-weapons had already been made. The missiles that would carry this deadly cargo were already in place, waiting to be launched. Scientists had prepared toxins that would only affect humans. All plant and animal life would be unaffected, and buildings and technology would remain equally unharmed.'

'So those countries bordering Hainan were bio-nuked?' I asked.

'Think of it like a fire,' she said. 'Remember the Great Fire of London? 1667, I think it was. Ironically, it ended the Great Plague of 1666. They had no hosepipes, helicopters or any of our modern fire-fighting technology in those days. All they could do was to create a fire break in a circle around the affected area. Gunpowder was used to blow up a ring of buildings, creating a gap across which the fire was unable to spread. Those buildings were in perfect condition. They weren't on fire and their owners were pretty pissed to have them destroyed like that, but it was done in the interest of the greater good, which was to end the fire. And that, Iggy, is how the Annihilation was justified. Phase One created a fire break two hundred miles wide, surrounding all the affected areas on Earth, in which all human life was extinguished. It then poured its bio-poisons into the central area of that circle, ensuring no one remained alive, healthy or otherwise, within the zone of infection. It was done with no warning. It was completed within twenty-four hours of it starting. Those of us who were fortunate enough to live in the States just woke up one morning to learn that a third of the planet's population had just been sacrificed in order to save the rest of us. The Annihilation wasn't just a few million people, Iggy. This was two billion souls. The majority hadn't even yet caught the plague.'

'Two billion?' I gawped the words, too stunned to make an intelligent comment.

'Two billion,' she repeated. 'I'm talking about almost the whole of Asia. We lost China, Japan, parts of Russia, half of India, Hong Kong, Taiwan, Indonesia, New Zealand and Australia, Pakistan, Afghanistan, and dozens of other places that now I can't even remember. How horrible is that? So many wiped out that we can't even remember them.'

I poured another glass of wine for myself. Her story put all of my troubles into perspective. The plague and humanity's attempts to control it had cost the planet a third of its population. Now I thought I understood the apparent reversing of technological progress.

'So is that why there's no Internet? No gasoline? No food in the stores?'

'Exactly. When we wiped out Asia, we lost the factories that make everything we needed for modern life. We lost the expertise of China's manufacturing sector. For too long we'd been dependent on them. It was all down to greed. We just had to save a buck or two, and when the supply of those things ceased, we were screwed. We couldn't fill the void, especially with the new political fanaticism for pruning the population, forcing everyone to transfer down their job to the lowest common denominator.'

'But we have factories in the States,' I pointed out. 'Couldn't they fill the void?'

'Remember the iPhone?' she asked. 'Great American product. Trouble was, the components came from all over the world. Without chips, circuits, sensors and screens, production stopped. Boeing jets – all assembled in the

Boeing factory, but from components built elsewhere. The same with car manufacture. No country made every part of their cars. The technology was too complex. Without imported electronics, production ceased. Even oil refining and power generation depended on machinery and technology that was no longer available. The shrinking populations helped to stretch the remaining supplies a little longer, but ultimately they had to run out. We couldn't replace the skills and factories at a fast enough rate to combat the inevitable decline, and the further we regressed, the more important it became to get on with supplying people with the basic necessities and forget about those luxuries upon which we used to depend. Without people to spare for research and development, progress halted. Time ran backwards. We fell back into the Dark Ages. And here we are.'

'So it's kind of the same story here in Europe, too?'

'Precisely. Population decline. No imports. Not enough food. A downward spiral in health, wealth and morality.'

That night I slept in my chair while Tania slept on the sofa beside me. Two lonely souls, lost and adrift in life, comforted only by our proximity. I quietly yearned to snuggle against her on that sofa, to have that security of holding her tight against me, but despite her revelations about Pascal it seemed inappropriate to make any kind of personal advance so soon after his demise. By keeping my distance I gave her the kind of respect that she probably no longer expected. I was a relic from the old days and it felt good to maintain that small connection to the standards and values with which I grew up.

Unfortunately my values were not shared by the people who used a log to ram open the front door of the chateau at first light.

Chapter 14

It wasn't the intruders who woke me, however. It was Tania, shaking me vigorously and slapping my face in an effort to disperse the intense dreams into which I had sunk as my exhausted body indulged in a few hours of precious healing. When I looked into her concerned eyes I couldn't for a moment understand how she was making the noises I could hear. There were heavy footsteps, shouts, slamming doors.

Then I realised.

'Follow me,' she whispered, helping me to my feet. 'They've started to search the house.'

She pushed open the doorway in the panelling through which she had made a surreptitious entry to the room the previous evening. I glanced back at the other door that led to the hallway, and could see the handle beginning to turn. We were out of time. We slipped through the opening and closed it silently behind us.

The void was almost devoid of light, save for the merest hint of a glow that leaked through narrow splits in ancient oak planks to our sides. I was pressed tight against Tania's chest, our two hearts now beating as one.

'We have to go up,' she said, directly into my ear with a soft breath that tickled the side of my face.

As my pupils adjusted, I was able to make out a steep set of stone steps in front of us, barely eighteen inches wide, squeezed inside the thick-set interior walls of the chateau.

'You found this last night?' I asked, as I followed her upwards.

'Shush,' she replied.

I shut up. There was no need to question her. Once again, she had been my miracle. At the top of the staircase we were hemmed in on all sides, forcing another tight intimacy to which I had no objection. With the lightest touch, Tania pushed a section of oak boards. It swung open to reveal a horizontal passage between the upstairs rooms. More cracks of light along the sides hinted at discrete doorways into the bedrooms. Something told me that whoever designed this castle had a penchant for night-based, bedroom-swapping antics.

The voices were still audible to us, leaking through the oak panels from the rooms and corridors of the chateau. They definitely sounded French to me, although I wasn't sufficiently conversant with the language to be sure that it was us they were shouting about.

Tania took my hand and led me along the dusty passage. I didn't know what made her think this hidden space was any safer than the secret staircase. It seemed to me that we were vulnerable to discovery in either part. This void was secret, but not that hard to find.

We turned a right angle corner to find our progress halted by a dead end. No light penetrated here. The walls surrounding us were made of stone. There was a distinct chill in here, and an unmistakable odour of antiquity.

'What now?' I whispered, astonished at how much my soft voice could echo within these walls.

She put my hand against the wall in front of us. I felt the texture of rough iron.

'Ladder,' she replied. 'Climb it.'

I squeezed around her and climbed the rungs, aware

that this was a new strain on my weakened frame and one which would further test my limited endurance. I was also concerned that she was climbing beneath me without waiting for me to complete my ascent. The iron ladder wobbled loosely and disconcertingly. A few more steps and I reached a gap in the ceiling. I climbed through it into a circular room. A thick wooden hatch lay on the floor. Light streaked in through vertical arrow slits spaced evenly around the room's circumference. We had made it to one of the turrets. I looked for another entrance, but could find nothing else. The floor, walls and vaulted ceiling were made of solid stone.

'Help me,' whispered Tania, now inside the room with me and attempting to lift the iron ladder up through its guide rails. I took one side of it while she took the other, and together we slid the ladder up. She lowered the oak hatch across the hole in the floor through which we had climbed and bolted it with a steel bar.

'Panic room,' she said, now speaking in a normal volume. Clearly she considered us to be untouchable in here.

'You mean like my friend Dan has behind his library?'

'Precisely,' she replied. 'Only this is the real deal. The original mediaeval version. Found it last night while I was exploring this place. With the ladder up and the hatch closed, there's no way in or out of here.'

We were physically safe, but there were no supplies and no electronic monitoring systems. However, through the arrow slits in the walls we could see down to the grounds of the chateau, giving me my first glimpse of the intruders and the true horror of their intentions.

'What the hell is that?' I asked Tania. She looked through the slit towards the front of the chateau where I had spotted the unusual goings-on. 'What are they doing in that oak tree?'

'Shit,' she replied. 'They mean business. This could be a long siege.'

I looked out again. On a level branch of the tree someone had prepared a noose and was checking the knot.

'They don't like strangers round here, I guess,' I told her. 'How do you think they found us?'

'Must be the fire,' she replied. 'Even though we lit it after dark, it was a clear night. Someone must have seen the smoke from the chimney lit against the moon or the stars.'

'Or maybe it was still smouldering in the morning,' I said, still staring out at the noose. 'It doesn't matter now. There's an angry mob after our blood.'

Tania lay down in the dust and stretched her limbs.

'Care to join me?' she asked.

'What are you doing?'

'There's no way they're going to find us. Watching them won't make them leave any faster. Come and lie next to me.'

She patted the stone floor. It didn't look comfortable, but it made sense to rest while we had no other option anyway. As I lay down beside her she slid an arm behind my neck, cradling me. I tentatively placed my hand on her waist. She grabbed it and pulled it all the way around her, forcing us into a tighter embrace. My nose pressed against hers. She smiled and kissed me, before spinning the other way and leaving me huddled against her back in a cosy and affectionate spoon position. I closed my eyes and enjoyed her warmth, feeling protected by her aura of love.

The shouts and sounds of excitement coming from outside didn't prevent me from falling asleep. I felt safe with Tania. I relaxed and sank back into the realm of dreams that my overstretched body needed me to occupy in order to give it time to repair itself.

This time I was the one to wake first. Tania was asleep in my arms, too far gone to notice the black smoke that obscured the light from the arrow slits and began to fill our hiding place with acrid particles. The intruders couldn't reach us, but they could smoke us out.

'Shit,' she said, as soon as her eyes opened. 'They don't give up easily, do they?'

'Who the hell are these people? Why do they want to kill us?'

'Fear of strangers,' she replied. 'Ever since the plague hit, no one welcomes strangers to their towns any more. Visitors spread the disease. In the more rural backwaters it's common for paranoia of new faces to lead to witch hunts and summary executions. This is not a good time to be a backpacker, Iggy.'

More smoke began to enter the room. I noticed it starting also to seep in through the gaps in the oak hatch in the floor.

'How in hell are we gonna get anywhere if we can't show our faces without being crucified?' I asked.

'I've been giving that a lot of thought,' Tania replied.

'And what did you come up with?'

'Only that I'll need to give it a hell of a lot more thought. Come on. We have to get out of here.'

'But they have nooses waiting in the garden,' I protested. 'They'll hang us as soon as we step outside.'

'It's a chance we'll have to take. This chateau is burning. We'll cook in here if we don't suffocate first. Our only chance is to get out of the building.'

She unbolted the hatch and swung it fully open. A plume of smoke billowed into our faces from the passage below. I reached up and grabbed the iron ladder, sliding it down through its brackets.

'There won't be time to think,' I said. 'We might have to hold our breath.'

'We will,' she agreed. 'Move fast before we choke. They won't be in the building now it's on fire. They'll be waiting outside with their trap.'

I slid down the ladder first, into what felt like a sauna, and held my hands out to guide Tania down into the blackness. Sweat erupted all over my body. I tried to breathe normally, but the smoke tickled my lungs and triggered a coughing fit. There were no flames as yet in the hidden passages, but it was obvious that most of the surrounding rooms were ablaze. We stumbled down the steps and arrived back at the living room.

Now it was clear what the intruders had done. All of the chairs were burning vigorously. They must have targeted beds and chairs throughout the chateau to smoke us out. I was still coughing, and dropped to my knees to find cleaner air.

'Let's get down to the cellars,' I suggested. 'Nothing flammable down there.'

When Tania crawled beside me and pointed at the open door to the hallway, I recognised the flaw in my idea. Someone had dragged an antique sofa across the doorway, and it was burning fiercely. We wouldn't be able to move it or climb over it whilst it was in that state.

I watched Tania crawl to the door and close it. Maybe that would buy us some time by keeping out the smoke from that sofa, but we still had enough of a problem with the fires that burned where we were. Without apparent haste, she returned to my spot in the centre of the room.

I recognised a determined look on her face. She had a plan.

'They don't know for sure that we're here,' she said.

I hadn't considered that. It seemed a foregone conclusion

that they knew, given the efforts they had made to find us and kill us, but when I thought about it I realised that their evidence was circumstantial. They couldn't be certain that we hadn't already fled before their arrival.

'So what?' I asked Tania, failing to see the point of her remark.

'Open the secret door in the panelling,' she continued. 'Wedge it open with something.'

It seemed insane, but I had no better ideas. I opened it and dragged a coffee table across to prevent it from closing again.

'You've just made a chimney,' she said.

'But there's already a chimney,' I pointed out. 'A huge one.'

'Which is doing nothing, because the smoke is higher than the opening of the fireplace. This door provides the smoke somewhere to go. Up the stairs, along the passage, through the hatch and into the turret room, and then out through the arrow slits. Basic physics. Fresh air will come in through the chimney, and smoke will go out through that door.'

I got it. This was a fireplace in reverse. The room was burning, the fireplace wasn't. Therefore the flow of smoke and air was back to front. I now knew where this was heading. I crawled to the fireplace and stood up behind the mantel. The air in here was clear. The embers of last night's fire in the hearth were now cold and dead. Tania joined me and held my hand.

'Good call,' I told her. 'You think if we can wait it out in here, they'll give up on us?'

'If the whole chateau burns down, this fireplace will still be standing. The hotter the fire burns out there, the more cold air it will draw down this chimney and past us, keeping us cool.'

'You think it will get to that?' I asked. The stone walls were so thick I couldn't envisage a fire being able to destroy this chateau completely.

'No,' she replied. 'I think the furnishings will burn themselves out.'

'Shame we didn't get a chance to find out where we are.'

'Didn't we? You don't really think I spent all that time peeing last night, do you?'

'Well, peeing and messing about in secret passages. What else?'

'I found the library, Iggy. Thousands of books. All of which I ignored and went straight for the telephone. Underneath it was an old copy of the Yellow Pages directory. I know where we are.'

'Where?'

'Vitrac,' she replied.

Where the hell was Vitrac? I'd never heard of it. Didn't even sound French.

'The wine was a red herring. We're further north than the Languedoc. This region is the Dordogne.'

Still nothing of what she said meant anything to me. Landing in the Dordogne could have been wonderful news or a disaster – I didn't know what to think.

'You know anything about this place?' I asked. 'Is there anywhere safe we can go before the locals round us up with pitchforks and burn us at the stake?'

'They're already doing that, aren't they? If we can bluff them into thinking we've either escaped or been roasted in here, we should be able to travel undetected, as long as we follow sensible rules.'

'Which are?'

'No fires. No movement in daylight. And no kissing in public.'

'How about in private?' I asked.

She kissed me quickly.

'I think I can allow that,' she replied.

'But where should we go?' I asked.

'Home, of course. Back to the States.'

'I can't go back to the States. Society sucks there. Everything I ever valued has gone. It's just too dangerous.'

'But I have to go back, Iggy. My children are there. Our children.'

'What's the point? You won't be able to see them for at least fifteen years.'

She slapped me. I came to my senses.

'I'm sorry,' I said. 'I didn't mean it to come out like that. It's just that with everything being so shitty out there, people being tested and shot for failure all the time, it's not exactly a desirable place to be. You need to stay alive for your kids. What are your chances of surviving that long if you go back?'

'We're not exactly being treated like visiting VIPs in this country, Iggy. Things have changed. Life is cheap. Deal with it.'

I didn't want to argue with her. She was all I had. The last thing I wanted was for us to part company in this unwelcoming land.

'Say we try to make it back across the Atlantic,' I said, playing along with her wishes for now, 'how are we going to do it?'

'I don't know,' she replied. 'Look, we're inland,' she said. 'Pascal fired his gun after we crossed the ocean and hit landfall. Our descent happened entirely over France. So we're probably at least a hundred miles from the Atlantic coast. There are boats at Bordeaux. Maybe we can sail back?'

'You know anything about sailing?'

She shook her head.

'Me neither.'

I crouched down to look at the progress of the fires in the room. There were three main blazes, consisting of the sofa and two armchairs. Another fire had broken out on the fabric of a lampshade, but it had already run its course. The ceiling was completely obscured by an impenetrable fog, but the air inside our fireplace was still comfortable to breathe, drawn constantly from outside by the vacuum created by flames hungry for oxygen.

'Look, Tania, I want to help you all I can. When we make it out of here we'll find somewhere that's safe for us. We'll settle, learn what's going down around here, maybe find our niche and give it a few years for things to get better back home.'

'How is it going to get better unless someone makes it better, Iggy?'

'All I'm saying,' I said, 'is that we shouldn't rush this. If we need to learn how to sail, we take our time and get it right. If we need to hire someone to help us, we find enough gold or wine or whatever people will barter with. Crossing the ocean is a full-on expedition now. We won't be passengers. We'll need supplies, we'll have to navigate by the stars, we'll have to face towering waves with no hope of rescue if things go tits up. Planning and preparing something like that takes years. And while all that essential stuff is happening, who knows, maybe things will get better back home, anyway?'

'You can't sit and wait for things to happen,' she replied. 'When you want change you have to go and make it happen. You have to use the power within you to change the world.'

'I can't change the world. Nobody can.'

'I'm a nobody,' she said. 'And so are you.'

'Ha. You got me there,' I conceded.

'And you have already made small changes to the world. Just by being yourself. Every time things in history have changed greatly, for better or worse, it's been inspired, led, provoked or prodded by one person. We are all born equal, Iggy. Any one of us can be that person. The opportunity awaits anyone who chooses to take it.'

I had to admit she was inspiring. She had a charisma that I found hard to resist. She had a magnetic personality that I would blindly follow anywhere. I was hooked and she was a health hazard. Because whilst she was right that revolutions had always been brought about under the leadership of individuals, for every successful coup in history there were probably hundreds of failures. Those were the activists and revolutionaries forgotten by history. Killed in their attempt. Or thrown in jail to rot. I didn't want to follow that destiny. I wasn't the heroic type. Sure I wanted things to get better, but like most lazy-ass types I wanted someone else to get their hands dirty to make it so.

'Honestly, Tania, what can a guy like me achieve? I'm not a freedom fighter. I'm not a politician. I'm just a regular Joe six-pack who fell down the rabbit hole and ended up in Narnia.'

'Wonderland, idiot.'

'Whatever.'

'Anyway, Iggy, you are a freedom fighter. You've already fought for your own freedom. You've been inventive, you've been tough. You've come through against the odds. You're the kind of guy who can make a difference.'

'But what do you think it takes to end the current regime?' I asked her.

'It takes someone who has the brains and the balls to find who has been pulling the levers, where they base themselves, and throw them out on their asses and start doing a better job.'

'You make it sound like a walk in the park.'

'It's no harder than the life I've had to lead every day for the past few years,' she said.

She was right. I stood silently for some minutes, thinking about her ideas. It was unlikely that we'd even make it to the coast, let alone all the way to America. That put any plans we made for after our return to our homeland firmly into the realms of fantasy. And who was I to deny a girl her fantasy?

We stood in that fireplace for three uncomfortable hours. Finally, the flames in the living room died back. The furniture was reduced to ashes, along with the curtains, rugs and paintings, but the flagstone floor had resisted the spread of the fire, and the ceiling was sufficiently high to avoid suffering anything more serious than a layer of black tar.

Tania stepped out into the charred room first.

'Keep away from the window,' I whispered, following her.

The air was heavy, rich in flavour. Reminded me of pubs in the days before the smoking ban. My concern about anyone seeing us through the window appeared to be unfounded. The glass had remained intact, but was stained dark grey and offered only limited transparency.

We listened for voices. The grounds outside were silent. It seemed likely that we had been abandoned to our fate. The xenophobic mob had dispersed, but we still had to find a safe way out of the smouldering castle. I opened the main door to the hallway. The blazing sofa that had earlier blocked our path was now a pile of sooty sticks. We jumped it and threaded our way past various pieces of smoking detritus towards a back door. The smoke damage made it impossible to see out through its glass panes, but I foolhardily prepared to put my shoulder against it and push.

'No,' she said, stopping me. 'They could be waiting outside. We need a visual to be confident.'

'But all the windows are blackened. We can't see out anywhere.'

'Not every room has windows,' she replied. 'Remember the arrow slits in the turret?'

'Of course. I can see three sides of the chateau from in there. Wait here,' I told her. 'I'll be right back.'

I retraced my steps back to the drawing room, climbed the hidden staircase and found the iron ladder still in place at the end of the narrow passage. Everything was warm and sticky to the touch, and as I climbed the ladder I had to grip especially tight to prevent my fingers slipping off the rungs. I entered the turret space via the hatch and peered out through each arrow slit in turn. The day was bright and I had an unobstructed view of much of the gardens and the surrounding lands. I could see the hanging noose, swaying nonchalantly in the breeze. No one was near to it, or, more importantly, in it.

The picture was the same from other angles. Plenty of signs of recent disturbance, but no one had stuck around. I felt reassured and began to make my way back down. I was in the narrow passageway between the bedroom walls when I heard a woman scream.

Chapter 15

I froze to the spot. There was nothing I could do. Tania was in trouble, but I was powerless to help. I was unarmed and trapped in an unfit body that felt close to collapse. If I went charging downstairs to where I had left Tania, I would run straight into their trap and would suffer the same fate as her. So I climbed back up the ladder towards the turret. The weight of my guilt made the ascent doubly hard.

To appease myself, I ran through various scenarios in my mind. They might have killed her already, in which case there was nothing I could have done. Or they might take her into the grounds to hang her from the noose, which would give me the opportunity to spy how many of them I was up against, and would buy me enough time to run through the house in search of something that could be wielded at them. I thought of the heavy iron accessories next to the fireplace in the drawing room: one of them was a poker, a mildly ornate rod of metal with a spike at one end. Not quite a sword and not quite a spear, but nevertheless something to fear when caught at the business end of it. And when I looked through the arrow slits towards the shouts I could hear from outside, I realised to my considerable relief that neither scenario had taken place. Amid a huddle of five or six men dressed in dark brown robes, Tania was being spirited away from the chateau. I never glimpsed her face. She looked resolutely ahead, never back towards the turret in which I was hiding. She knew better than to imply that she had not been alone.

I had to move. In a few seconds the group of kidnappers would be out of sight. If I lost them, Tania would be gone for ever. I'd been separated from her too often. No more. I skimmed down the slippery ladder, skidded along the dark passage, ran down the steps into the drawing room and remembered to pick up the metal poker. Then I was out through the back door to the gardens. From the side of the chateau I could look down towards the road. The huddle of heads moved ponderously. Keeping up with them would not pose a challenge. I no longer felt the need to run, a decision for which my muscles were thankful. With the weighty weapon in my hands I felt less vulnerable, and I practised swinging it and jabbing it as I walked at their slow pace, keeping fifty feet behind them and on the other side of an overgrown and neglected farmer's hedgerow at the side of the road.

The route twisted through the hills for a mile or two. Occasionally I glimpsed a wide river flowing through a veil of willow trees, almost parallel to the road. For the first time, I saw a road sign. Vitrac Port. Tania had been correct. We had reached the edge of the village. This was a problem for me. I couldn't trail them through a populated area in daylight. I would have to hold back, and hope that somehow I might be able to track her down at a later date. It didn't seem too promising.

But the group of kidnappers turned as one to the left before we reached the first buildings, and scrambled down to the river. I hid behind a tree and waited to see what they would do next.

At first they did nothing. The group, still huddled tight

with Tania in the centre, stood beside the river. Tania made no noise. There was no conversation.

The boat arrived: shabby, varnish peeling, built from planks that looked as if they had seen better days, rowed by two men dressed in similar brown robes to those who had captured Tania. From my vantage point they looked like monks. It was certainly a strange new world if monks had become prone to kidnapping.

They loaded Tania and themselves on board, looking precariously overloaded. I wondered if she might have the sense to rock the boat and throw them all into the river, and I resolved to be there for her should she instigate such an attempt before they reached the other side.

But they were not crossing the river. When I stood with my ankles in the cool flowing water, I saw a bridge just a few feet away. If they merely needed to cross they could have used that. They obviously intended to travel along the river for some distance, and that gave me an idea. Rivers flowed to the sea. We could make our escape to the ocean by floating down the river. No power needed, no noise, and we could do it all during the hours of darkness. I just needed to remove her from the grasp of these odd monks.

The rowing boat moved as slowly as they had walked. It was almost as if all of their movements were constrained by reverence. I splashed along the bank, keeping my distance without losing sight of them. The river meandered left and right, flowing peacefully. In another age it would have been a paradise for kayaking. In parts, the river bank was blocked by foliage and I had no option other than to wade into deeper water and swim a short distance to the next section of bank. The first time this happened, I nearly drowned trying to hold on to my fireplace weapon, and I reluctantly dropped it into the water at the next deep stretch. I was always conscious of making too much noise by splashing, and the strain of trying to see but not be seen started to give me a headache. Why had Tania done nothing to instigate a capsize and escape in the ensuing chaos? She had to realise I would be tailing her and wouldn't simply abandon her to her fate.

After what seemed like a mile or so of river passage, the boat crossed to the far side. I crouched low and watched it tie up at a rickety-looking wooden dock. The monks and Tania climbed out. Behind them was a steep hill, and where one side of it had been eroded by the river over millions of years there were now vertical limestone cliffs, pocked with caves and irregular overhangs and protrusions. And perched at the top of these cliffs was an extensive stone structure, some kind of mediaeval defensive position at the crest of the hill. Maybe a castle. Maybe even a monastery. The latter fitted my perception of Tania's captors.

They appeared to be walking along a narrow path towards the base of the cliffs. I couldn't see where the path went: it passed behind a tree and then stopped. To my astonishment, the monks and Tania failed to emerge from behind that same tree. It was time to swim across.

The current in the centre of the river was stronger than I was expecting. Instead of cutting across in a straight line, I found I was marking a tangent, heading for a landfall at least a hundred yards further downstream than I was aiming for. I knew better than to fight the current. In my condition, I would only have wasted my strength and gotten into trouble. Far better to accept the unplanned destination and deal with it when I got there.

When I crawled, gasping for oxygen, onto the gravelly bank on the far side, I was so far down the river that the wooden dock and the adjacent footpath were out of sight, around a corner. I rolled on to my back and lay there, panting, barely coping with the over-exertion through which I had just put myself. On this side of the river I was more exposed. The bank was wide and open, and I risked being spotted at any moment. Ignoring the pain in my lungs and the desperate demands of my body for rest, I hauled myself up on my feet and started jogging for cover, looking for signs of the path along which Tania had vanished.

There seemed nothing special about this path when I found it. Stony here and there, muddy in parts, well-worn over hundreds, if not thousands, of years. I forced myself to keep running, imagining I was on the final mile of the New York marathon, turning that magical corner into Central Park and the finish line, smothering the pain with the joy and love of the crowds and using up every last bit of *va-va-voom* that I possessed.

Somehow I found the strength I needed. I climbed the path towards the tree where I had last spotted Tania. My observation of it from across the river had been wrong: the path did not end, it merely changed direction.

The path turned into the cliff itself. I gawped at the opening. It was a comfortable size, organic, yet with a suggestion that it had been augmented by human hands. I stepped inside. The cavern was unlit and uneven underfoot. Tania had to be in here. I would have seen her if she had gone anywhere else.

Stalactites brushed against my head. Cool water dripped onto me. My eyes adjusted gradually, but any additional sight they provided was negated by my progress further into the hill which took me away from my one source of light. The foolhardiness of my venture struck me: there could be a hole in the floor of the cave system that would plunge me dozens of feet onto an unforgiving and razor sharp stalagmite. But I had to follow Tania's trail; I had to take my chances. My compromise was to use my hands to take firm grips on the natural features of the cave as I passed them. It was like a horizontal rock climb. I always tried to be connected securely to something before attempting to move forwards.

A thought struck me. There ought to be a well-worn path through this cave. It would be easy to follow if I could find it. I crawled around until my finger sank into fine gravel. This had to be it. I remained on my knees and groped forwards, confident that the gravel path provided a safe passage through the cave system. It probably dated back to happier times, when it would have served as a tourist attraction for the area.

Progress became harder. I realised I was crawling up a steep incline. Then I hit a concrete step. And another. An entire staircase had been set into the cave. I looked up. There was a chink of light, maybe twenty feet above me. I rose to my feet and ascended the steps towards it.

A wooden door, so ancient I could see through the gaps in the planks, and – beyond it – a cloister. I was in the heart of the monastery. No one was in view. I pushed the door open just far enough to be able to squeeze out into the daylight.

It was completely deserted. I listened for voices, chants, bells, any sign of human life, but could detect only my frightened heartbeat, yearning to find a less-exposed position. With no further clues as to Tania's location my only option was a systematic search. I pushed open the first door I came to. Inside were bare limestone walls that seemed damp with sweat. I left it and tried the next one. It opened into a spacious corridor, lined with suits of armour, dusty tapestries, and a rack of brown hooded capes. I really didn't know what I thought I was going to be able to do in this ancient monastic fortress. The moment someone spotted me I would surely be captured and killed. The solution to that was not to be seen: I took one of the monk's robes from its hook and wrapped myself within it. I felt invisible. I could now search more closely, with a reduced likelihood of arousing suspicion.

Unless someone attempted to engage me in conversation, of course. And that is precisely what happened.

I had no idea of what the words meant. The tone of his voice did not seem aggressive, however. It seemed a monk had entered the corridor behind me and was asking me a question.

I turned round to face him. Without looking closely at me, he repeated the same words. I puffed my cheeks and mimed a chewing action, then pointed at my mouth and shook my head. The sign language for 'can't talk, I'm eating' was international. He should get the message.

He didn't. The man strode towards me, repeating the question with a heightened urgency in his voice. I didn't know whether to run, or hit him, or to continue to play mute. Surely he would recognise me as a stranger as he strolled closer? I backed off, maintaining our mutual separation of about twenty feet. That ought to do it.

The monk stopped. I breathed easy. But there was a breeze on my neck. I felt it all the more because I was soaked right through. Only it wasn't a breeze. There was a repulsive odour carried in that air. Someone was standing immediately behind me.

I looked to the sides for a way out. There was one doorway and I ran through it. Right into the group of kidnappers who had taken Tania.

Chapter 16

'Thanks for rescuing me,' Tania said.

I couldn't see her, but it was obvious that she was in the adjacent subterranean holding cell. Some might have called it a dungeon, but it didn't have the rats and the chains and the straw on the floor that you'd expect from a dungeon. Despite the antiquity of the building above, these rooms had been fitted out in more recent years: I had the benefit of a toilet and basin in the corner, a bed and a desk, plus a small Picasso-style chair. Not exactly the Hilton, but perfectly adequate accommodation.

'I didn't rescue you,' I replied.

'I was being sarcastic, dummy.'

'Are you hurt, Tania?' I asked, ignoring her wit.

'Don't worry about me. I probably gave them more bruises than they gave me.'

'How's your cell?'

'My cell? This isn't a cell, Iggy.'

'What is it?'

'I'm in a monk's bedroom. Only without the monk, obviously. These people like to keep things simple.'

'Who are these guys?' I asked her.

'Some kind of warrior monks,' she replied. 'They're not the ones who originally stormed our castle. They didn't set up the noose in the gardens. The crazy mob were the ordinary locals. The paranoid farmers. I don't really know what role the monks have, but they seem to be acting like some kind of police force, stepping in to resolve complicated situations.'

'Like the arrival of you and me?'

'Exactly.'

'Did they say anything about what they'll do to us?'

She said nothing. I took a gulp, automatically assuming her silence to imply the promise of a very grave outcome for us both.

'Did you hear me?' I called out again.

'Shut up,' she replied. 'Someone's coming.'

I heard voices and footsteps approaching. Talking to Tania had partially assuaged my fears. These were the good guys. Maybe they were pissed that we'd damaged their crops by crashing a Concorde into their fields. Maybe we were in trouble for raiding a little wine from the abandoned chateau. It was nothing that a little charisma and bonding couldn't fix. We just needed to get them on our side. Tania's door was unlocked, and seconds later mine opened, too. A monk stood there and motioned for me to follow him.

'Hi,' I said, holding out my hand and forcing a tone of civility towards these assholes that I was absolutely not feeling within. 'How's it going?'

He kept his hands by his sides and repeated the nod of the head in the direction that he wished me to go. Tania was already walking next to another monk. I wasn't tethered or cuffed, and in theory I could have run away, but the risk of losing sight of Tania again was too great.

I started walking.

The grey stone floor of the corridor echoed under our reluctant feet. Sunshine burned through occasional slits in the upper walls, but generally the space was shadowy and gloomy. We climbed a set of spiral steps and passed through an arched doorway into our destination.

A courtroom.

Not in the modern sense like I'd seen on *Boston Legal*. This looked like the refectory of the monastery, converted in haste by rearranging the tables into a U-shape. Severe-looking monks sat around the outer edges of these tables, and raised slightly above them, in the centre at the far end, was their equivalent of Judge Judy. An elderly woman, the sole female in the room apart from Tania, dressed in the same brown robes as the men, but marked as different by a red sash. So this was a group of monks led by a woman. Things certainly had changed.

The diffused light that shone through the stained-glass windows was enhanced by burning candles on iron candelabras. I felt as if we'd tumbled through a time warp and landed in the Dark Ages.

Tania and I were made to stand in the middle of the room, visible to everyone. We had no chairs to sit on and no pulpit or lectern against which we could lean. And, I realised as the full gravity of our situation sunk in, we had no legal representation, no idea of the charges and insufficient knowledge of their language.

A monk stood and addressed the old woman. I assumed he was explaining the circumstances of our arrival and capture. She nodded, listening carefully and eyeing us with the same curiosity that a visitor to a zoo observes an animal in a cage.

'Your names,' she said in almost impeccable English.

I glanced at Tania, momentarily considering inventing a false name. It wasn't as if we'd been travelling with passports, after all.

'Tania Burton,' she stated, calmly and clearly. Someone wrote it down with a pencil.

'Ignatius Inuus,' I said, wondering if the court's scribe had the faintest idea how to spell my name.

'You have been brought to the court of Domme to answer the charges that you did enter the domain of Vitrac and Domme without permission or legal justification. This domain has a zero tolerance policy against outsiders entering our lands. The local people wanted to execute you both immediately. We are fair and reasonable, however. We brought you here to permit you the opportunity to answer the charges against you. I should warn you that execution may be the most likely outcome. No one has ever entered our lands and been permitted to live. The villagers are outside these walls now, waiting for our verdict, itching to carry out the executions on our behalf. How do you plead?'

We both mumbled words to the effect of 'not guilty'. I found it hard to accept the authority of this kangaroo court, but I didn't think it would help my situation to question or criticise their right to hold this trial.

The monk who had made the initial address to the judge now spoke some more. I had no clue what he was saying. The old woman nodded and listened patiently before translating for our benefit.

'The prosecution has made the case that you were found in the Chateau de Belet, two kilometres inside the private and regulated domain of Vitrac and Domme. Have you anything to say in your defence?'

'For Christ's sake, we crash-landed here!' I screamed, amid rising panic at the direction this trial seemed inevitably to be taking.

Tania looked at me sternly, silently reprimanding my choice of words. I'd forgotten that this was a religious institution.

'We were on a jet plane that had technical problems. We were forced to make an emergency landing,' said Tania. 'I'm sorry the pilots chose your territory to make their landing, but they did and they're dead now, so we can't ask them why they did it. We are the only survivors. We were passengers. We had no say over where we landed. We have no wish to stay here, we don't request any of your resources, and if you let us leave we will travel back to the United States and forget all about this.'

'Right,' I said.

The judge shook her head. We were not doing well.

'An interesting defence,' she said, 'but it does not negate your illegal presence here. I sentence you both to be handed to the people of the village so that they may mete out the level of justice that they see fit.'

'No!' shouted Tania. 'Let us go. We don't want any trouble!'

'Take them outside,' said the judge.

A huddle of monks moved as one towards us. Meanwhile the scribe approached the old lady with his piece of paper and whispered in her ear.

Tania and I were surrounded, nudged towards an exit route.

'Wait!' shouted the judge. We all stopped and faced her. 'The male. Your name again, please.'

'Ignatius Inuus,' I repeated for her.

She whispered something to the scribe. He nodded. She looked back at me.

'Is this true?' she asked.

'Guess so,' I replied, not really understanding her point.

'You have immunity to the plague?'

'Guilty as hell,' I told her.

'And you are the father of the new race?'

'That's me,' I said.

'The court is dismissed,' she said.

There were dissenting tones amid the mumbles of the

monks as they left the chamber, but any forcefulness or aggression against us ceased. I was incredulous. Had my fame been sufficient to ensure our freedom? Tania smiled at me. Then she threw her arms around me, no longer caring to respect the twisted version of the institution from which we were now free to leave.

Our celebrations proved to be premature, however. There were shouts in the main hallway. Heavy feet were running in our direction. The mob had broken in.

A line of monks held them back for a moment while the judge attempted to address them, but such was their fervour that they would not be silent. These people were intent on meting out their own justice and I had no intention of waiting to find out what that would entail. I took Tania's hand and dragged her through the door farthest away from the crowd. The line of monks was busted. The raging peasants were on our tail.

I slammed the door shut behind us, but there was no visible means of securing it. We were in a corridor, and to one side was a line of high windows that I recognised. On the other side of them was the cloister into which I had emerged from the cave system. We tore to the far end, rounded a corner and found a dead end. There was no doorway into the cloister from here, and the crazy guys were gaining on us. We had no way back.

'Jump up, and I'll push you over,' I told Tania, pointing up at the open window. It started about five feet off the ground.

'But how will you get up? You'll never make it.'

'Just do it.'

She launched herself high enough for me to grab the soles of her feet. I thrust her higher, giving her sufficient momentum to pull herself through the window and out into the cloister.

I was screwed. There must have been twenty local guys, each holding knives or home-made spears. The absence of guns was reassuring. I guessed it had something to do with the supply of ammunition. Once it was gone, it was gone.

'Run to the cave!' I shouted to Tania through the window.

'What about you?' she screamed.

'I, I don't know. Just go.'

The mob slowed. They approached cautiously, as if unsure whether I had any weapons secreted within my clothing. I resigned myself to my fate.

'Iggy!' shouted Tania. She was still there, refusing to abandon me even though there was nothing she could do physically to help me. 'Repeat after me: *j'ai la peste*. You got that? *J'ai la peste.*'

What was she thinking? Had she gone insane? This was no time for French lessons.

'Huh?' I shouted back.

'*J'ai la peste!*' she screamed, desperately. 'Shout it at them, Iggy. *J'ai la peste.*'

'*J'ai la peste,*' I said, nervously and softly at first. The men in the front of the mob ceased shuffling towards me and stopped. '*J'ai la peste,*' I repeated, much louder this time. The entire mob arrested their progress.

'Keep saying it!' called Tania.

'*J'ai la peste! J'ai la peste!*' I yelled.

The mob came no closer. Those at the rear turned and ran in the opposite direction. It was no more than a second or two before the rest of them span on their heels and sprinted the other way.

Without really understanding what had just happened, I followed them for a short distance, slipping out into the cloister at the earliest opportunity. Tania was at the entrance to the cave.

'Come on,' she said. 'Don't think we should stick around.

We scrambled and crawled through the cave and emerged on the path overlooking the river. A rock landed with a disturbing thud on the path next to me. I looked up, suspecting a rockslide. People were leaning over a rampart high above, at the edge of the village. They began throwing rocks, bricks and stones at us. I felt a burning sensation as a stone glanced off my shoulder.

'Shit!' I shouted.

There was no need for us to discuss the ensuing escape plan. We had no other options. We ran as one down the path towards the river. The row boat was still there, tied with a single rope to the wooden dock. We were out of range of all but the most determined rock throwers. A brick crashed through an adjacent tree, snapping a branch clean in two. I untied the rope and we climbed in. Tania sat at the stern, and I took up a position on the central bench from where I could row. A rock landed just in front of the boat, causing a plume of displaced water to splash over us. I pushed us away from the dock, towards the middle of the river. One last stone came whistling at us. I cringed helplessly, hoping for it to miss. Another second and we would be out of range. There was a small explosion. Shards of wood sprayed around us. The stone had penetrated the bottom of the boat, halfway between where Tania was seated and my feet. The clear water of the river began to seep through a jagged hole.

I had to ignore it. I set the oars in their rowlocks and rowed for our lives. Every stroke was harder than the last, as every inch of water added pounds of weight to the boat. Tania began scooping it out with her hands, but it was so ineffective that she quickly tried something more imaginative. She ripped off her top and stuffed it into the hole. Our rate of sinking slowed. I rowed harder than ever and, carried by the flow of the river as much as by my efforts, the hilltop fortress of Domme receded from view.

Tania continued her scooping efforts. It was a battle she could now win.

'What does *j'ai la peste* mean?' I asked her, in between short breaths.

'You didn't know?' she replied, sounding astonished. 'I thought you said it beautifully, as if you meant it.'

'Meant what?'

'It means "I have the plague".'

Chapter 17

A few miles downstream we switched the leaky boat for a kayak. We'd found it sitting, upturned, on the river bank, apparently abandoned. A brief inspection of its aluminium hull suggested it would give us a drier ride than we had previously experienced. I was prepared to let the row boat float downstream without us, but Tania had a better idea.

'Leave the row boat here on the bank,' she said. 'They might find it and assume we're on foot now. That will stop anyone searching for us downriver.'

'Like it,' I said. 'But we need to hang on to the oars. Don't see any paddles with this kayak.'

She grabbed her jacket from the hole where it had provided a reasonable service as a bung, and helped me to set the kayak into the water. We climbed inside, holding one oar each. This time Tania sat in front and I took the rear seat. My shoulder was bloodied and hurting like hell, and I didn't want Tania worrying about it by having to stare at it throughout our journey. After a few minutes of zig-zagging across the water, we found our co-ordination and kept the kayak pointing straight down the centre of the river.

'This is the Dordogne river,' Tania announced, looking back over her shoulder.

'How can you tell that?' I asked.

'Saw a sign. But this is good. I hoped we were on this one.'

'How come?'

'The Dordogne leads to the Atlantic coast. Bound to be lots of boats there. And downhill all the way.'

'Look, we're too exposed here. I think we should lay up somewhere until nightfall. Find some shelter, then head off under cover of darkness.'

She looked back at me and nodded agreement. The choice of where to stop was easy to make. At the next bend in the wide and lazy Dordogne was an island, thickly wooded and offering the chance to hide the kayak and ourselves with minimal risk of discovery. I jumped out and dragged the kayak with Tania still seated. When it was stable on the sand, she climbed out and helped me to carry it into the clump of trees. I sat next to her on the damp ferns that grew all over the island's interior. She must have noticed how I winced from the pain in my shoulder, because she shuffled around behind me and started fussing with the wound, trying to clean it.

'You were lucky with that stone,' she whispered into my ear. 'Another couple of inches to the side and it would have gone into your skull. You just took a glancing blow. It hasn't cut very deep. Mostly grazing. You'll be fine.'

'I'd like to stick around to feel it healing,' I said. 'Please don't put me in another coma while it gets better!'

She laughed, and hugged me gently.

'I think we should spend the afternoon naked,' she said, without expression or passion.

If I had been drinking something I would have choked.

'How come?' I asked.

'We're both covered in dirt and blood and God knows what else. We should clean ourselves and our clothes in the river, hang up our things to dry, and only put them on in the evening when we're ready to head off. Right now we stick out a mile as strangers anywhere we go. At least if we're clean and less stinky we might have a chance of not attracting so much attention. And clean people offer a less intriguing scent to local dogs.'

I shrugged. I had no counter-argument to her logic. The surrounding lands were rural, largely uninhabited. All we could see from our island were trees and fields. It wouldn't be taking too much of a risk to jump into the water for a few minutes to wash our clothes and ourselves.

'You go first,' I said. 'I'll keep a lookout in case you need to make a quick retreat.'

'I know what you'll be looking at,' she quipped. 'Don't worry. I don't expect you to be a saint. You've waited eleven years, after all.'

She took off her shoes and waded into the water, fully dressed. While I scanned for signs of humans approaching she took off her clothes one at a time and scrubbed them in the river, before emerging onto the bank completely naked and carrying a wet bundle. I took some of the items and helped her to wring out the water before hanging them to dry from a tree.

Before I could take a proper look at her, she ushered me back to the river and partially hid herself behind a tree from where she could be my lookout. I scrubbed myself and my clothes, and felt more comfortable and energised as a result.

'Get down!' she shouted, just as I was about to return to shore.

I ducked below the water, holding my bundle of clothes tightly to my chest. I hadn't seen anyone, but I had to trust my companion completely. With just my eyes and nose above the water line I scanned left and right. And then I spotted them. Two children skipping along a track that bordered one of the fields adjacent to the river. They hadn't seen us and weren't looking in our direction.

It was difficult to ascertain their ages from such a distance, but I doubted that they could have been older than four or five. A mother then followed, some distance behind, struggling to keep up with their enthusiastic pace. It made me think. Could they be mine? Was it possible that I had encountered the first of my many offspring?

Such reflections would have to wait. Any contact with strangers had to be avoided. Keeping low in the water, I reversed away from them, making my way to the other side of our tiny island. With a dense cover of the trees between myself and the family I exited the water and met up with Tania amongst the ferns. We hung my clothes next to hers on the tree and then stood awkwardly, Adam and Eve, chilly and embarrassed. We tried not to stare at each other but with nothing else to distract our eyes we had little choice.

Tania made a modest effort to cover herself with her arms for the first few minutes, as did I, but we soon accepted the futility of such modesty.

'For god's sake, Iggy, I'm cold. Come here and give me a hug,' she ordered, holding out her arms to embrace me, and revealing the full magnificence of her body. No artificial enhancements, no overly-toned muscles, just the natural beauty, curves and stretch marks of a mother in her early thirties.

I walked towards her and self-consciously held out my arms too. Looking down at myself, I mumbled, 'You gotta remember, that water was cold.'

She laughed and took me in her arms, taking care not to rub her hands on my sore shoulder.

Making love in the ferns that afternoon changed me. I had only ever done it in bed or in a car before. Rolling naked with Tania in the mud and the weeds and the leaves was a more powerful sexual experience than I had ever encountered. The intense entwinement with nature somehow boosted the sensations and the excitement. Nothing was sanitised. We were two animals, uninhibited and wild. Unstoppable.

By the time we were done, the sun was beginning to dip towards the hills. Soon we would have to leave our miniature paradise and face a perilous journey into the unknown. I had suffered greatly these past few years. I had been deprived of all the normal things that should have been part of my life. But now I had known Tania none of those losses seemed to matter. Her physical presence and contact held me in a healing aura. It was too soon to be thinking such things, but I truly felt that I had fallen in love.

Checking for any other strangers, we cleansed ourselves once more in the river and returned to the trees to shake ourselves dry and put on our clothes. They were still damp, but the freshness was unmistakable.

Dusk had arrived. It was time to resume our journey.

The kayak slid silently through the water, needing only the lightest of strokes with the oars just to keep it pointing the right way. I was in high spirits. With Tania on my side I was invincible. We had tackled everything this twisted world could throw at us, and we had come through. As night took over the valley of the Dordogne, I felt confident. We were more than two individuals. We were a team.

The night was cloudy and starless. We floated on a river that became as invisible as the sandy shores, muddy banks and stone bridges around us. I couldn't even see Tania's silhouette two feet in front of me. After several accidental bumps into unseen obstacles and brushes with the soft, dangling branches of willow trees, we learned to navigate by tuning our ears to the sounds of the water, ensuring that there was an equal balance of river noises in both ears at all times. Any imbalance usually meant we had veered to one side. There was no sense of time, no sense of distance. It was as if we were stationary and the world simply turned beneath us.

'Those kids we saw today,' I said. 'You don't think, do you ...?'

'No, Iggy. I don't think. France devolved into hundreds of mini-states years ago. When that happened they lost centres of excellence, medical services, law enforcement, food distribution, all that kind of stuff. Hospitals capable of providing IVF services now only exist in the major cities. I don't think rural backwaters like this would have been major customers for your unique exports. So don't even think about it.'

She was right, but that didn't stop me thinking about it. And I carried on thinking about it right up until we hit the first set of rapids.

It began with a sickening downward lurch. Gravity let go of me for a moment, and my stomach moved up to my chest.

'Shit, what was that?' I called out.

'Like I said,' she replied, 'downhill all the way.'

'Hope there are no more of them. Not sure my stomach can take it. Makes me seasick.'

Contrary to my wishes, the river held plenty more whitewater sections in store for us. These were not the kind of extreme rapids where people would wear lifejackets and helmets and hurtle down them in big rafts on the understanding that they would have a fifty-fifty chance of making it to the other end in one piece, but when you can't see the turbulence ahead it makes the slightest unexpected motion completely terrifying. Not

172

knowing which way to steer, and having no clue as to when the river will flatten out again, makes for an uncomfortable ride.

'If we get thrown out, try to keep hold of the canoe,' said Tania. 'If we lose our grip, it will float downstream and we won't be able to find it.'

'Right.'

Once more we attuned our ears, this time not caring about grounding the kayak on the sands in the shallows of the river, but listening out for each set of rapids that filled the quiet night with a roar that would envelope us, throw us around and then spit us out into calmer waters on the other side. We must have been through three or four of these in quick succession before we hit the one that was too much for us.

The roar of the angry waters was more intense this time. We braced ourselves and started paddling backwards, as we had attempted previously, in order to slow our pace through the rocks and the funnels of accelerated water. The kayak smashed into a rock with a jolt and a bang that could easily be heard above the noise of the river. We were thrown sideways into the fast and twisting waters, sucked downstream and bounced over smooth – but nevertheless painful – boulders. Holding on to the kayak was impossible. It was as much as we could do to keep our heads above water. Despite an average depth of probably no more than two feet, the river bottom was too slippery and the current too strong to be able to stand up. We had to go with the flow, occasionally shouting each other's names for reassurance, and answering whenever there seemed to be enough breath to spare. Finally the river slowed and became once more the innocent, benevolent entity that it had initially pretended to be. I dragged myself, breathless, to the shore and listened for Tania.

Hearing nothing, I threw away any sense of caution and shouted her name.

'Tania!'

There was no reply. I stood up and shook myself like a wet dog. I couldn't see where the land finished and the river began, and to spot Tania in amongst the infinite blackness was impossible. I shouted again and stood still, listening for a response.

The voice was weak: like she was almost a mile away, on the other side of the river. It was possible that she had found land on the opposite bank, but it couldn't be that wide. I held my breath and listened again.

'This is almost a lake!' I heard her shout.

'Huh?'

'I'm on the other side,' she continued.

'How can it turn into a lake? I thought you said this river went to the sea?'

'It does. They must have put in a dam before the sea. The river is much wider here. It's too much to swim. One of us needs to find a boat to get across to the other. Then we'll need to proceed on foot.'

'A dam?' I repeated. 'In that case, keep walking. Forget about boats. Stay on the shore, and when we get to the dam I'll cross over to you.'

'Iggy?'

'Yes?'

'This section of river could get even wider,' she said. 'We won't be able to see or hear each other, maybe for hours. We won't know if the other is in trouble. So I just want you to know that I don't regret a minute of our adventure. Being with you was amazing. And if you make it home without me, please look up our kids and tell them mummy loved them.'

I felt a lump in my throat. There wasn't time for sentimentality.

'Sure,' I croaked. 'Come on, let's do this. See you soon, I promise.'

I started the long and lonely trek around the bloated river. After about an hour, the clouds parted and my path was lit by a reticent moon and a patchy collection of stars. I gazed out across the shining black lake, hoping to see a hint of Tania on the other side, but she had vanished into the night. I pressed on, negotiating complicated detours whenever my path was blocked by fences or untended hedgerows. I thought about Tania, alone on the other side of the water, and hoped she was making unhindered progress. I thought about her kids: having two was special; it meant so much more than the ridiculous notion of having two million of them. What were their names? Scarlet and Bert. Not my first choice of names, but then if it were up to me to name all of my babies I'd have run out of original names after the first few thousand. I would have been forced to call one of the boys Bert and one of the girls Scarlet eventually. Probably several times over. Sharing this historic connection with Tania was profoundly meaningful. We had kids together. I was crazy about her. We were a family ... but only, I realised, in my fantasies. Some serious changes would have to take place in America before we could bring those kids home. Some kind of revolution was essential.

Despite her inspiring words, I didn't think I was the kind of guy to bring about a new political order. That didn't mean I shouldn't strive for it, though – maybe find others to take the lead, put the right team in place. Use my fame or notoriety or whatever it was I seemed to have to push people in the right direction.

A line of arches emerged from the gloom, spanning the

full width of the river. Not a dam, but a bridge. I clambered up the steep bank and climbed a brick wall. I was standing on a disused railroad, its rusty rails steadily disappearing beneath the weeds like an unintended copy of New York's High Line park. I walked across the bridge, and from the centre I could see the dam, about fifty yards further downstream. This was no Hoover Dam, but it would have presented a challenging obstacle for our kayak, had we still possessed it.

I reached the other riverbank and looked into the murky night for any sign of Tania. My biggest fear was that she would have walked past the railway bridge and attempted to cross the dam, leaving us both on opposite sides of the water again. A feeling of tiredness washed over me as I waited for her. The adrenaline was gone and I was empty. I hadn't eaten in ages. I was dehydrated. I needed to rest. I closed my eyes, just for a moment, giving in to their demands.

'Iggy!' I heard, whispered sharply into my ear. 'There's a light coming this way. We have to get out of here.'

'Tania?' I opened my tired eyes and saw the vague resemblance of my miracle woman.

'Get up,' she continued. 'We have to move.'

'I just closed my eyes for a minute,' I said, struggling to my feet.

'A minute? I've been standing guard over you for two hours. You were out cold.'

'I was?' I asked, ashamed of my weakness.

'I had to let you sleep. You've been through so much. But come with me. Someone's over there with a lantern. I don't like it.'

I looked where she was pointing. A weak light swung left and right, suggesting it was being held to light the way of someone out walking.

'We need to get away from the bridge,' I whispered. 'This is the only crossing for miles.'

She sighed. In my semi-awake state, I was virtually repeating her instruction and thinking it was my idea. We moved away from the bridge, seeking shelter far from the approaching light. A section of ancient, crumbling stone wall was perfect. We dived behind it and waited for the nocturnal traveller to pass.

It was only when the glow from the lantern could be seen illuminating the underneath of the leaves above us that I felt the overpowering urge to sneeze. There was little notice. My mouth erupted faster than I was able to move my hand towards it to muffle the sound. The sneeze echoed off the wall in front of us and disappeared into the valley. I heard voices reacting to my incompetence: at least two voices, maybe three. We lay low, hoping the problem would go away, but the travellers were curious. They split up and walked to both ends of the wall at once. The weak glow of the lantern appeared to our right, and another voice cried out to our left. We were trapped.

I saw Tania rise slowly to her feet with her hands in the air. I followed her moves.

'It's them,' said the man with the lamp.

'I didn't expect to find them this easily,' said the other.

This didn't make sense. These guys spoke with American accents. They were wearing khaki and black coloured clothes. They couldn't have come from the monastery at Domme.

'You're more than sixty miles from the crash site,' said the lamp carrier. 'At this radius we thought we'd never catch you. You can stand easy, Mr Inuus. We're here to take you home.'

I lowered my arms. It seemed too good to be true.

Tania's body posture also suggested a deep suspicion of our companions.

'OK, who are you guys?' I asked, faking a confident tone in my voice.

'Smith,' said the lamp man.

'Jones,' said the other.

Tania rolled her eyes. They obviously hadn't gone to very much trouble to think of their pseudonyms. I looked at their faces: Smith seemed early thirties, Jones was in his twenties. They had short hair, verging on crew cuts. They looked like they worked out. Everything was pointing to military men. Smith confirmed my theory.

'Marines,' he said. 'You're too valuable to the United States. We have to bring you back from France.'

'What am I, Private Ryan?' I asked.

'Might as well be for all the trouble you've caused us,' said Jones.

'Who's your friend?' asked Smith.

I sensed Tania shaking her head next to me, but I didn't need to look. I knew she distrusted these guys and wouldn't want to be named.

'Are you Tania Burton?' asked Jones.

She made no response.

'Sure looks like her,' said Smith. 'Ma'am, you're a hero. You could be up for a medal for your part in saving Inuus.'

'I am?' she asked, surprised.

'You guys did the job that we should have done,' explained Jones. 'You foiled the kidnapping. There's a lot of people back home wanting to shake your hand.'

Still she appeared unconvinced, and I could tell she was considering whether to attempt to run away. But I had seen the guns holstered on their waists, and I was pretty certain she had, too. We wouldn't get far against those. Besides, if this was a genuine rescue mission, we would be mad not to go along with it. I was aware that it would bring us back to the heart of the corrupt and amoral political system that had filled the vacuum in America these past few years, but if we were going to crack that system and get Tania's kids back, we needed to take advantage of the chance of a safe passage back across the Atlantic.

'Follow us,' said Smith, walking back towards the bridge and keying something into the kind of electronic location device that I didn't expect to see any more.

'How did you guys get to France so quick?' I asked, struggling to keep up with the pace of men who were better fed and more muscular than me.

The distant thud-thud of rotor blades negated the need for them to answer that question, at least for now. As the shadowy shape came in to land on a level field adjacent to the Dordogne river, I could see other lights moving towards us from several directions.

'Other marines?' asked Tania.

The lights were moving fast. Then we heard the sound of horses' hooves, clattering along the road at high speed. They would be with us very soon.

'No,' said Smith. 'Local farmers on horseback. Already killed four of our men. Quick. Into the chopper.'

The four of us piled into the loud beast. The inside was cramped and utilitarian, all unnecessary weight and comfort stripped out to maximise fuel economy. We sat on the floor and held on to webbing straps as the helicopter took off over the heads of the approaching horsemen. I could hear the clatter as stones and spears hit the body of the aircraft. The small window in the side door cracked upon being impacted by a small rock. I winced and cowered from this intrusion into our flying refuge. Moments later we were high enough to be out of range of the primitive weapons wielded below us. Our rescuers relaxed and high-fived each other. Tania was still emotionless. I wondered if we had made the biggest mistake of our lives.

'Where are we going now?' I shouted above the engine noise.

'Carrier,' replied Smith. 'Just over the horizon off the coast at Bordeaux, out of sight of the locals.'

'I didn't think you guys had any hardware like that still in service,' said Tania, with a notable hint of accusation and suspicion in her voice.

'Believe me, it's nothing impressive,' said Jones. 'It's the only one left, and we only manage to keep it going because it has no computer systems or modern technology.'

After twenty minutes in the air I felt the helicopter begin its descent. I could see the sun peeking above the hills to the east, but beneath us now was the Atlantic Ocean. The chopper settled on the carrier's deck and adopted its gentle swaying motion. It felt disorientating to have landed and yet still be moving. The door with the cracked window was opened from outside, and we climbed down to the deck.

I stretched and yawned and looked around me. The bridge of the ship was just ahead. I could see the vessel's name plate, and blinked to read it clearly.

'*Intrepid.*'

I felt almost as if I was home already.

Chapter 18

'If I'm a national hero and you've been rescued, why have they locked us down here?' Tania asked.

I didn't have an answer to that. I was too distracted by what had seemed like the sound of children crying and playing as we were led down into the bowels of the ship. I didn't think kids were normally part of the crew on a navy carrier. It was another change to the modern world that I would have to get used to, I guessed.

'You heard those kids, didn't you?' I asked. Occasionally I could still hear the faintest scream penetrating the steel walls of our cabin. They must have been on the deck above us, perhaps in a larger compartment that would give them space to run around and play.

'Smith said it was for our own protection,' said Tania, still focused on our own predicament. 'I don't buy that. We should be VIPs on board. Dining with the captain. Touring the facilities. Free to explore and stuff.'

'We have a bathroom,' I pointed out.

'Big deal,' she replied.

'So if it's not for our protection,' I asked, 'then why are we locked in here?'

'I think they are trying to hide something from us,' she said, 'but I don't know what.'

I spread myself out across my bunk and tried to get comfortable. There was no room for us to share a bed on this voyage. She had the lower bunk and I was up above. Frankly I was too exhausted to care about the locked door or the fact that the sailors seemed to have brought their families with them. I needed recovery time. I intended to sleep for days on end, if necessary. I had no idea how we were going to carry out our vague plans once we reached American soil, but the more I rested and recovered before then, the greater would be our chance of success.

'How long do you think it will take to cross the Atlantic in this thing?' Tania asked.

'Don't know. Depends what speed it can do. At twenty knots we should be able to make three thousand miles in seven days, give or take. Ocean liners usually take about a week. Or used to, I suppose. So treat this as a cruise. A vacation.'

'Not my first choice, Iggy. A windowless cabin, probably below the water line, and not even a double bed in which I can snuggle with you. Hardly a dream vacation, is it? But at least they put me with you. That means a lot.'

'So what does a girl like you normally do for a holiday?' I asked.

'It's been so long I can't even remember. I used to do all sorts. Water skiing. Cycling. Kitesurfing.'

'Don't you ever just sit on your ass and read a trashy book?'

'I'm not that kind of girl, Iggy. Sorry to disappoint you.'

'No, I think it's great. You're an action chick. That's cool.'

'So how about you? Can you remember much from before your comas?'

'Sure. I was into cooking. Always fancied myself as a celebrity chef, only without the celebrity.'

She laughed. The implied role reversals between us

were obvious.

'Don't you do anything physical?' she asked.

'I used to run. Completed a few marathons. Not much else, though. When you're working hard and socialising hard, there's no time left for anything else.'

'What about a special woman?'

'That's you, Tania.'

'I'm not special. And I mean before me. There must have been someone before the plague changed everything.'

'Don't think there was. Not right then. I'd been dating a little, but I don't remember any of them getting serious. Too late now, anyway. Don't expect any of them will have waited for me. And that's good. Because now I've found you I don't want to lose you again.'

She stood up against my bunk and gave me a slobbery kiss.

'I'm glad I found you too,' she said. 'But I mean it when I say I'm not special. You can't afford to get involved with me.'

I felt a weight in my stomach like it was suddenly full of lead. 'I already am involved with you,' I protested.

'Iggy, we have to be realistic. It's not going to lead anywhere. Our destinies were set to cross paths, but not to share the same path for long. If the State doesn't force us apart, we have to face the possibility of one of us not making it. We're playing a dangerous game in a dangerous environment. Live in the moment, Iggy. Enjoy the present. There may not be a future.'

'I don't think I can enjoy the present when you're saying stuff like that. I've had to accept a lot of shit in my life, Tania, but enough. If we want something to happen, we're going to make it happen. If we want to stay together and the world doesn't allow it, then we'll change the world.'

There was something about her smile that suggested she was satisfied with my words, almost as if she had set me up to make that speech. I sensed that she was goading me towards a direction that suited her. She was playing with my mind, making a freedom fighter out of me. There were plenty of things I would fight for, but she knew that the risk of losing her was a more powerful motivation for me than anything else.

'If they split us up,' she said, 'if one of us is arrested, if we lose each other in a crowd, if circumstances keep us apart for any reason at all, then we have one backup plan. At midnight on new year's eve we will look for each other in Times Square, where they used to drop the ball.'

'But there are thousands of people there at new year,' I pointed out. 'I would never spot you.'

'New world, remember? No one celebrates it any more. No one has hope. People keep low profiles. We would be the only ones breaking the curfew by hanging out there.'

We slept on and off for the rest of the day, rocked by the ship in our bunks like babies in their cradles. In the evening, a sailor arrived with food and drink for us. He was civil and pleasant when he opened the door and offered us the trays, but I could see an armed military policeman standing a couple of feet behind him. I thanked him and passed one of the trays to Tania. I listened as he locked the door once more and departed.

Halfway through our meal I noticed something odd. The motion of the ship had changed. There were none of the broad undulations that were typical of a passage on the open sea. The carrier was in calm waters, moving slowly. I even thought I could hear bow thrusters juddering the ship sideways. Minutes later all movement stopped.

We had docked somewhere.

I looked at Tania's face. We both knew this wasn't an American port. We had been travelling for less than a day, and at twenty or so knots that gave us a range that could only mean we were still on the French coast to the north, or on the Spanish coast to the south. Soon after the ship stopped moving, I realised something else. The sounds of children playing and shouting had ceased. I thought maybe they were asleep, as it was late in the day.

An hour later the ship fired up its bow thrusters once more and made its way back to open sea. When the sailor returned to collect our trays I quizzed him about the recent stop.

'Bilbao,' he said, after checking with his guard that it was permitted to reply.

'Spain?' asked Tania.

'It was our prime destination before we were diverted to your rescue mission,' replied the sailor. 'All objectives are now accomplished, and we are returning home.'

He closed and locked the door once more, leaving us alone for the night. Tania shared the tiny shower with me, and we tried to share the lower bunk for a few minutes before giving up and going our separate ways for the night.

We didn't notice the absence of noise from the children's deck the next day. It was only when we were three days into the voyage, probably halfway across the Atlantic, that Tania mentioned the silence that had reigned above us consistently since Bilbao. I listened intently for a few minutes.

'You're right,' I said. 'I hadn't noticed before. Those kids are gone.'

'Two possibilities,' she declared. 'Either they have been moved to another part of the ship where we can't hear them, or they were offloaded in Bilbao.'

'And why was a US ship visiting Bilbao in the first place?' I asked.

'I hate to come to this conclusion, but it seems to me that the children were offloaded there.'

'Why?'

It was clear that the conclusion she had reached sat uncomfortably within her. Bert and Scarlet were in the hands of the Government. Was this what the Government was covertly doing with the children in its care? Exporting them without the knowledge of the mothers? Selling to foreign powers for profit? It was a ghastly prospect, as bad as the old ways of the slave trade. I didn't want to pursue this theory with her for fear of exacerbating her concerns for our shared children, but she was determined to debate the worst case scenario.

'What if Bert and Scarlet were on this ship all along?' she asked. 'What if we've just left them behind in Bilbao?'

'How many kids do you think have been taken by the Government?'

'It's somewhere between a hundred thousand and a million,' she told me.

'Right. And how many could there have been on this ship? A thousand at most, I'd have thought.'

'But how many other ships have been exporting American children?' she asked.

'We don't know for sure that any kids were sold to Spain,' I said. 'We're in the realms of hypothesis right now.'

'The Government still regards you as extremely valuable. Diverting a warship and risking their marines on foreign soil means they still stand to make a fortune out of your sperm, but it won't last. Your value will plummet to zero once your boys reach puberty, and that's less than a decade away. One million teenage boys will be able to do what you've been doing. And given that you'll then be a figurehead and a father figure to so many around the world, that is going to make you a very powerful and influential person.'

I hadn't thought of that. The idea of wielding power and influence was appealing.

'Cool,' I said.

'No,' she countered. 'Of course it isn't cool. The Government won't let you become a threat to their authority. When you cease to have commercial value, you will cease to exist. It's obvious. An assassination or a forced accident is inevitable.'

Tania really had the ability to make me see things as they were. She saw right through the smokescreen of state propaganda. She understood how things worked and what motivated people. And she must have realised that if I wasn't already champing at the bit to get started with trying to change things for the better, I was certainly ready now. She was right. I was doomed if I trusted the government doctors and agreed to stay on as a sperm donor. I had nothing to lose by fighting back. I could curl up and die in a shitty country, or I could die in the effort to make it better for my kids, and especially for Bert and Scarlet. And there was a miniscule chance that I might even live to see the consequences.

PART THREE

Chapter 19

The familiar judder of bow thrusters indicated our arrival in a port. The elderly ship rattled as it moved sideways through the water. We had been at sea for seven days since Bilbao, and we were therefore confident that this would be our final destination.

We said nothing to each other as we waited uneasily to be escorted from our cabin – gladiators about to enter the arena, athletes about to compete for gold. Death or glory. And it started now.

As the key turned in the lock I nodded at Tania, and she nodded back to me. There was nothing to discuss. We had no plan. We had goals and we had a destination, but we had no map to show us how to get there. Of course, we had spent some of the long hours of the voyage talking about what might be in store for us, but the many unknown factors made any kind of planning impossible. So, despite having had enough time to concoct a strategy for taking over the country, we had nothing. It all depended on our circumstances when we reached land. Would we be split up? Freed? Incarcerated? Drugged? Each scenario presented its own challenges. And even if we were able to escape the clutches of the system, how would we start to fight back? Was there some equivalent to the Death Star with a clear vulnerability that would guarantee us victory? I knew life wouldn't be like that. There was no black and white. Only grey.

The same sailor who had brought our meals invited us to follow him. Two guards hovered in the shadows.

'Where are we?' asked Tania.

'Just docked in Norfolk,' the sailor replied.

'And where are you taking us?' I wanted to know.

'That's on a need to know basis,' he said, 'and I don't need to know. So you don't, either.'

There was clearly nothing more we could get from him. We dutifully followed him along the corridors, up the steep steps and eventually emerged blinking into the early morning light of the harbour at Norfolk naval base in Virginia. It was the first daylight we had seen since France. There was something inspiring about this light as it washed away the darkness and started a fresh day full of potential and optimism. We were back in America and we were alive. After what we had been through, we couldn't have asked for a greater start to the next phase of our journey through life.

But things rapidly went downhill from that moment. While two military policemen gently held me back, Tania was taken to a gangway and made to walk across it to the dock. From there she was marched into a nearby building and she disappeared from sight.

My fate was entirely different. The officers led me to the helicopter in which I had arrived on the carrier the previous week. I climbed inside and strapped myself to the seat. A marine was already strapped into the other seat. I offered no resistance. There was no point turning against armed military guys in the middle of a naval base, and I was too consumed with the loss of Tania to think about making any kind of escape.

The door closed from the outside. It looked like there were only going to be two passengers: me and the marine.

'It's gonna be OK,' said a voice next to me. I turned to

face the marine in the adjacent seat. He was dressed in a uniform that looked immaculate, like it was straight from the dry cleaners. The kind of shiny outfit those guys wore to dazzle the ladies in the bars, not to engage the enemy. His features were strong, and his face – and presumably the rest of him – had been chiselled free of fat by intense exercise. On his top lip, he wore a thin moustache, and it was this that threw me. I tried to picture him without it. I knew this guy. But how?

Then it came to me. The photo on Dan's shelf. His only son, taken on the day he joined the military. No moustache back then, but given that he was only sixteen when he signed up it wouldn't have impressed anyone if he had tried to grow an upper lip warmer so soon in his career. What was the kid's name? I'd met him a few times back in Grand View-on-Hudson, but he was about ten years younger than me, so we'd never really hung out together. And even were we to have, I doubted that I would have had much in common with someone so determined to follow in the violent footsteps of his father's former line of business.

I remembered the kid's name: Marty.

'That you, Marty?' I checked, talking loudly above the noise of the engine as the helicopter took off.

He nodded. Either this was a strange coincidence, or he had been placed on this chopper flight with me for a reason.

'Flattered you remember me. Not many people do. Usually I fly these things, but I've been assigned to accompany you today. That's a cool assignment, because everyone knows who you are, these days. You're like a pop star, or the leader of a world religion. But I guess you probably know that already?'

'I was getting a hint of it. Some crazy old lady in

France even knew who I was.'

'Must be kinda cool, huh?'

'Marty, the Government stole eleven years of my life. I just woke up and a whole decade had slipped past, and then it happened again and I lost another year. You think that kind of shit is cool? It's so not cool, my friend.'

I looked outside at the receding naval base. We were flying over Chesapeake Bay, heading inland.

'I know Dad helped you out, didn't he?' Marty asked.

'Your Dad saved my ass. How's he doing? Managed to get back to writing yet?'

'No chance. I don't think he'll ever write another novel. It's a shame, because I know he still has stories to tell. There are war missions from years ago that he wants to fictionalise. You know, change the names and the places, but still base it on the events he lived through. I think he finds it frustrating that he can't do that any more.'

'So is he just trying to grow enough potatoes to see him through the winter?'

'Pretty much. I think he misses the old action hero days, too. Lives it vicariously through me, I guess.'

The chopper was now over the Potomac River, Washington dead ahead.

'OK, Marty,' I said. 'Let's cut the crap. Why am I sharing a helicopter ride with the son of my old neighbour?'

'I'll be honest with you, Iggy. They're taking you back to hospital. The one in Washington where Doctor Tang kidnapped you. Security's been tightened, so you won't have to worry about that kind of thing happening again. And everything will be different this time. I'm here to explain it all to you.'

'Out of the fucking frying pan, huh?' I mumbled.

'No, Iggy, not at all. You won't believe the package they've authorised me to offer you. Man, everyone in the country is gonna be jealous of what you have in store.'

He looked out of the window, and I followed his eyeline. The landmarks of Washington stood out clearly in the morning sun. We flew low over the city centre, and soon I could see a large 'H' painted beside a sports field, behind a group of buildings. It seemed we had arrived.

'I thought the country was dry,' I said, as I followed him out of the aircraft.

'Dry?'

'I mean out of gas. There are no cars anywhere. How come the Government can afford to move me around in choppers and on a carrier?'

'We have reserves, obviously, and we've been trading with other nations to get their reserves, too. It's enough to keep the infrastructure of control running. Probably sufficient for a couple of decades at least.'

More military police were waiting at the heliport in the hospital grounds. The moment to attempt an escape had still not come. Marty showed me the way to a meeting room. There were flowers on the table, home-made biscuits on a plate, a jug of mineral water and pots of hot water to accompany the decidedly ancient-looking tea bags that sat in the cups. The police waited outside in the corridor, and Marty shut the door. He invited me to pull up a chair and help myself to refreshments.

I noticed there were metal bars across the windows. Aspects of this warm welcome were decidedly cold.

'I heard about Tania,' said Marty, with a cheeky grin. 'She good?'

I suppressed the immature instinct to nod in agreement, choosing instead to adopt a tone of nonchalance. He was trying to bond with me, to gain my trust. It was obvious. And I wasn't going to give in to his charms that easily.

'None of your business,' I told him. 'Now, the thing that *is* your business is her well-being. Because I'm telling you now that if your people so much as move a hair out of place on her head, I will never co-operate with you, never trust you, and I will do everything in my power to take you all down to hell with me.'

That was quite a speech, I thought, proudly. I felt bad coming down heavy on this guy. I knew I wouldn't want to do anything to hurt him, because it would hurt his father. Equally, I knew I was powerless, anyway, it just made sense to bluff a little strength at the beginning of whatever this meeting would turn out to be.

'Relax, Iggy. Like I said, everything is gonna work out fine for you. I know you've been badly treated in the past, and that sucks, but you gotta understand that these were exceptional times. They needed exceptional ideas, brave actions. Pretty much everyone was in agreement that if you had been given a choice, you would have agreed to everything that happened.'

'Bullshit. Where's Tania being taken?'

'Think about it, Iggy,' he continued, ignoring my question. 'You had what it took to give the world a chance. You fathered the next generation, and they're going to be strong enough to withstand a new plague. You're not seriously suggesting you would have turned down the chance to do mankind such a great service?'

'Marty, they stole ten years of my life. It should have been the best bits. I had no choice. It doesn't matter what they think I might have chosen, because I wasn't asked. And if they think I'm going to lie down and let them do this to me all over again, then they're crazy. And I certainly won't let them do anything to Tania.'

'I know mistakes were made, Iggy. Listen to me. Tania is being looked after. Don't worry. And as for you, it will be different this time. It's going to be a job. You will get paid. Shitloads of money.'

'I thought money was worthless?'

'The old dollars, sure. Only good for wiping our asses. Bitcoins are the thing you need today. Either that, or gold. Anyhow, you'll have a luxurious apartment in the hospital, rent free, and full of any consumer items you care to own, provided we can source them. And you will be awake. That's a key part of the offer. No more induced comas. They said something about the sperm quality being higher if you're active, getting some sunshine, and generally happy. And that brings me to the greatest of the fringe benefits: a supply of hot nurses to help you deliver your daily sample. And – as if that wasn't enough – you will be granted lifetime immunity from the text message challenges.'

I'd heard this kind of empty promise before from Doctor Tang, getting me to think with my dick instead of with my brain, but I was prepared for it this time. I remembered Tania's prediction: I would be killed as soon as my exclusivity expired. One million masturbating teenagers would wipe out any advantage I currently possessed, and would seal my death warrant. Would I really be stupid enough to choose a life of luxury, followed by an inevitable, early death, like a pig that's invited to spend a year in the farmhouse before being sliced for breakfast? Of course not.

'Look, Marty, you're a nice guy. I owe your father, big time, and I appreciate that you probably mean well and you think that what you're offering me is pretty tempting, but I know better. Maybe you're brainwashed; maybe you have unquestioning loyalty to the monsters that are running this nation – that makes it all the harder for you to understand the simple fact that I don't believe a word you're saying.'

'Iggy, follow me. There's something you need to see.'

He stood up and opened the door, and we passed through it to the door opposite, watched closely by the military police. Inside was a luxurious apartment. It looked as if millions had been spent renovating it. The living room boasted a cinema screen. There were guitars and a drum kit set up in the corner. Through to the open-plan kitchen-dining room, and I was blown away by the quality and design of the kitchen. It was stocked with every gadget that could still be found these days, and the shelves were piled with fresh produce. The bathroom included a spa bath, large enough for four. In the next room I found a gym, with a treadmill and exercise bike. In the bedroom was the largest bed I had ever seen, and seated on the edge of it were two nurses, both dressed in uniforms that were too small to contain their breasts. They looked like strippers at a stag night.

'Real nurses?' I asked Marty, unable to hide the tone of disgust in my voice.

'Well, specialists at what they do,' he replied.

He didn't get how I felt about Tania. He didn't comprehend that she meant everything to me. 'And what about Tania? If I'm so important and you'll do anything for me in return for my daily donation to the women of the world, why can't I live here with Tania?'

'Well you could, but think about it, Iggy. Your relationship would have to be platonic. We can't afford any wastage, if you know what I'm saying. And then there's the jealousy issue. You know what women are like. She won't be happy with you enjoying a daily session with our sample retrieval specialists.'

'You mean hookers?'

Marty ushered me out of the room, embarrassed that I had been so rude in front of the scantily-dressed females.

'Come on, Iggy, get real,' he said, leading me to the living room and patting a huge and luxurious sofa for me to sit on. 'These are tough times for the world. Billions are dead. Those who have survived the plague have inherited a changed world. We don't have luxury now. We don't have security. We don't have it easy. You could have all those things.'

I settled into the plump sofa. I couldn't deny that this was a dream apartment, but I knew this was the devil tempting me to sell my soul. In the corridor outside were two armed military police. They would never leave, and they wouldn't allow me to make a free choice. I had no choice. So what was the point of this hard sell from Marty?

'Why don't they just knock me out again and keep me in a coma until I die?'

Marty shook his head. 'I told you: bad for sperm quality, and also bad for PR. Customers have been paying well for your exports. They trade with gold and oil, mostly. Sometimes food. Some use Bitcoins, if they have any. They want to know more about you. They want to see you going about your normal day.'

'So what is this apartment, then? A cage in a zoo for people to gawk at me? Is it going to be like the *Big Brother* house on television? A modern freak show?'

'Look, they don't expect much from you. Just lie back and let those ladies get their samples every other day. Apart from that, your time is your own. You can watch any movie ever made, cook any meal you want, have lessons on any musical instrument you can think of, learn a language, play video games. The hospital has its own generators, so the power stays on twenty-four seven here. You'll be treated like a king. And the only other thing you might sometimes have to do is give a friendly wave to visiting customers. That's not asking too much, is it?'

'And what if I refuse to go along with this?' I asked.

'I should point out that we saved your ass in France. You would not have survived more than another day or two out there, and even if you had made it to the coast there was no way for you to get home again without us. Your country has helped you, Iggy. It's time to do your duty.'

I noted with interest that he avoided answering my question directly. He was an accomplished politician in that respect. So I treated him as such and simply repeated my question.

'And what if I refuse to go along with this?' I asked, again.

'Iggy, please don't go there.'

'You're giving me the option of living in a gilded cage, with no freedom and without the person I happen to be in love with, or what? You haven't given me any alternative.'

'Come on, you know the truth. There is no alternative. We didn't save your ass for fun, you know.'

I walked over to the window. The apartment was on the second floor. Metal grilles made it impossible to open the windows fully. Outside I could see a car park that was overgrown with weeds and being used to store piles of logs for the heating furnaces. I turned back to look at Marty. He was right. I had no alternative. I would have to appear to accept the deal, and then work hard to find a way out of here. It meant studying the routines of the military police or any other security people they decided to place in the corridor for my protection. It meant taking the time to calculate all the different routes out of the hospital. And it meant building myself up physically and mentally so that I would be ready to make my move with no notice, as soon as an unexpected opportunity arose. At that moment I created clear and achievable goals. I would get out of here. I would go find Tania, and then we would strike back against the system. Together.

'All right, Marty,' I said. 'I give in. I'll take this apartment, and you can sign me up for the rest of the stuff you talked about.'

'Good decision, Iggy. I know you won't regret it.'

Chapter 20

The days quickly merged. I soon found that having every movie at my disposal made it impossible to choose anything to watch. Having endless boys' toys and musical instruments and a free diary in which to enjoy them made me not want to play with any of them. The busty nurses only filled an average of fifteen minutes of my time on sample collection days, and after their visits I would snooze and then pace guiltily at my enforced two-timing of Tania. I was beginning to tire of that apartment and it had only been a week. I made mental notes on the layout of the hospital, based on the limited views I had available to me and the noises of approaching cleaners and nurses. But there was always a contingent of military police in the corridor, and their changeover times varied each day.

I was getting nowhere. I had made no progress in my plans to get the hell out, and I had no clue as to where Tania might be even if I did manage to escape. I didn't even know which month it was, but there were healthy leaves on the trees and the water in the Dordogne river had not been too cold, so relying on meeting Tania in Times Square at New Year would probably require a wait of at least five months. I couldn't even be sure that I could survive on the run without her help and ingenuity for that long.

An assortment of important-looking visitors came by each day, asking me dumb questions like how was I feeling, how were the facilities here, was I proud of my job, that kind of bullshit. These people, I was informed, were the overseas buyers of my unique product. There were Oriental faces, South American and European accents, African representatives. One customer, a bearded visitor from Italy, seemed vaguely familiar. I wondered if he had been a soccer player or some kind of celebrity in his former life, but I didn't ask any questions. I didn't want to step out of line in any way. I played along – all forced smiles and faked contentment. The Italian told me what a wonderful job I was doing, and then looked out of the window and remarked on what a grand view I had. He repeated his comment about the view from the window several times. 'It is a grand view,' he said, in his mildly comical Italian accent. It made no sense, because all I could see out there was a disused parking lot, some neglected properties and a few trees.

Whether it was this odd Italian guy or anyone else, I told them what they wanted to hear, spoke about the daily deliveries of fresh food and drinks that I received, mentioned the privilege of an electricity supply that was on twenty-four seven, told them about the cleaners and tutors who took care of my environment and my mind every day, gave them a tour of my high-spec living accommodation. They all seemed to go away looking satisfied at the pampering I was receiving. Some even expressed jealousy at my situation, just as Marty had hinted. The Italian joked that it was so nice here that he might come back to visit me again, and to watch out for him. Weirdo.

There were enough of these visitors to convince me that the distribution of my DNA around the globe was no longer about saving the world. That motivation was long gone. It was obvious to me that I was simply a cash cow.

These were paying customers, and they paid well. And the more they seemed to pay, the angrier I became.

I picked up the electric guitar for a few minutes each day – a Fender Stratocaster, classic weapon of choice for generations of rock stars and wannabes. It made a sound that must have been horrendous for any passing doctors to overhear, but I got a small buzz from it as I mastered a few chords and managed to thrash my way clumsily through a song or two. I needed to enjoy something, I realised. I could easily go insane in this bizarre captivity if I didn't let my hair down and bellow out discordant renditions of old Beatles hits. Music was a way to release the demons that clattered around the inside of my head. I could scream away my frustration in the guise of a song.

There was another reason for maintaining a façade of contentment with my situation. The happier I appeared to be to the doctors and the security contingent, the less likely it was that they would consider the possibility of an escape attempt. And if no one seriously expected me to try to break free, I was more likely to succeed in that venture. Two weeks in, and already I could see that the military police on duty outside the apartment carried none of the tensions and seriousness of their first couple of days on the job. They joked with nursing staff, they read books, and they even spiced up their shifts by daring each other to do dumb things, like flirt with the next person who came along no matter what sex or age that person turned out to be. As I watched them from my cocoon, I almost wished I could join in their games.

By the end of my third week, everything started to change. The signs were subtle at first, and it took me a while to notice them. It started with the food delivery. One day it contained only half of the usual supplies, and nothing in the basket was fresh. The next day I received zip. That night I went to the bathroom to pee and the light wasn't working. I checked the apartment and the power was off everywhere, and the next morning I noticed another change. There were no more visitors. After the flurry of buyers in the first fortnight, all visits from VIPs abruptly stopped. The cleaners failed to show up. No tutors attempted to enlighten my mind. I sensed a slow abandonment. Something was about to happen.

And when it happened, it happened fast.

The night was stormy. It had taken me longer than usual to get to sleep due to the whistling of the wind and the battering of rain against my barricaded window. I was dozing lightly in my sumptuous bed when I heard the first sounds. A saw. It took me some moments to focus, and then I knew the noise came from outside. Probably workmen in the grounds of the hospital, cutting down a tree. It was odd to be doing that at night, and during bad weather, but maybe a tree had fallen down and needed to be cut up and cleared away? I went to the window to see if they were nearly done.

I blinked. A man in black nodded at me as he hung from a rope and attempted to hack his way through a metal bar. I nodded back, as if this were a routine greeting. We could barely see each other in the darkness. The power was off in my apartment, and from what I could tell from the view it seemed the entire wing of the hospital was currently in blackout. A stormy night during a blackout. I couldn't have chosen a better night for a breakout myself.

One of the bars was already missing, and the suspended man's hacksaw was making short work of the second. Two more bars would be enough for me to squeeze through.

He held up two fingers to me. I took that to mean he

needed two more minutes. I gave a thumbs up and began a frantic scramble to prepare myself. I threw on my jeans and dragged a T-shirt over my neck. I had no idea if it was inside-out or back-to-front. I groped in the invisible closet and found a jacket to protect against the rain. I pulled on my sneakers, blindly lacing them, then returned to the bedroom window and watched the stranger complete his audacious task. I had no idea who this person was. I didn't yet know his motivation for busting me out of there. He might have been another Doctor Tang, ready to sell me from one slave master to another. Frankly, that didn't bother me. I was getting nowhere here. Another location might offer me more opportunities for escape. And, as had happened before, the mere fact of being abducted from one location to another gave me a chance to break free.

The gales and the rain dampened any noises created in the removal of the bars from my window. The only chance of detection was if a passing security guard happened to point a flashlight up at my window, but my experience to date suggested that such an event was improbable. I'd never noticed any beams shining into the bedroom before, and the inclement weather was likely to discourage the security team from venturing outside more than necessary.

It was unlikely to delay my detection, but I filled my bed with a line of pillows and clothes to imitate my outline, just like I'd seen done in a dozen movies. When I returned to the window the bars were gone. The man passed me a rope with a loop around the end, and I squeezed myself into it. The rope supported me under the shoulders. I climbed halfway out, into the relentless onslaught of rain, and tugged at the line to test its safety. When I was convinced that it would hold, I climbed fully outside, closed the window behind me, and dangled uselessly in the night. I couldn't see the ground. There was no indication as to how high we were. So far I hadn't said a single word to this person. The storm gave us excellent cover, but words could travel far in the quiet hospital grounds. I waited to see whether there was someone on the roof who would lift me up or lower me down, but for the moment there was no movement in either direction. Then the man turned to me and spoke softly.

'It is a grand view from here,' he said.

I recognised those words. Right, I thought, hanging in the surreal blackness, lashed by a summer tempest, looks as if I'm going to Italy this time.

The Italian fiddled with his rope and mine, paying out the lines and slowly lowering both together. Before my feet touched the ground, however, I heard a generator firing up. Lights began to appear randomly across the façade of the hospital like the console of a computer from a sixties sci-fi series. I checked the face of my rescuer or my abductor – I had yet to deduce which he was – but there was no expression visible through his woollen balaclava.

'Don't worry,' he whispered. 'They won't notice you're gone just yet.'

Now I was really confused. There was no hint of the amusing Italian accent that I was expecting to hear. This was plain New York speak. If this wasn't the guy I thought it was, it could be anyone, but there was no time to quiz his identity. I heard the window opening above us. Shouts emanated from my room. We had been rumbled.

'Brace yourself,' he said. 'This might hurt.'

He loosened his tight grip on the ropes, causing us to fall direct to the ground, slowed only slightly by the friction and heat that seared into his gloves. I bent my legs and absorbed the hard landing with my thighs.

More lights came on in the surrounding buildings, and street lights appeared as if from nowhere.

'Hope you've got a fast horse,' I shouted, as he unclipped us both and we sprinted away from the military police who had burst out of the hospital entrance.

'Horse?' asked the man. 'I think we can do better than that.'

He guided me through tight alleys between hospital departments, through a hedge and down to a sports field. I had a flash of recognition. The helicopter pad was adjacent to this field. And then, through the sound of raindrops and fast-flowing drainpipes, I heard the whine of the jet engine and the slow thud as the blades began to turn.

I heard more shouts behind us and a gun being fired. Surely they wouldn't shoot at me? I thought I was too valuable for them. It had to be a warning shot. I could safely ignore it.

The helicopter sat on the pad, flicking rain water away and itching to take off. It was dark this far from the main buildings, but it looked like the same kind of helicopter that had delivered me here some weeks ago. So how come the marines were plucking me out of the hospital like this? That made no sense. They were being shot at by the military police. They should be on the same side – unless this wasn't an official operation … but there was no way for the underground movement to get hold of a chopper like this one, let alone fly it.

The side door was already open. More shots sliced through the wet air around us. I dived in, closely followed by my rescuer. He slammed the door shut, breathing heavily. The rotors accelerated. We lifted into heavy skies. The helicopter must have been invisible from the ground within moments as we rose into the clouds.

There was no communication with the pilot. Flying solo in conditions like this, and – I guessed – without functioning GPS to assist him, he was probably sweating profusely. Compass, map and altimeter only. Screw up for a second and we'd be impaled on the Washington Monument or bouncing off the wall of an office block. It was too soon to breathe easy. I wasn't out of danger yet and I still had no clue as to who these people were and why they would risk their lives for me.

'So are you guys gonna tell me who you are, now?' I shouted over the noise of the blades as they swam through the rainclouds.

No response. I leaned closer to my fellow passenger to repeat the question, assuming he hadn't heard me through the balaclava that was still covering his head. There was barely any light in the cabin, but I could see he was slumped in his seat. The guy was out cold.

I released my safety belts and searched the cabin for a light. I couldn't help him if I couldn't see much. There were various switches and levers, but I didn't want to touch anything that could result in an open door or launched missile. It was time to distract the pilot. He needed to know he had a sick passenger.

'Hey!' I called over his shoulder. 'This guy back here is out cold. Thought you should know!'

'Dad? Shit! Strap yourself in, Iggy. We're going down.'

I felt the machine lurch sickeningly as I sat back down and pulled the belts tight around me. Looking out the window, I could see no visual clues as to our location. Only patches of dark and patches of even darker. I had to trust that this pilot knew what he was doing. I gritted my teeth and waited for the descent to stop. It felt like we were going down far more than we had risen in the first place, like we were dropping down through the mouth of hell. Then the heavy clouds parted and from the helicopter's own landing lights, I could see trees. Lots of them. There was a spray of branches and wood chippings, a cloud of sawdust, and then the spinning started. The body of the chopper span out of control, turning over a couple of times before coming to rest on its edge. The engine shut down and an unsettling silence enveloped us.

The cabin seemed intact. I wasn't injured, just disorientated. My seat position was now parallel with the ground, and my fellow passenger hung from his straps above me. Something was dripping onto my face. At first I thought it must be fuel, but it was too warm to be kerosene. It could only be blood. But nothing had broken loose in the cabin, and we hadn't struck any surfaces during the crash landing. It was then that the pieces came together. My rescuer had been shot. He had been losing blood since we had taken off, and he had said nothing about it.

The pilot extricated himself from his seat and climbed back to release me.

'Help me get him out,' he said, fiddling with the injured man's straps.

I opened the door, which was now in the roof, and climbed up, ready to take the weight of the casualty and lift him through. Rain poured in, drenching the man and making him heavier. A waft of kerosene filled my nose. Panic began to rise within me. We were sitting on a potential bomb.

The pilot pushed the unconscious patient towards me with what seemed like superhuman strength, and I did my best to match his heroic effort. We climbed down to ground level, dragging him unceremoniously away from the wreck.

'Keep going,' he shouted. 'I'll get the med kit.'

Going back inside seemed like a bad idea – that thing could ignite in a moment – but before I could say anything he was splashing through the puddles back to the crash site. I laid my rescuer down at a spot that I deemed to be far enough from any shrapnel, should the worst happen. The forest floor was soft and wet, and I had to find a log to support his head and prevent it slipping back into the mud. Without a light I could see virtually nothing. The wound could have been anywhere. I pulled the balaclava from his face and put my ear to his mouth, listening for breathing. It was weak, but he was hanging on.

Light came unexpectedly from behind me. I saw a ball of fire rise up into the towers of rain. The fuel had ignited. The pilot hadn't returned. I wondered whether he was part of that fire that now lit up the woodland so dramatically. I forced myself to focus. I now had light. I could locate his wound, and maybe stop the bleeding with a tourniquet. I looked him up and down. There was blood everywhere. The tumbling motion of the crash had caused it to drip all over him. I loosened his clothing until I found the hole, to the side of his stomach, just above the belt line. A hideous sight, despite its small size and neatness, and not something I could fix with a tourniquet after all.

I heard a rustling. The pilot skidded to a halt next to me, tearing open the first aid kit and chucking liberal amounts of antiseptic powder over the wound.

'Come on Dad, stay with me,' he shouted.

This was the second time I had heard the pilot use the word 'dad'. I looked at him properly. The moustache and the face were now unmistakable. Then I took my eyes away from the injury and looked at the unconscious features of the patient.

'Dan? Marty?' I asked. My pleasure at recognising them was counter-balanced by the gravity of Dan's condition.

Marty stapled the wound a couple of times, stuck a padded bandage over it, then rolled his father on to his front. There was the exit wound. It was four times larger, surrounded by jagged flaps of skin and gristle. Marty calmly and quickly sanitised the wound, closed the skin with sticky strips, then stapled the wound closed and covered it with an even larger bandage than before. Next, he selected a bag of saline solution and got me to hold it up while he found a vein in his father's forearm. I was impressed with the quality of his medical training and the efficiency with which he exercised it.

When Dan was stabilised and there was nothing more to be done, the ice-cool marine began to crack.

'Shit! Shit!' he shouted at himself, marching in tight circles. 'Why did I have to roll it? Why did he have to get himself shot at the last minute? We were so goddamn close!'

I didn't know what to say to that, and offered nothing more than platitudes.

'It wasn't your fault, Marty. You did your best.'

'I threw away everything for this, Iggy. My career, my home, my friends. There's no going back for me. All I came away with was this helicopter, and now even that's just a goddamn bonfire.'

'You were lucky you weren't inside it when it blew up,' I pointed out, trying to find something positive with which to appease him.

'That wasn't luck. I set it off myself. Knew we needed light to work on him, and wasn't sure the torches would last. You can't get new batteries these days, you gotta remember.'

'Is he gonna be OK, do you think?' I asked.

'This was his dream, you know? One last mission. Death or glory. Putting the old skills back to use while he still had them. I don't know, Iggy. I just don't know. The old man's lost a lot of blood. He may have kidney damage. Internal bleeding. It doesn't look good.'

He sat and cradled his father, waiting for a sign of life.

'Should I squeeze the saline drip? Get it into him faster?'

'It's on maximum flow rate already. Anything more than that does more harm than good.'

'Marty, now isn't perhaps the time, but I need to know something. How come you've deserted from the marines to come and rescue me with your father? I mean, last time I met Dan he didn't want to get involved in the underground movement that was helping me. And you're the one who sold me the idea of co-operating with the doctors and staying in that apartment.'

'I was lied to, Iggy. The whole apartment thing was a sham. A shop window for your international customers. Once they had all the orders they needed for the next few years, they planned to put you back in a coma, and when you ceased to be of value to them, they would ensure that you never woke up again. I found this out from the military police. They were going to inject you tonight. That's why we had to act fast, me and Dad. We had to get you out of there.'

'And how come Dan wanted to help out?'

'In his old career, he often went undercover. He was a trained master of disguise and accents. He came to visit you last week dressed as an Italian dignitary. Did you notice?'

'The guy who kept telling me I had a grand view? Now I get it.'

'He was there to look at the security arrangements. He worked out the size of hacksaw he would need to get through your bars. He studied the layout of the hospital and its grounds during his official visit. Looks like the disguise worked. If you didn't catch on that it was him, despite his unsubtle references to his village, then he would have been able to charm anyone in that hospital.'

'Do you think anyone is coming after us?' I asked, looking around, nervous that the fire would attract attention.

'In this weather, no. GPS satellites started to go offline one at a time years ago. Now there's only two left in service, and that's not enough to get a fix. I flew too low for radar. So there's no way for the authorities to track where I took their chopper, and no chance that they can navigate in this weather to try to find me. We should find shelter, though. Dad needs to warm up. Pass me the drip and take the foil blanket out of the med kit.'

I handed him the bag and rummaged amongst the bandages for the foil blanket. It was exactly the same as the one I had been given at the finish line of the New York marathon. Folded up, it occupied no more space than a pack of cigarettes. I opened it out and spread it over Dan's damp body, tucking in the sides as tight as possible.

'What else can I do?' I asked.

'Go and scout for a house or anything we can use for shelter. Don't be shy. We'll take anything now. If it triggers any shit we'll deal with that later.'

'Can you give me any idea where we are?'

'I was following compass reading zero-four-zero and flying time was approximately twenty minutes, airspeed of one-eighty, so we're sixty miles north-east of Washington – between Baltimore and Philly. From the terrain I'd guess this could be Susquehanna State Park.

The Susquehanna River should be north-east of here. If you find the river, you'll know I'm right, and you can look for park buildings.'

'Right,' I said. 'Which way is north-east?'

He handed me a pocket compass. I glanced at it in the fading light of the flames behind me, then set off in that direction. There was no way to check it again once darkness enveloped me, but that turned out to be unimportant. After just a few yards I could hear the sound of the flowing river. I turned back.

'We're almost at the river,' I gasped, not stopping as I ran past Marty.

'Roger that,' he mumbled.

I slowed down as soon as it became impossible to see. After only a minute of groping through the undergrowth I could hear water again. I retraced my steps.

'River's on both sides,' I reported.

'Hell, we've come down on one of the islands. Probably Spencer Island. River's real wide, here. Good news is we're safe from detection. Bad news: no food or shelter.'

'How's he doing?' I asked.

'Hanging in there,' Marty replied. 'Typical of Dad not to tell anyone he'd taken a bullet.'

'He was a great man,' I said.

There was a cough. We both looked at Dan.

'I'm not dead yet, young man.' He coughed again, before adding, 'Don't write me off that easily.'

'Dad? I knew you'd make it. Do you need something for the pain?'

'Pain? Don't feel any pain. Thought you'd already jabbed me with the morphine.'

Marty shot me a worried look. I knew this was not good. Lack of pain from an injury as severe as Dan's could mean paralysis, hypothermia or the gradual shutting down of a body that was no longer viable. The bullet wounds didn't look as if they were close enough to the spine to have caused paralysis. Either he was fading fast, or he his core temperature had dropped to a dangerous level. Whichever way it panned out, Dan's condition was critical.

'Iggy, go find shelter. A shack. A log store. A boat. Anything you can.'

I ran back to the first contact with the river that I had found. An island should have a boat dock on it. There could be a covered structure next to it. Maybe even a boat. I started to follow the outline of the small island. From my earlier explorations I guessed it was no more than a hundred yards wide. If there were any form of shelter on the island, I would surely find it.

Marty had been right. There was a boat dock: it was a wooden jetty, sticking out into the flow of the river, but there was no building adjacent to it, and no boat moored there. I started to sense despair. Dan wasn't going to make it. That was a tough fact to swallow.

I saw a light bouncing off the trees around me and thought it must be the burning remains of the helicopter, but the crash site was a little too far inland to be visible from here.

'Stick 'em up where I can see 'em,' said a gravelly voice.

I raised my hands and turned slowly around. Holding a flaming torch in one hand and a shotgun in the other was a woman. She wore what looked like dirty rags, and the deep lines in her face suggested she must have outlived most of her contemporaries.

'Please,' I said, 'there's an injured man. He needs shelter. Can you help?'

'I heard you coming,' she replied in her ungracious,

manly voice. 'Knew you'd come for me in the end. I've been living off-grid for a long time. Well I ain't going down without a fight.'

'No, listen, we haven't come for you. We're off-grid too,' I pleaded. I wasn't entirely sure what she meant by 'off-grid', but I guessed it had something to do with evading the text messages and living a self-sufficient life, staying beyond the clutches of any kind of government. 'We were escaping from the military police. One of us was shot. Can you help?'

At last the message got through. The shotgun lowered.

'Them police here on the island?'

'No, they were back in D.C. We came in a chopper and crash-landed. No one was trailing us.'

'Lead on,' she said, following me through the trees to the where I had left Marty and Dan.

When we found them, the patient had fallen silent once more. Marty was still cradling him. When he saw us, he wiped a tear from his eye and shook his head slowly. I felt a lump in my throat and couldn't speak. This generous, kind old soldier had sacrificed himself for my freedom. I knew I had to honour his memory: I would achieve my goals; I wouldn't let him die for nothing.

'Too late, huh?' asked the old woman. 'That sucks. Cover him over. I'll bury the poor man in the morning. You two should come with me. Reckon you could use a drink.'

Marty laid his father down respectfully, and I helped him to spread the space blanket over the face. We stood there in silence, heads bowed, letting the rain drip from our noses. We were waiting for one of us to break ranks. It was Marty who finally turned away.

'Let's go,' he said.

The old woman took us down a path that I hadn't

spotted previously. In less than a minute we were at a log cabin in the centre of the island. It would have been invisible to anyone on the mainland or even passing by on the river. She opened the door and we stepped inside. I pulled the door closed behind me and she lit an oil lamp.

'Wipe your feet,' she ordered.

I looked at the room in which we stood. The pale light was generous to it, but squalor of this degree could not hide so easily. We went through the motions of wiping our feet, even though the floor inside appeared dirtier than the ground outside. There was one window, covered with a wooden shutter. Furniture was a single garden chair and a plastic table. Boxes and crates of food were stacked around the walls, reaching as high as the ceiling in places. In normal times, she would have been considered a hoarder.

She picked up a couple of plastic beakers and poured something into them from a glass bottle.

'They called this moonshine in the old days, I guess,' she said, offering us each a measure of the unappetisingly cloudy liquid. 'You boys look like you sure could use it.'

We didn't resist. Somehow it was helpful to let another human make decisions for us while we were wet, drained of energy and in shock. I felt sorry for Marty. I knew what he must be going through. Even though Pops had been dead for a decade, to me it seemed like only a few weeks ago that I'd learned of his passing, and the feelings were still raw and unhealed. The drink tasted vaguely of vodka, but with a hint of engine oil and gasoline. It was grim, but the insanely high alcoholic content was a welcome buffer against our reality.

'It was his plan,' sighed Marty. 'This whole rescue was his idea. When I told him what I'd discovered from my contacts in the military police at the hospital, his eyes lit up. I knew he was planning something. Back when the plague thing started and everything went bananas, he never wanted to perpetuate the problem, but he didn't want to be part of the solution. Until now. He believed in you, Iggy. He refused to let them put you back into another coma because he knew you would never wake up again.'

'But why did you go along with it?' I asked, pausing to slurp some more of the eccentric home-brew. 'You've stolen a government helicopter and thrown away your entire career for this.'

'Sounds like you boys truly are off-grid,' butted-in the old woman.

'I've seen what's been happening,' said Marty. 'I didn't like it any more than the next man, but I didn't think there was anything I could do about it. You're not trained to question authority when you're a marine. The whole system breaks down as soon as people start to think for themselves. Dad had been out of the military for long enough to see things for what they really were. He showed me a way forward. Saving your ass is the first step. Then we kick some ass.'

The ass-kicking stuff was the thing I had planned to do with Tania. But whose ass? Where was it? The coward in me wanted to skip that bit, find a relatively safe country and leave America to fester in its own corrupt shit. But somehow I knew I wouldn't let myself off the hook that way. I was in this until the end. With or without Tania, with or without Marty, I would find a way to kick that ass that needed kicking. However small, however large, I would make a contribution towards putting this country back on the right path.

'You boys gonna kick some ass? Now that I'd like to see.'

We looked at her as if she were intruding on our

private conversation.

'We just want to change the way things are,' I explained to her, thinking patronisingly that she wouldn't really understand our aims. 'There's something rotten in the state. People shouldn't be forced to live in fear, or to have to hide like you are. I don't know how we can change things in the absence of any democracy, and I don't even understand how the current system of government even functions. But we'll find out.'

'Well it sure doesn't function the way it was designed to,' she told us. 'It's gone rotten to the core, like you said. What started out as a way of filtering out the weakest to make society stronger seems to have turned into a game for sadists. They're inhuman. It's got nothing to do with saving the human race these days.'

'What do you mean by a game for sadists?' I asked her.

'The original make-up of the emergency government was bad enough, but it created a system that's riddled with evil. Enshrining the survival of the fittest in law gave a green light for bad guys to take control. And now it's entrenched and we're stuck with it.'

'But who are the bad guys?' asked Marty. 'Where can we find them?'

She laughed at the question. 'Why, they're everywhere. In every goddamn square mile in the country there's a bad guy controlling his little patch.'

'Why can't the police stop them?' I asked, knowing that it would trigger more whimsical amusement in our host. But it was Marty who responded.

'Because they *are* the police. But they're not really bad guys. They're just doing what they're paid to do. It's the laws that suck, but you can't change the law unless you can change the people who make the law. And that's the strange thing. We don't know who they are or where they are.'

Now the old woman broke into hoarse laughter. 'That's the point,' she said. 'No one knows. They sure as hell ain't in Washington no more. You need to find where the machinery of government takes place. Who pays the police. Who pays the army. Who collects the taxes. I may be isolated out here, but I have contacts. I hear stuff. But could you boys imagine that a crazy old woman like me would know where to look?'

We both responded with polite silence. Of course we didn't think she would have any idea who was running the country or where they were based. I decided to change the subject slightly.

'Marty, do you know where to find Tania?' I asked, hoping that he might have had access to intelligence as to her whereabouts. 'Last I saw of her, she was still at the naval base with the military police.'

'They let her go,' he told me. 'Right after we took you to the hospital. She was going back to New York City. So that's where I was heading. Actually, to the bunker she was previously hiding out in, not far from Manhattan. She mentioned that she hoped it was still habitable. It's the only lead I had.'

'Manhattan?' asked the old woman. 'That's a good choice. Seems you know more than I thought. But it's a mighty long way to travel these days.'

'I'm aware of that,' said Marty, rather officiously. 'We still had a hundred miles to cover.'

'Then you'll be needing a boat,' she announced.

'I didn't see any boats on your dock,' I pointed out.

'That's because I keep it in the house,' she replied, pointing at a cardboard box next to the sofa. 'Leaks a little, but you won't have to go far to get to the marina across the river. You folks can rest up until the morning if you want to. Always happy to help a fellow off-gridder.'

'That's kind,' I told her, 'but I think we need to travel by night.'

'No,' said Marty. 'I can't just leave my father.'

I took him aside and whispered into his ear. 'Marty, the helicopter wreckage will still be smoking come daylight. This island is gonna be discovered. Look, she doesn't have a fireplace here. She prefers to freeze rather than risk detection. I lit a fire for Tania in France. It was night, but someone saw the smoke in the morning and we were in the shit big time. If we stay until morning we won't be able to travel until tomorrow night, and someone is bound to investigate the smoke by then. We'll get reported. This poor old woman is gonna be found out, too.'

He thought about what I'd said for a few moments before responding. 'Shit, you're right. Help me with this dinghy.'

We laid out the rubber boat on the floor. The old woman passed me a foot-pump, and slowly the boat took shape. It was tiny, barely enough for two, and it was covered in patches where holes had previously appeared.

'You'll be going with the flow of the river,' she told us, holding open the door. 'You'll need to paddle to the left bank. No more than a couple hundred yards. You'll see the marina. Most of the motor boats are abandoned. Not much use if you can't find gas.'

I was pleased to note that the rain had finally cleared. There were breaks in the cloud, and faint starlight was lighting our way.

'How are we gonna take a boat a hundred miles up to New York without gas?' I asked.

'Leave that to me,' she replied.

We arrived at the old boat dock, and placed the dinghy in the water. The woman tied a mooring line from the bow of the dinghy to the dock.

'Get in,' she said, 'and wipe your feet.'

As we clambered into the inflatable boat she disappeared.

'Iggy, when I said we had a hundred miles to go, that was flying distance. If we go by boat, we're talking at least four times that. This river leads south to Chesapeake Bay, and we won't be able to turn north until we're right back at the Norfolk naval base. That base has got to be two hundred miles to the south, and if I go anywhere near it, I'm dead. I deserted, remember? I stole a helicopter. We can't travel to New York by boat. We'll just use it to cross this river, then we'll work something out from there.'

The old woman returned with a paddle.

'Only got one,' she said.

'You think we can row to New York?' I asked.

She shrugged, and vanished a second time. On this occasion, her absence was longer, and I could tell Marty thought she wasn't going to come back. The mooring line was straining under the flow of the river. The boat was impatient to move, and so was Marty.

'Let's go,' he said. 'Don't wanna hang around here. She's not coming back.'

I nodded. I could tell the presence of his father's body just yards away amongst the trees was disturbing him. He wanted to move on. Marty reached forward and began to unwind the rope from the cleat on the dock. He had almost set us loose when I heard the squelch of the old woman's feet in the muddy ground. She was weighed down by something. When she reached the dock she placed two heavy containers down with a thump.

'Five gallons in each can,' she said. 'Give or take.

Reckon one of them is more full than the other. Take it slow and steady in a small boat and you should make a hundred miles, easy.'

'Where do you keep all this stuff?' I asked her.

'You don't think I live in a one-room shack, do you?' she replied. 'That's just my cover. The bunker is beneath it.'

'Do you have any more fuel down there?' asked Marty. 'We've done some calculations. To get to the sea, we'll have to head south as far as Norfolk, and that's gotta be two hundred miles before we can start heading north. So it might be as much as three or four hundred miles to New York by boat from here.'

'Why would you do that?' she asked.

'Because that's where this river goes,' he replied. 'We have to reach the Atlantic to go north.'

'Yes, but there's a canal just a few miles away that takes you to Delaware Bay,' she said. 'Don't they teach you anything at school these days? Cuts a couple of hundred miles off the journey. You'll still be needing more juice, though, and that's a problem, because I got no more gas. Hmm.' She walked away into the night, apparently pondering something.

Marty reattached the line and climbed out on to the dock. He passed the jerry cans to me, and I placed them carefully on the floor of the dinghy. Marty stood on the dock and waited.

Minutes later the woman returned with bags full of chinking glass bottles.

'Always thought my brews could power a rocket,' she said. 'Gotta be enough alcoholic content to move a boat engine.'

'You serious?' I asked. 'Doesn't that kind of thing damage engines?'

'She's right,' said Marty. 'In some countries they used

to run cars on alcohol made from sugar because it was cheaper than gasoline. If the spark plug can ignite it, you're in business. Sure, it won't do the engine any good if it's not tuned and set up for alcohol, but it might give us the extra miles we're looking for.'

'How do you know that kind of stuff?' I asked.

'We're trained to improvise in the marines. There's always a way to get home if you know how. I've been trained to by-pass the ignition key and get an old engine running on practically anything.'

He took the bags of bottles and passed them down to me. The waterline was now uncomfortably close to the topsides of the boat, and Marty had yet to clamber back in.

He gave the old woman a hug and she hugged him back. I guessed they both needed it.

'Come on, Marty,' I said, gently. 'Watch your step when you climb in. Not much room left for you.'

As I paddled off into the strong flow of the river, the woman waved and called out something. I wasn't entirely sure what she was saying, but it sounded like 'Freedom Tower'. I thought nothing more about it, being more mindful of the grim task we had left for her, and how unfortunate it would be if she succeeded in burying Dan's body only to be raided by police the same day. She might have been able to shovel sand or mud onto the remains of the chopper to prevent any more smoke rising into the sky, but such a task would probably be beyond the capability of one person. I couldn't help thinking we had taken advantage of her generosity, but there wasn't time for lengthy reflection: within moments, we were in sight of the small marina tucked into the side of the river behind a long pontoon.

I tried to paddle close to the pontoon. If we missed it,

225

there was no second chance. The current was too strong to row upstream for a second attempt. Marty leaned out and tried to grab hold of the pontoon, but it was wet and slippery, and we bounced off it, back into the flow.

'Paddle closer!' he shouted. 'I'm gonna lasso the next post.'

It seemed a long shot to me, and unsurprisingly Marty's attempt to be a water cowboy was a complete disaster. I paddled hard against the current to slow us down, attempting all the while to stay close to the pontoon. There was one more post ahead of us before we floated past the marina altogether. Marty focused on it, but he didn't bother with the rope this time. He leaned over, arms outstretched, and clamped his upper body around it as we passed. The drag of the boat against the current caused a violent backwash to build up and flood the sides. The bottles of home-brew started to float around.

'Pass me the rope!' Marty shouted.

I did as instructed, and he got the boat tied securely.

'Get on the pontoon, and I'll pass the bottles,' I told him, throwing the paddle onto the dock. 'We're gonna lose them otherwise.'

We lost a couple of bottles in the messy transfer from the flooded dinghy, but we still had the gasoline jerry cans and the majority of the home-brew. Marty sat, panting, next to them while I walked around the jetties, looking for a suitable boat. He hadn't complained, but I guessed he was badly bruised from his impact with the post and strained from the effort of holding the mass of the boat against the current.

In the distance, I saw some flashlights. It seemed as if our arrival had not gone unnoticed by the locals. There was no time to choose our boat carefully. I jogged back to

Marty and helped him to his feet.

'Company,' I said, pointing at the lights. There were two of them, moving as if held by people walking. And they were getting closer.

We picked up the fuel and ran to the nearest boat. Whatever it was, it would have to do. Marty peeled back the canvas boat cover while I loaded the fuel. It seemed we had inadvertently picked quite a machine. Leather-effect seats that once would have been quite sumptuous, had the vessel not sat neglected for years. Sleek radar arch. Cup holders everywhere. Cabin at the front. Drinks table at the rear. I could just about make out the brand name on the radar arch: Chaparral. Then I found the fuel filler cap and encountered the first problem.

'Fuel cap needs a key!' I called over to Marty. He was busy down in the cabin, and emerged carrying a toolkit.

'So what?' he asked, casually producing a hammer and a screwdriver. He whacked the screwdriver into the keyhole, gave it a twist, and the cap opened. 'Fill her up. Just the proper gasoline for now. I'll sort the ignition.'

As I began my task, I thought about the state of the battery.

'How are we gonna crank the engine? The battery is gonna be dead,' I said.

'Boat like this has two batteries, and there's an isolator switch that stops them discharging. If we switch them both inline together, there's a good chance of getting just enough to get this baby running.'

He lifted the engine cover and reached down into the spacious compartment until he found a switch. The engine was monstrous, almost six litres in capacity. Satisfied, he closed the cover and returned to the driving position where he rapidly unscrewed the panel, revealing the wiring for every control on the boat.

I finished pouring the contents of the first container and was about to start with the second when I saw another flashlight approaching, this time from the other direction and already much closer than the first two.

'More company,' I told him. 'Real close. You ready to try this thing?'

There was no backup plan. If we couldn't get this Chaparral to start, we were screwed.

'Ready,' he replied. 'Undo the lines.'

I disentangled the ropes that held us to the pontoon while Marty touched together the wires that he hoped would start the engine. I heard a weak cranking noise beneath the engine cover.

Then nothing.

There was just one more line to release. Already the boat was starting to swing away from the dock, held in place only by a line at the bow. Marty tried the ignition wires again. This time the result was even more pathetic. Those batteries were no good. But I had an idea. I jumped onto the pontoon and ran back to where we had tied the dinghy. The paddle was still sitting on the dock, where I had left it. I grabbed it and ran back before Marty could even question what I was doing.

The first of the flashlight holders was almost upon us. I untied the final line and jumped on board. The current immediately pulled the boat sideways, towards an empty pontoon a few feet away. I stood on the swim platform at the back and paddled. It made very little difference, but there was a sense that we were moving further out towards clearer waters. When the Chaparral slammed into the dock, I pushed against the wood until we reached the free-flowing waters. Whoever had come to investigate stood helplessly on the pontoon as we drifted silently into the night, steered badly by me at the back using the paddle as a rudder.

'We need to get this engine started,' I called to Marty.

'How come?' he asked.

'Looks like they've got a boat and they're coming for us,' I told him. I could see them clearly on the water, about fifty yards to our rear, but their engine made no sound. I guessed they had access to a boat with an electric engine, charged either from the sporadic mains supply or by solar panels.

'I've never tried this,' said Marty, 'so I don't know if it's gonna work, but we need to get the engine turning over, so turn the boat around to face those guys.'

Without understanding why, I twisted the paddle the make the boat turn in the river until we were floating backwards.

'Run to the front and drop the anchor,' shouted Marty, now fired up and tense, ready to test his theory.

I did as I was told, dropping the anchor and chain. It rattled and banged as it played out, until it stopped the boat with a sudden jolt.

'Here goes!' shouted Marty, as he put the throttle in gear and touched the wires together again.

I couldn't believe it. The engine turned over, coughed, and then started. We moved forward against the flow of the river, dragging the anchor chain beneath us.

'Force of the water turned the prop, which turned the engine,' he explained. 'Like push-starting a car. Lose the anchor and let's move!'

But there was no quick-release for the anchor. I pulled at the chain, slowly reeling it in. The electric boat was now beside us. I could see three men inside. Dressed badly, like they had been dragged from their beds in a hurry. They seemed nervous. And that could make them dangerous.

One of them grabbed the side of our boat and received a whack on his knuckles from an ex-marine armed with a boathook. The intruder yelped and released his grip. Marty reversed the engine and tried to swing around, away from the electric boat. The motion caused the anchor chain to slip from my hands, and it fell into the river once more. I continued to pull at it while Marty motored forwards to provide slack for the anchor. Finally, I heard the anchor smack against the hull and we were free.

'Up!' I shouted at him. 'Let's go!'

Marty pushed the throttle hard ahead and turned downstream again. There was no way the little electric outboard could keep up with this beast. The powerful Chaparral lurched forwards, then decelerated unexpectedly before continuing at a slower pace. I came close to being thrown over the side, but managed to clamp my fingers around the guard rail. When the boat stabilised I rejoined Marty in the open cockpit. He pointed at the stern and shrugged his shoulders. I saw what he was pointing to and didn't know how to react, either.

The electric boat was keeping up perfectly, effortlessly, and it was doing so because its occupants had managed to secure a tow rope to a cleat on the stern of the Chaparral. The three men inside were sat back, apparently enjoying the ride. One of them waved at me.

'What do you guys want?' I shouted.

'We want to come with you,' returned one of them.

'Don't trust them!' yelled Marty. 'I'm AWOL, remember? The price on my head is enough to buy a small city. Untie their line and leave them behind.'

That seemed to be a sensible precaution under the circumstances, I decided, and began to fiddle with the knot they had applied with subtle dexterity.

'No, don't do that!' shouted the same man as before.

'We don't want to hurt you. We're not cops. We're not even armed. One of you is Ignatius, right?'

I looked back at Marty. He slowed the engine. I left the knot in place.

'What makes you think something like that?' Marty shouted at them.

'We heard Ignatius was sprung from the hospital. When we saw the chopper go down on Spencer Island we thought this could be our chance.'

'Chance to do what?' I asked them.

'To go off-grid. Join the underground. Be part of the fight back.'

They sounded genuine, and they looked young enough to be idealistic fools. Marty put the throttle into neutral and waited for the river to push the electric boat up against ours. Two of the three young men climbed aboard, and the final one removed their lightweight electric outboard and passed it up to his friends, before cutting their boat loose.

'Well, Iggy,' said Marty, 'looks like you just got your first three recruits.'

Chapter 21

We hit open sea before sunrise. The swell made me queasy, but my empty stomach kept it under control. I poured the contents of the second jerry can into the fuel tank and Marty steered a course far from land, keeping us invisible to anyone on the coast. He kept the speed low, in order to conserve as much gas as possible. There were still the bottles of home-brew, but we had low expectations of what that source of fuel could do for us.

Our new recruits had slept for most of the journey so far. Two were down below in the cabin, and one was curled up on the sunbathing bench at the rear of the boat. Marty and I still knew nothing about them, not even their names. I could tell he was on edge, refusing my offer to take the helm and give him the chance to sleep for an hour or two. I sensed he was planning to interrogate them when they woke up.

'Something's been bugging me,' he whispered, trying not to wake his passengers.

'What's that?' I asked.

'These guys knew about us and wanted to join. The odds of us happening to come down close to their homes are vast. So I got thinking, what if we had come down ten minutes earlier? Or ten minutes later? Would we be in a similar situation, only with different recruits?'

'You think there's a massive groundswell of support for us?' I asked.

'Not among the older generation. They're too scared to stick their heads above the parapet. But the young ones are the dreamers, the idealists, and they are everywhere. We could have more support than we realised.'

But that possibility wasn't occupying my thoughts. I was confused by how quickly these kids had learned about my escape from hospital when I thought there wasn't supposed to be a public news service any longer, and even if there was a radio or television channel broadcasting stories I would have expected news of my escape to have been censored. It was time to wake our companions. I needed answers.

I nudged the youth dozing on the sunbathing bench. He opened his eyes and threw up.

'Sorry,' he muttered, wiping the seat with his sleeve.

'We need to talk,' I told him. 'Go get the others.'

He roused them from their cabin and for the first time Marty and I could see the faces of our recruits in daylight. They all appeared to be teenagers, seventeen at most. One of them had a wispy beard and was wearing a rather effeminate ring on one finger. One wore thick-rimmed glasses that made him resemble Buddy Holly. The other was fresh-faced with bleached hair. All looked healthy, and all were dressed in old jeans and shirts that looked like they had never seen a washing machine or an iron. The three boys sat across the rear seat, looking scared and excited in equal measure.

'Right,' I said. 'I want names.'

'Jody,' said the one with the beard and the diamond ring.

'Jake,' said the Buddy Holly lookalike.

'Jim,' said the blond one.

Marty and I shared a look of despair.

'Come on guys,' Marty said over his shoulder. 'They

can't be your real names?'

'They're not,' said Jody. 'We've been planning our revolution for months. These are our freedom fighter names.'

'You deliberately chose names all starting with J?' I asked.

'No,' said Jake. 'We thought them up separately, but we kinda like it.'

'You're all jerks,' muttered Marty. 'You're the goddamn J Team. How old are you?'

'Seventeen,' said Jody, and the others nodded that this number applied to them also.

'That's too young,' said Marty. 'This is too dangerous. When we make it to shore I'm gonna drop you guys off, and you're gonna go back home. Got it?'

The three of them looked crestfallen.

'How old were you when you joined the military?' I asked Marty.

'That's different. I was joining a well-structured organisation. I got training before I ever saw combat. These three will be a liability.'

'We can shoot straight,' said Jim. 'We're all top level snipers. And archers.'

I could see a flicker of respect on Marty's face.

'Top level, huh? And what does that even mean? Where did you learn that stuff?'

'Nintendo,' said Jim. 'Jake's got an old Wii.'

'I took it apart and got it working,' boasted Jake.

Marty's laugher was devoid of sympathy. 'Shit, I might as well throw you overboard now,' he groaned. 'But I don't want your deaths on my conscience. I've got enough shit to deal with as it is. And that's why you're not coming to New York with us.'

'But Marty, there's only two of us. We don't know

what we're up against. We're gonna need some help.'

'But learning to shoot on Nintendo? Come on, give me a break.'

'What difference does it make?' I asked. 'We don't have any weapons, anyway.'

Marty thought about my observation. He looked the three youths in the eye, one at a time, before asking them another question.

'Your parents know you're doing this crazy shit?'

The boys looked at the deck. I sensed a possible bond of orphanage amongst all of us on board.

'Dad failed his text challenge last year,' said Jim.

'Mum was caught out just a few weeks ago,' added Jody. 'This was her engagement ring. She wanted me to have it if anything happened.' He stuck out his hand and showed us the impressive diamond ring squeezed onto his little finger.

'Lost both mine to those bastards,' grumbled Jake.

'And what do you guys intend to do about it?' asked Marty.

'We'll follow you,' said Jody. 'All the way. Right?'

The others nodded.

'You'll follow us?' I echoed. I looked at Marty and shared a knowing grin. 'You think we know what we're doing, huh?'

'You know the end game is gonna be in New York,' said Jim. 'We know that too. Everyone in the underground knows it. All the off-gridders know it. There's been a buzz about that place for more than a week. Word is spreading.'

'How does the underground share this information?' asked Marty. 'And how the hell did you all know about Iggy's escape from the hospital so soon after it happened?'

235

'CB,' of course, said Jody.

'Citizen's Band radio?' I asked.

'Breaker breaker one-nine this is rubber duck and all that crap?' asked Marty.

'It was used by truckers in the seventies to avoid problems with the cops,' explained Jim. 'And that's exactly why it was re-introduced after the law of the jungle came back. Not many of the old sets survived, but plenty of people found themselves VHF radios. We all needed to avoid cops. Gradually the network of CB users grew. A new code language evolved. Unlike cellphones, CB radios were hard to trace. People trying to stay off-grid got help from everyone in the neighbourhood. They always had prior warning when the cops were coming.'

'And when you busted out of that hospital in DC,' said Jody, 'someone who worked there got on to their radio and told the underground and the off-gridders in Washington. They spread it, a mile or two at a time, until the news had covered the country. Ignatius had been freed. It was the spark.'

'The spark?' I asked, feeling a heavy sense of pressure weighing down on me, forcing me to live up to a set of ambitions that I might have been a little hasty in planning.

'This is where it starts. If we all fight together, we have a chance,' Jody continued.

'And what do you guys know about New York being so important in all of this?' asked Marty.

'Because that's where it started,' said Jake. 'According to the recent rumours, anyway. That's where they're based. We think it's in a complex built beneath Ground Zero. Under the Freedom Tower. Everything comes from there. All the shit that happened since the plague. All directed by those bastards.'

'And who do you think those bastards are?' I asked.

'No idea,' said Jim.

'How many are there?' asked Marty. 'Are we talking like a bunch of knights of the Round Table? A dozen dudes to take down?'

'No one knows,' Jim added. 'And I get the feeling you guys didn't know any of this. So how come you're going to New York?'

'I have to find someone,' I said.

'Would that be Tania?' asked Jody.

I nearly fell over. How could this kid from a backwater town possibly know this stuff? He was creeping me out.

'Hope we can all get to meet her,' said Jim. 'I had a poster of her on my bedroom wall.'

'What the hell is going on?' I asked. 'Tania is a member of the underground. No one is supposed to know about her.'

'The only person more famous than Tania is you, Ignatius,' said Jody.

I was having difficulty assimilating everything the boys had been saying. I picked up one of the bottles of the super-strength home-brew and took a swig. Marty shook his head and pointed at the fuel gauge. We were running on fumes. It was time to test the old woman's alcohol on our engine. I gave the refuelling task to my new team. They poured the contents of the bottles into the filler pipe while I listened to the engine for a change in pitch.

The change was obvious. The sweet-running purr of the engine switched in moments to a rattling knock. Our speed dropped. Vibrations shook through the hull, but the propeller kept turning. Marty powered down the throttle and gave a thumbs-up. The pistons didn't like their new fuel, but they kept on firing. The engine would be damaged beyond repair eventually, but we just needed it to limp ahead for a few more hours.

'The engine knocks because there's water in with the alcohol, so it doesn't combust as well as it should,' said Jody. 'I can adjust the carbs to reduce the knock.'

'You can?' I asked, impressed.

'Won't last for ever, but if it runs smoother it will take longer before it blows up.'

Marty put the boat into neutral while the lads opened the engine cover and made space for Jody to make his adjustments. With the knocking noise substantially reduced, we resumed our progress. We all took turns at the wheel, giving Marty and me time to get some sleep down in the cabin. Despite the forceful rocking motion of the boat, I slept deeply. When I woke up, I had no sensation of time. Marty was no longer in the cabin. I climbed back up to the deck.

Ahead were tall buildings. A skyline I recognised as home. The alcohol-fuelled boat had done its part. Now I had to do mine. It took me seconds to get my bearings.

'Looks like Coney Island over to the right. And we're a couple of miles south of the Verrazano Bridge,' I told everyone. I pointed at a small island ahead of us. 'See that? It's Hoffman Island. Man-made. Used to be a quarantine centre for diseased immigrants. Left abandoned since the war, so it should be uninhabited. We should hide up there until nightfall.'

'Put you in a quarantine centre? Damned appropriate,' said Marty, with a sly grin.

'Uninhabited?' asked Jody. 'Only in the legal sense.'

'What do you mean?' I asked.

'You crashed landed your helicopter on Spencer Island in the Susquehanna River. Bet you thought there was no one living there, huh? But that's where you found old lady Marian living off-grid. And you can bet your life there will be off-gridders on Hoffman too. And on any patch of land where the regular cops can't patrol easily without wasting fuel.'

'We'll moor the boat there, anyway,' I said. 'We can't go ashore to the mainland yet, and we might get spotted if we stay in open waters like this. We have no choice. We'll just have to be careful.'

'You kidding?' asked Jim. 'There'll be off-gridders there. They'll help us. Might even join us.'

'But how do they know we're on their side?' asked Marty. 'They won't know that we mean them no harm.'

'CB radio,' said Jody.

'But we don't have a CB,' I said.

Jody pointed inside the cabin. I looked inside. Clipped to a shelf was a marine VHF radio.

'They use the same frequencies?' I asked.

'You have to know which channel is most likely to be monitored,' Jody explained. 'In this part of the country we're looking at channel seven.'

'How do you know this stuff?' asked Marty.

I could tell he felt side-lined. All those years in the military should have made him aware of this kind of thing. And yet he didn't get the real reason. This covert radio network existed purely to by-pass the kind of police and military structure of which he used to be a part.

'This revolution has been years in the planning,' replied Jody. 'We've done our homework.'

I let Jody into the cabin. He turned on the radio and selected channel seven, and then listened to it for several minutes. I heard mostly static, punctuated by occasional bursts of a language that was completely incomprehensible. Finally Jody pressed the transmit button on the handset and spoke. It sounded to my ears nothing more than utter gibberish. He released the button and waited for a response. Again, more distorted words blared through our speakers, making no connections in my brain, but Jody appeared satisfied. He switched off the radio.

'They've been expecting you,' he said, emerging from the cabin.

Chapter 22

Neglected for a century, the wooden docks at the side of the island had almost vanished. Enough posts remained protruding above the water line for us to secure the Chaparral, however, and we swam from there to the rocky shore.

I couldn't see anyone waiting for us. No welcoming committee. No garlands of flowers. Just ruins and trees. Like a lost Mayan city in the jungle, this place was the picturesque result of nature reclaiming man's abandoned edifices. Around the perimeter of the island was a wall, and it seemed appropriate to position ourselves within that wall as soon as possible. Once inside, we threaded a path through rubble and bushes and sections of wall towards the middle of the island. The five of us sat on the ground in a circle and waited. I was tense. This didn't feel right. We could have walked into an ambush. From Marty's expression I could tell he was beginning to think the same.

When I heard the scream, I nearly jumped into the air with fright. I hoped Marty couldn't hear my heart pounding. Each of us crawled to the cover of the nearest tree. Still no visual evidence of the inhabitants of this island, but then footsteps approached, seemingly from all sides. Voices again, this time laughing, not screaming.

A young girl ran into the clearing and looked at the five self-conscious and uncomfortable men around her.

'Which one's my daddy?' she asked.

I rose to my feet. Could it really be that, at last, I had met one of my own? She was beautiful. I stepped towards her.

'What's your name?'

'Cindy,' she replied.

I tried to suppress my reaction to the choice of name. It wasn't her fault. Maybe I was projecting my imagination on to her too much, but I was convinced she had my features.

'What do you get if you cross a plague survivor with a lesbian?' came an adult voice from behind me.

I span round. Two women stood hand-in-hand. They were in their late twenties and looked as if they hadn't seen a bathroom for a year. Their black outfits were shredded, and peeled repair patches hung limply in places.

'I don't know,' said Jake, entering into the spirit of what seemed to be a lame and predictable joke, 'what do you get when you cross those two things?'

'Damned if I know,' laughed one of the women. 'Cindy, I guess. Never thought she'd get to meet her father.'

'She really is one of mine?' I asked them. 'How come you still have her here?'

'That's the reason we're off-grid,' said the other woman.

I tried to tell which one was the mother, but I had been so obsessed looking for my own features on the little girl that I now found it impossible to spot anyone else's.

'Did you know about this?' I asked Jody.

He laughed. 'You obviously don't know the language of the underground,' he said. 'Guess that proves it works, huh?'

I turned back to Cindy. She had already lost interest in

242

me, and was skipping merrily in her own world of make-believe.

'Hey Cindy,' I said, crouching down to her level and trying to win her attention, 'I'm Iggy. I'm your daddy. So how old are you, little girl?'

'Five,' she replied. 'And a half.'

'Don't forget the half,' I said. 'That's real important. Do you have a favourite toy, Cindy?'

'Huh?' she asked. 'What's a toy?'

I looked back at the women in disbelief. They took my expression to be one of disapproval.

'Hey, don't judge us, Ignatius,' said the first woman. 'We're doing our best here. It's not exactly a life of luxury for us, hiding out here with just the food we can grow and the water we can collect. We're doing this for Cindy. Gotta stay off-grid as long as we have to, until things get better.'

I stood tall and proud. This was my daughter, and she was living in squalor and deprivation in order to avoid being separated from her mother. And there must have been hundreds of thousands more like her across the country, if not across the world, suffering and toiling daily to remain off-grid, to stay together. This was the reason I was on this journey. To make life better for people like her.

'I've come a long way,' I told them. 'I know what needs to be done. Things are going to get better. I promise.'

'I'm Valerie,' said the first woman. 'And this is my wife, Leslie. And we are both counting on you.'

Darkness fell slowly across the bay. Leslie and Valerie took us to the part of the island where they had created their home and their hidden farmstead. A vast basement beneath the floor of a razed accommodation block, built originally for the containment of immigrants with contagious diseases, now provided the storage space and the shelter they needed. Above ground, trees provided the bulk of their food, with irregular-shaped vegetable patches and other isolated edible plants supplementing their diets. All arranged haphazardly, to prevent detection of their presence from the air.

We dined frugally with our hosts, picking at nuts and berries and fruits, washed down with fresh water. I watched Cindy playing intuitively, alone, gaining more fun from her own limitless mind than a room full of dolls and computer games could ever provide. But happy though she seemed, it wasn't fair. She had no friends, no interactions with other kids, none of the wide range of experiences that she deserved to have in her young life. And then something happened that was as odd as it was beautiful. Cindy came and sat on Leslie's lap, loosened her mother's shirt, and began to suckle.

Instantly I recognised the good sense in a prolonged period of breastfeeding. Nutrients were scarce on this island. Breast milk would be the healthiest product available to Cindy. In the culture we had lost, this would have been eccentric behaviour. Now it was a basic necessity.

'How long have you guys been off-grid?' asked Jody, trying not to stare at Cindy's source of food.

'Since Leslie became pregnant,' Valerie replied.

'We're new,' Jody continued. 'Just went off-grid yesterday.'

'It's a hard life,' said Leslie. 'But we're not alone. More and more of the population are finding ways to escape the tyranny of the text message challenges.'

'It's ironic when you think about it,' said Valerie. 'The

244

whole point of the text messages is to ensure only the fittest survive. But actually, it's the fittest who forge their lonely lives. They become independent and self-reliant. They escape the texts and they prosper away from the system.'

'The underground is growing, Ignatius,' said Jim. 'All our friends would have come with you if they could. And it's the same across the nation. The country has had enough. People are ready for change.'

Everyone nodded agreement, except for myself and Marty. He had spent years cocooned within the bubble of his military life, disconnected from the rising groundswell of sentiment that was starting to appear, and I was having trouble believing what I was hearing. My first experience with the underground had only been a year ago, and they'd seemed to be isolated and few in number. I recalled Pascal and Tania telling me that there was plenty of sympathy for their cause amongst the general populous, but the penalties for being caught were too severe to contemplate. It was beginning to dawn on me that there must be a point of equilibrium, a moment of realisation that every citizen must reach, when it became obvious that the risks of playing along with the system were just as great as the risks of hiding from it. That must be especially true of the weak, the old, and the women at risk of having their children taken from them.

This evil regime was burning itself out. It was time to smother that fire for good.

Chapter 23

The boat was going nowhere. The batteries were fully charged, but the engine wouldn't catch. Jody wasn't surprised.

'It's fine when the motor is warm, but it's cold now. That alcohol won't be enough to fire it up from cold,' he said. 'Turn off the ignition. Save the batteries. We're gonna need them to run this outboard.'

He pointed at the little electric outboard motor they had retained from their own boat the previous night.

'Jake, you fix it to the swim ladder,' said Jody. 'Jim, you hold open the engine cover while I run cables to the batteries.'

Marty looked at me and shrugged. He let them carry out their alterations to the Chaparral before quizzing them.

'That outboard can't be more than a couple of horsepower,' he said. 'How's it going to push a boat like this? That gasoline engine down there chucks out three hundred horsepower.'

'Probably not as much as two horsepower,' said Jody, 'but the thing has a propeller. It turns and the boat will move. Unless you're in a hurry, it will do the job. We have two batteries down there. Both fully charged. Both capable of one hundred amp hours. This motor uses thirty amps an hour. That gives us a potential cruising time of eight or nine hours. We might only make half a knot in speed, but that's enough to get ashore. Mind if I drive?'

Jim lowered the engine cover, jamming a fender beneath it to avoid damaging the cables that connected the outboard motor to the batteries. Jody climbed onto the swim platform at the back of the boat and twisted the throttle on the motor. It sounded as if nothing was happening, but then I sensed a tiny forward movement. Jody twisted the throttle to full power and the boat glided silently away from the island, soon lost in a dark sea.

There were no shore lights to guide us. The evening's power cut had already begun, and New York's southern skyline was a mere boxy blackness against the stars behind it. Soon we could see the outline of the Verrazano Bridge above us, marking the entrance to the Hudson River.

'You want to go find Tania, now?' asked Marty.

'Sure. That was the whole point of coming to New York,' I told him. 'I don't know where else to look for her.'

'Look, Iggy, I can't keep this from you any longer. I need to tell you something about her.'

'What do you mean? You told me you let her go. No one knows where she is, right?'

'I'm real sorry, Iggy. You're wrong on both counts.'

I felt like I had been stabbed in the stomach. I almost wanted to punch him. 'What the hell are you talking about?'

'They didn't let her go, Iggy. She was too dangerous to the State.'

'So what did they do to her?'

He looked down at the deck. I felt sick. 'Iggy, they made the problem go away.'

That was the worst possible news. There were no prisons any more. The only punishment was total and irreversible. The bastards must have killed her. I took that news hard. In this grotesque world, she had become my sole motivation, my beacon of beauty and love. And she was gone.

I sat in silence. Marty had tried to get me to New York in spite of what he already knew about Tania. That meant he knew more about what was going on than he had let on. Whether it was from Dan or other sources, he knew where we needed to begin our fight back.

· I knew it wasn't Marty's fault. He had lied to give me hope, because without hope it was all too easy to give up. Suddenly the world felt empty. The absence of light and noise and normal nightlife became oppressive. I was hurting. I wanted out of this whole foolish mission. But where could I go? I belonged nowhere. The people on this boat with me were all I had. Sticking with them would probably lead me to an early grave, but then so would any other course of action. Any which way I turned, I was doomed. And that knowledge took away some of the worry. Because it didn't matter what I did or where I went. I remembered Cindy, and I thought about Bert and Scarlet. With or without Tania by my side, I still had to try to make things right for those children and the millions of others who were growing up in this twisted universe.

'Right,' I said. 'Where are we making landfall?'

Out on the open water with such an underpowered craft, it felt as if we were making no headway. It turned out I was correct.

'We need to make for land right now,' said Jody. 'We're hitting the outflow of the Hudson. It's too strong for this motor. We'll end up going backwards.'

'Lower Brooklyn,' said Marty. 'That gives us the shortest distance on foot to Manhattan.'

'What does that mean in real terms?' asked Jody, from

the improvised helm.

'Turn right.'

An hour later we were grinding the sea defences at the side of the Belt Parkway. Jody held the boat steady against the rocks while we climbed out.

'No point keeping the boat, is there?' he asked.

'No,' I said. 'Push it out to sea. It's served us well.'

The six lanes of the Belt Parkway carried nothing more than the sound of our feet. The asphalt was cracked and sprouting weeds, and in one or two places I even spotted young trees beginning to grow. Society truly had a long way to go before normality could resume. We marched north, following the highway as it slowly curled towards Manhattan. It was the perfect route to pick, avoiding all urban areas and divided from them by a band of trees along the entire coastal section of the journey. The young lads were elated, propelled forwards by their sense of adventure, whilst Marty and I lagged behind, each anchored by our private grief.

I was also aware that we had no hope of making it in one night. Travelling by day was too risky: there would be phone inspection checkpoints. We had to find somewhere to hole up until the next night.

The need for cover became more urgent as we reached the point where the Belt Parkway merged with the Gowanus Expressway. There were residential neighbourhoods to our left and to our right. The highway was raised between them. The rising sun was beginning to burn a deep orange colour into everything around us. We were exposed. We had to find a shelter.

But we had left it too late to stop before being spotted. A man jumped out from behind a road sign. 'You took your damn time,' he whispered. 'The girls on Hoffman Island radioed ahead. Figured you might be trying to get to Ground Zero. Hurry. This way. I'm Blakey, by the way.'

'Another dumb underground pseudonym,' said Marty into my ear. 'Whole damn country doesn't know who they are any more.'

'But they all know who we are. Should we trust him?'

'Don't have much choice, do we?'

Blakey walked hurriedly, but with a limp that suggested he was in pain. I guessed his age at about forty, but the etches in his face revealed a man who had lived a hard life, and the problematic leg implied that he had suffered injuries that would make him likely to fail most text message challenges. A man like him had no choice but to stay off-grid.

He took us through shadowy alleys and under a loose, barbed-wire fence to an abandoned industrial building close to the old docks, a relic of this area's long-forgotten maritime prosperity. The interior was vast and empty, containing only the echoes of our feet as we stomped up the steel steps to its upper floors. We climbed three flights of steps until we reached a closed door. Blakey, by now wheezing and rubbing his sore leg, knocked rhythmically on the door. Seconds later it opened and we were ushered into another empty space by an old man. He appeared to be delighted to see us, and tried to shake each of us by the hand as we entered. Blakey slid back a hidden partition in the wall. It reminded me of a modern, industrial version of the hidden passages at the French chateau. Behind it was another staircase, much narrower this time, leading up to an attic above the warehouse.

The space inside reminded me of photos I had seen of Londoners taking shelter in the subway stations during the war. Rows of people, lying in sleeping bags, precious possessions at their sides. Lost. Frightened. Needing a miracle.

'These people are all off-grid?' I asked Blakey. He nodded. 'How do they survive up here?'

'The local community supports them,' he replied. 'They are the weak ones, those who the law of the jungle is supposed to eliminate. None of them are capable of surviving a text message challenge.'

I gazed across the lines of faces. They were the people that modern societies were supposed to take care of. The grandparents, the sick, the injured. It was like visiting a large scale version of Anne Frank's hidden attic. The sight was sickening – it shouldn't be necessary – yet it was equally heartwarming to see that communities had come together to undermine the authorities and protect their vulnerable neighbours and friends. And that protection was now more important than ever: a new impetus was driving the police force, a fresh sense of urgency to eliminate the weak from the neighbourhood. The news came from Blakey.

'It's back,' he told us.

'What is?' I asked.

'The plague. Brazil. A million dead already. Word of it is spreading fast. Just like the disease.'

'Shit,' said Marty. 'People are fleeing, I suppose?'

'Heading in every direction,' replied Blakey. 'I won't be surprised if we hear news of its arrival in New Mexico or Arizona before long.'

'Unless the same thing happens as last time,' said Marty.

'Another Annihilation?' I asked.

'We still have the military capability,' he replied. 'We could annihilate the whole of South America within a few days. They wouldn't stand a chance.'

'That's awful,' I said.

'Is it?' he asked. 'Would you prefer the disease to spread to our homes and families?'

'Well no, of course. Still, it's a tough call for anyone to make. I wouldn't want to be the one who has to push the button.'

I tried to think no more about the situation in the southern half of the continent. I distracted myself by speaking with many of the people hiding in this attic. Learned their stories. Found out about the curfews and the legends about the Freedom Tower. Filled in some of the vast gaps that existed in my knowledge of the past eleven years.

We left them at sunset, equipped with tools and maps and clockwork flashlights, ready to continue our mission. I came away with a sense of hope. Brute force would never succeed against the might of the State, but our small band of determined guerillas could achieve some kind of hit. With subtlety, elegance and brains, we were sure that anything was possible. Ordinary people had faith in what we were trying to accomplish, and they gave me a feeling that America was ready. Enough was enough. Provided there wasn't another Annihilation, or outbreak of the plague on American soil, then if I could only pull the trigger, America would do the rest.

Once again, we followed the deserted and unlit road north, towards Manhattan, crossing the Brooklyn Bridge unchallenged. We were all on the lookout for cop patrols. Every few minutes one of us would lie flat on the road, and we'd all copy unquestioningly. I spotted a few patrols myself, and took pride in leading the dive to the floor. But the cops we saw were in the residential neighbourhoods, some distance from the highway. Most were on foot or on bicycles, some cruised silently in electric cars. They seemed to have little motivation to patrol the disused highways – the population was supposed to be immobile, in any case. It was like they knew the souls of the people were broken, making it inconceivable that anyone would be out on the highways at night.

'They say the Freedom Tower is the most heavily guarded place on the planet,' I told Marty. 'And yet apparently no one has been seen entering or leaving it in the past ten years.'

Marty shrugged. 'Must make some damn good chocolate in there,' he quipped.

The road down from the Brooklyn Bridge into lower Manhattan provided adequate cover where it terminated at City Hall Park. From there, we could connect to St Paul's churchyard on Vesey Street, and that provided cover all the way to the edge of Ground Zero. There was just one wide road junction to cross before we could reach the church. The open crossing would be risky; a large group like ours would be too easy to spot.

'Let's go one at a time,' I suggested, 'over to the church, hide behind the pillars, and wait for the next. What do you think?'

The idea was accepted. Taking responsibility for it, I went first. New York at night, without power and without people, was a most unsettling place to be. We had not seen anyone break the curfew, and since we had made our way down from the Brooklyn Bridge, we had seen no police patrols either. I wished I had Tania beside me. Her streetwise confidence would have given me strength.

The Woolworth Building towered above to my right, its peak mingling with the stars. I crept nervously across the junction. There were seven-foot high iron railings around the church and its graveyard, capped with unhelpful spikes. The entrance gates were shut. I looked urgently along the length of those railings for a vulnerable point. It wasn't ideal, but I found it, a later addition protruding onto the sidewalk: a steel-framed sign, showing a map of lower Manhattan. It rose to the same height as the fence, but without the spikes. I climbed upon it, tottered nervously, then leapt down the other side, into the hallowed grounds.

I waited for the next person to join me. One by one, they appeared, and I waved them all towards the metal sign that would enable them to jump over the railings. We ran through the dark, wooded graveyard that filled the entire block between Fulton and Vesey. Across the street I could sense the presence of something vast. It cut a black swathe through the stars, like a rip in the fabric of the universe.

The Freedom Tower. I mouthed the words, in awe.

'It's not called Freedom any more,' whispered Marty. I must have elucidated my thoughts more loudly than I realised. 'The building is just One World Trade Center now.'

'So how come people think America is being run from there?' I wanted to know.

'Guess it's the strongest, most bomb-proof, most up-to-date and secure structure anywhere,' said Marty. 'The security presence begins at the boundary of the old Ground Zero construction site. You can just about see the wall across the street. Don't go anywhere near it.'

The wall he was pointing to was unlit, and not visibly protected.

'With the power off at night, there's no way for them to have any automated security systems,' I said.

'You really think they would cut the power to themselves? Just because you don't see lights, doesn't mean they're not there.'

'Why do they say no one is ever seen going in or out

of the area?' I asked.

'Could be all sorts of reasons,' Marty answered. 'They were still developing parts of the site when the plague hit. They could have altered the plans to make it easy to keep people hidden. The underground tunnels here go on for miles. There are layers upon layers of basements. Public subways don't run any more, the last train ground to a halt about five years ago, but the old tunnels are still there.'

'So you believe the rumours of an underground base that the emergency government created here?' I asked.

'It might sound like a conspiracy theory,' said Marty, 'but these rumours are all we have to go on. It they're true, then you're looking at the source of the new laws. All that is fucked up about this country emanates from here: the machinery of justice, paying the police and the army, and making all the dumb decisions that have been made – all from this place.'

'So what happens now?' I asked. We had literally hit a brick wall in our plan. I had been counting on having Tania by my side when we planned an operation like this, and without her I just didn't know how to move forward. All I knew was that I needed to get over that wall somehow, to make a strike against the Government on behalf of all those who were counting on me.

'Putting your head over the top of that wall would be like showing yourself to the enemy in the opposite trenches in World War One,' said Marty. 'You'll lose it. We can't–'

He stopped speaking and dived to the ground, shuffling behind the cover of a gravestone. We copied his movements and waited.

A police car hummed quietly past us, patrolling the perimeter wall. The two officers inside failed to notice the five motionless black shapes in the shadows. When it had turned a corner, we retreated to the centre of the churchyard.

'We need to go down,' said Jody. 'Subway entrance is right here on Fulton.'

He pointed. I knew that subway entrance. It had been sealed up since 9/11. Before I could point out the obvious challenge of getting into it, the three youngsters had hopped over the iron railings into Fulton and Jim was tackling the locked door to the subway entrance with a range of tools from their kit. Marty and I followed them. The door swung open. A waft of stale air hit our faces. We were in. Jim passed us each a wind-up torch.

'Use sparingly,' he said. 'You won't get much out of each wind-up.'

I flashed mine for a moment to ascertain the position of the staircase down to the ticket hall. I glimpsed a dusty poster showing the subway route map. Then I realised something.

'This is the A and C line. It doesn't go to the World Trade Center.'

'But it goes to Canal Street,' said Jody. 'And from there you can take the E line direct to Ground Zero.'

'Do you know how far it is from here to Canal Street?' I asked the group.

'Come on,' said Marty. 'Talking about it won't make it any shorter.'

We walked among the rats and the litter and the grime for two hours, flicking on a flashlight for a second or two every few steps, just to make sure we weren't about the fall into a hole or trip over an unseen hazard. On arrival at the World Trade Center station, the platform was bricked up. Only a small steel door provided any hope of access.

The boys set to work. Jim seemed to take the lead in tackling the lock. In less than five minutes he announced that the lock had been broken and we could pass through.

'You seem very comfortable breaking into places, Jim,' I remarked.

'Dad was a locksmith. I used to help out. Taught me everything before the cops murdered him.'

The corridor behind the wall was unmarked. We had no way of telling which way to go. Jody started marching in one direction, and we had no reason to disagree with his choice. A set of steps led up a level to a barren concourse. Flashlights blinked at the walls. Now there were signs. One World Trade Center was clearly indicated.

'Look at the floor,' I said, shining a light at Marty's feet.

He looked down. Our feet had left perfect footprints in the dust.

'Shit,' he said. 'Any goddamn idiot could trail us now.'

'No,' I countered. 'Look around us. Apart from our footprints this floor is unmarked. No one has kicked this dust around for years. No one ever comes here.'

Marty appeared to ponder my comments for some moments. He shone his torch in every direction, seemingly desperate to disprove me.

'Fuck,' he eventually declared. 'Fuck and shit and fuck. I was so certain this was the place. Those rumours are everywhere, Iggy. Everyone has started to believe this is where it's at.'

'The rumours must be based on something,' I said.

'Sure. They're based on total bullshit. I can't believe we're almost at the Freedom Tower and no one ever sets foot in this space,' continued Marty. 'Shit. No one is running the country from here.'

'Maybe they have another way in and out,' I said.

'There must be,' said Jody. 'I've heard so much about what goes on here. It can't just be a fairytale.'

Marty was kicking up clouds of dust in frustration, thinking fast and not appearing to like the direction that his thoughts were taking him. Then he stopped abruptly, pointed his finger through the dense air and grinned.

'Or maybe they don't come in or out,' he announced, waving the dust cloud from his face. 'It's the chocolate factory thing. No one comes in because they're already here. And once they're here, they never leave.'

'That's what the rumours say,' said Jody, 'but they would have to have a route for obtaining supplies of food at the very least.'

'Normally, yes,' said Marty, 'but think about it: they have over a hundred floors to themselves in this great tower. It's the tallest structure in the country. That's got to be enough room for some indoor planting.'

'If you think about it,' said Jim, 'it doesn't even need to be that obvious. If you can deliver water through a pipe, you can deliver food.'

'Yuck,' I said.

'Of course,' said Marty. 'Don't mock it, Iggy. What do you think kept you alive for all those years you spent in the coma?'

'I know, but I wouldn't choose liquid food if I was conscious, would I?'

'We've come this far,' said Jody. 'Might as well rule it in or out.'

I led the march to the base of the tower. I felt more relaxed. The blatant lack of people down here reduced the likelihood that this was the right place to begin a revolution, but it also meant we were out of danger, for a while at least.

We climbed a silent and motionless escalator to the

concourse of the tower. Our flashlights picked out the vast slabs of white marble that covered the walls, rising fifty feet to the ceiling. The layer of dust remained uniformly thick with every step. This had to be the wrong place. No politicians could work here without leaving footprints, and if they did work here, they would have got someone to clean the place up, anyway.

If further evidence of the absence of life were needed, we found it in one of the four elevator lobbies. A vending machine stood against the wall, visibly packed with snacks, some of which had turned mouldy. It seemed out of place amid the grandeur of the building. Jake set about the front panel with a screwdriver, seemingly determined to indulge his desire for chocolate, despite the obvious health risks.

'Where is everyone?' asked Marty. 'All that security at the perimeter can't be for nothing.'

'But there's no security inside this place,' said Jim. 'Don't you think that's weird?'

'Maybe we should go?' Jake said as he sorted through the unappetising array of confectionary in the machine. 'If the dust is undisturbed on the floor, I don't think there could be a clearer indication that this is not the centre of government for this country.'

'Or maybe that's what they want us to think?' said Marty. 'Maybe there isn't a congress chamber or any of that kind of shit, but something else that they don't want us to find? Something they're keeping on one of the upper floors.'

'I think we should check a few of the floors for signs of life,' I said, pressing the call button on the elevator. There was no apparent response from the button. 'No power here, guys. Guess the rumours about this building were wrong.'

'The Hershey's are still good,' said Jake, strolling back towards us in the centre of the lobby. 'I left the machine open if anyone else wants one.'

I shrugged and wandered over to it. Something about the odour in the vending machine nulled any appetite I may have previously experienced.

'Maybe I can find the control room and reactivate the elevators?' suggested Jody.

'What's that noise?' Marty asked. There was a hissing sound coming from the walls, accompanied by a mechanical grinding. Two metal security blinds were descending from the ceiling, designed to seal off the elevator lobby at both ends.

'A trap!' I shouted. 'I must have set it off with the elevator button!'

The blinds were descending steadily. One of them was coming down adjacent to the vending machine. I could now smell something sweet, counteracting the stench of decaying food. Gas filled the air around us, and I felt instantly lightheaded and yawned. My reactions slowed.

'Shit! This could be the same gas they used in the Annihilation!' screamed Jim.

'If it was Novichoks we'd be dead already,' said Marty, calmly. 'Get down to the floor.'

We were all too groggy to sprint beneath the descending security blind. As my vision began to blur, I acted on instinct. I strained with all my weight and managed to tip over the vending machine, causing it to block the path of the security blind. The electric motor in the ceiling screamed in protest and the metal grille buckled, but our escape route remained open. We crawled lethargically beneath it and collapsed in the main concourse. Jody fell asleep. The rest of us sat and yawned breathlessly, trying to inhale clean air and to wake ourselves up.

'I don't know what gas that was,' panted Marty, 'but I'd guess it was an anaesthesia. Sevoflurane, most likely. If we'd been trapped in there, we'd be out cold, maybe for days or even weeks if the gas keeps coming. We'd die of dehydration before that stuff wore off, and if the concentration was too high we'd never wake up anyway. Thanks for knocking over the vending machine, Iggy. Good work.'

'If pressing that elevator button really did trigger their automatic defence system,' I said, 'then there's definitely something up there that someone doesn't want us to find.'

Jim patted Jody's cheeks. Gradually he came round.

'That was pretty cool,' he said.

'There are other elevator lobbies,' said Marty, 'but we don't want to make the same mistake. Can you guys find the control room down below and get one of the elevators to work properly?'

'Only if we can identify and disable the defence systems,' said Jake. 'Otherwise we're taking the stairs.'

I sat in the dust with Marty and waited while Jake and his friends retraced their steps down the dead escalator to the basement level.

'What if the machine floor is booby-trapped, too?' I asked.

Marty looked at me.

'Shit,' he said. 'Let's go.'

We dragged our tired bodies down the stairs to the basement level.

'Jake?' I called out. 'Where are you guys?'

'Here!'

I followed the sound to a nondescript door. Inside was a room with a low ceiling, packed with machines that hummed softly.

'Is this it?' I asked, oblivious the function of the racks of gear before me.

'No,' said Jake. 'Not exactly. The elevators are controlled from here, but not the defence systems.'

'What use is that?' asked Marty.

'Some of the elevators go down to this floor,' said Jody. 'They're the service elevators. Five of them. That means if we can summon one of them from in here, we might be able to bypass that whole security thing in the ground floor elevator lobbies.'

'Good thinking,' I said, stepping back into the corridor to wait. The whirring noise and the 'bing' sounded before Marty had even joined me. With handshakes and pats on the back, Jody guided us to the elevator he had reactivated.

'Top floor, please,' I told him, and braced myself for the acceleration.

'Take this,' said Jody.

He passed me a rope.

'What's this for?' I asked.

'I'm tying it to the hand rail, and we're all going to tie it to ourselves.'

'What good will that do?' Marty asked.

'I've seen that Bond film. *The Spy Who Loved Me*, wasn't it? The floor could drop out of this elevator when we're a thousand feet up,' Jody explained.

'Makes sense,' said Marty. 'We have no reason to believe that the booby-trap in the lobby is the only defence inside this building.'

I looked at the floor of the elevator car. Seemed solid enough to me, but nevertheless I tied myself tightly to the others and gripped the handrail until my knuckles were white as we rose swiftly into the sky.

The floor remained intact, but when the elevator

squeaked to a halt and the doors remained closed, I found myself hugging the handrail until it was in danger of breaking off.

I looked around me. The other four were holding the rail with equal ferocity. Some stared at the floor; others at the doors.

'Gas?' asked Jim.

'Don't hear any,' I replied.

'Maybe it's going to release the cable and let us fall,' said Jake. 'How high are we?'

'I think this is the fastest elevator system in America,' I told him. 'So we have to be near the top already, but we can't fall: elevator safety systems make that impossible.'

'Oh I remember,' said Marty, 'didn't you use to work for an elevator repair company, Iggy?'

'So you know about this stuff, huh?' asked Jody. 'What do we do now?'

'Try to climb through the roof, I guess,' I said. 'That's what they do in the movies.'

'I don't see a hatch up there,' said Jody. 'So how do we get the elevator to move, or get the doors open?'

'That wasn't really my specialty,' I confessed.

'But Marty just said you worked for an elevator repair company,' said Jody.

'Sure,' I replied.

'So take charge,' continued Jody. 'Get us out of here.'

I tried to force open the doors, as if success in such an attempt would compensate for the disappointment the others would shortly feel about me. The doors were solid.

'Use your engineering skills,' said Marty. 'There must be a trick you know for getting the doors open.'

'Not really, Marty. And I don't have any engineering skills.'

'But it's true that you worked for the elevator repair

company?'

'In the accounts department,' I announced, head bowed.

Jim broke the uncomfortable silence that ensued. 'Anyone notice what floor we reached before we stopped?' he asked.

We all shook our heads. The display screen was blank. That could mean we were between floors. Even if the doors could be opened, they would not offer a way out. The only way was up, and that ceiling looked as solid as the floor.

'This doesn't make sense,' I said, as Jake and Jim began hoisting Jody to the ceiling like a pathetic human pyramid. 'Before you break your necks, come down and think about it.'

Jody jumped back to the floor, causing the elevator to wobble and triggering a rekindling of our former close relationship with the handrail. I steadied myself and continued.

'If this elevator is booby-trapped to kill us, we'd be dead already,' I said. 'Same in the lobby. If they'd wanted to kill us outright, they would have used a more deadly gas. And when have you ever seen something as downmarket as a vending machine in the lobby of such a prestigious building as this? It wasn't there to serve the needs of the tenants of this tower. There aren't any tenants.'

'You saying the vending machine was put there deliberately to provide a way out?' asked Marty.

'Exactly,' I replied. 'But only for anyone who can think and act fast enough in difficult circumstances. This tower is protected, but it has loopholes. We got through a metal door from the subway system to the basement network. The platform had been bricked up.

Did you even question why the door was there? Why didn't they seal the whole platform with bricks? And why keep the elevators here at all? Why not seal the stairs and elevator shafts with concrete? These traps have been designed to allow people through, but only if they are smart enough.'

'I guess that fits with the idea of the survival of the fittest,' said Jody.

'I think so too,' I said. 'There may be a hundred traps in this tower. I bet there's something in the stairs and even on the roof if anyone arrives in a chopper. But each one must have a workaround, if only to allow whoever owns whatever is up there the chance to go back if they want to. So before we go risking our necks in the elevator shaft, I think we should at least inspect the electronics behind the screen.'

The control screen for the elevator car was flush with the wall. I yearned for the old style buttons on a panel held in with screws. This was too high-tech to be likely to provide a simple solution.

'Don't see any way in,' said Jody.

'Probably need to access it from the shaft outside,' said Jim, who then attacked the display screen anyway with a screwdriver. There were no obvious ways to remove it from the wall. The only option was to destroy it. The glass cracked and then shattered. He poked the pieces out and forced a small gap between the brushed steel frame and the circuitry that sat behind it.

'What good will that do?' asked Marty. 'We have no touch screen now. Even if you get it moving, we can't control it.'

'Shut up,' said Jim. 'Flashlight.'

Marty suppressed the disquiet he must have felt at being spoken to like that by someone so much younger than he. To his credit, he simply wound up his flashlight and held it up for Jim.

'See anything?' I asked.

'Sure. Bunch of circuits. Nothing's been added. I'm looking for something out of place. All looks normal there.'

'Can you hack it?' asked Marty.

'No.'

'So what the hell are we gonna do?' Marty's frustration was now beyond his capacity for self-control. 'If we don't get out of this elevator we're gonna die in here.'

'I gotta pee,' said Jake.

'Oh shit,' said Marty. 'Just when I didn't think this could get any worse.'

Without Tania in my life, I was prepared for death. I had had plenty of time to ponder my approaching demise during the sea voyage in the Chaparral boat and the exhausting march to get here. Life had become cheap. I knew the odds were against me succeeding in this insane attempt at an unarmed revolution. I was not afraid to go down in a blaze of glorious heroics, hopefully inspiring others to pick up the baton of freedom from where I fell. What I was not ready to accept, however, was a protracted death, stuck in an elevator car, eventually rotting in our own faeces and urine while the world remained ignorant of our story. There had to be something we could try.

A memory came to me. Something a colleague at work had once said.

'Anyone got a lighter or a match?' I asked. Jody rummaged in his pockets and produced a plastic lighter. 'You guys give me a leg up.'

Jim and Jake hoisted me to the ceiling.

'If you break through the roof you should use a

flashlight,' said Marty. 'It's more powerful than a flame.'

'I don't think it's possible to get through this roof,' I replied. 'I have a different idea. Brace yourselves.'

I lit a flame and held it close to a circular sensor in the ceiling. Nothing happened. Jim and Jake began to lose their strength and were struggling to hold me there. I wafted the flame around the sensor for a few more seconds.

And then it happened. I felt weightless. The car plummeted faster than any elevator I had ever experienced. Our screams filled the compact space, echoing off the walls. Then the deceleration began. The speed fell rapidly, weight returned to our bodies, and the elevator car came to a gentle halt.

The doors opened. We were back at the basement level.

'What the hell did you do?' asked Marty as we all stumbled into the corridor.

'Maybe I don't know how to fix a broken elevator,' I replied, 'but I've hung out with a few people who do. Anyone prefer to use the stairs this time?'

'The staircase?' asked Marty. 'Seriously? There's got to be a hundred floors in this building.'

'You got any better ideas?' I asked.

'Hell no. But like you said, there could be more booby-traps. We'd better tread carefully.'

We climbed fifty flights without incident. After the first ten, our paranoia diminished as fast as our energy. We checked a few floors along the way – the mechanical floors that housed the services needed to run a building of this size filled the first dozen or so levels. They were silent, dusty, abandoned. Above these were empty office spaces, so many of them that we stopped checking after a while. On the fiftieth floor we resolved to take a break.

My legs were throbbing. My lungs were struggling to harvest sufficient oxygen for my body. I lay prostrate, not caring what the others thought of my fitness.

'How come there are no traps in the staircases?' asked Jody.

'You complaining?' asked Marty.

'No, of course not. It's just weird. Fifty floors we've climbed, and there hasn't been a single problem waiting for us yet.'

'Why does this stupid thing they're protecting have to be so high?' asked Jim.

'Hard to attack, I guess,' said Marty. 'Mediaeval castles were built on the highest hills. It tires the enemy before they can begin their attack.'

'That's it,' I said, sitting up as I suddenly realised why we had been afforded an unimpeded journey up so many steps. 'The next booby-trap. It's the stairs themselves.'

'Huh?' asked Marty.

'One hundred flights of stairs,' I continued. 'There was no need to set a trap on the lower part of the staircase. The height of the staircase itself is the deterrent.'

'So there won't be another trap until we get to the top?' asked Marty.

'Not if I'm right. I think their plan is to weaken intruders by letting them climb the entire building, and then hit them with something.'

'Let's go check it out then,' said Jake. 'We'll be ready for it, huh?'

I nodded and raised my aching legs from the floor. It seemed I was right. The next hour of stair-climbing was pure, painful monotony. Our pace slowed. We rested more frequently. We covered a mere thirty-five levels in that period. Conversation ceased. We saved our breath. We pressed on.

The trap was waiting for us at the top of the ninety-ninth floor. No one saw it – by then we lacked the strength to look up. Jim was the first to fall.

'Shit,' he said, teetering backwards down the stairs and grabbing his head.

'Huh?' asked Jody, before doing exactly the same.

The rest of us stopped. I reached up. A concrete ceiling had been installed across the staircase. The stairs just ran into it and stopped.

'Could be worse,' I said, sitting on a step and panting.

A piercing noise hit us from unseen loud speakers. In the bare concrete stairwell the sound was unbearable.

'It's worse!' screamed Marty, finding the capacity to descend two steps at a time. We followed him down to the ninety-eighth floor. The shrieking sound stopped abruptly.

'If they didn't know about us before, they certainly do now,' puffed Jake.

'Who?' asked Marty. 'The Oompa Loompas?'

'They must have sealed themselves up there for life,' said Jody. 'Unless they have a chopper on the roof or they're keen mountaineers.'

'Or unless they're not there at all,' I said. 'Do you guys really think someone would seal themselves away from the world at the top of a skyscraper?'

'Ever heard of Howard Hughes?' asked Jim.

'Well, whether there's someone up there or not, they'll have to try harder than that,' I said. 'Jody, Jim and Jake – you guys check out the other two staircases. See if they're blocked too. Marty, you check this floor for something to protect our ears. This looks like another mechanical floor. There should be tools and safety equipment here.'

'What are you going to do?' asked Marty.

'I'm looking for something else,' I replied, following him into the maze of pumps and generators and heaters.

The noise erupted again. The teenagers had set it off by attempting to climb the other stairwells. Moments later they returned and the noise ceased.

'Blocked,' said Jody. 'All three stairs are sealed.'

Marty had found a single pair of ear protectors. He offered them to Jim.

'Think you can chisel through the concrete if you're wearing these?' he asked.

'That could take weeks,' I pointed out. 'It's too risky. We need a quicker solution.'

'Such as?' asked Marty.

'I don't know. I'm still working on it.'

'Well whatever is above us, I want to see it even more badly,' said Jody. 'To go to this much trouble, the top floors must be hiding something awesome.'

'And what if there are crazy dudes with guns waiting for us?' asked Jake.

'Jake, there are crazy dudes with guns waiting for us all over America,' I replied. 'This could be our only chance to do something about it.'

I left them and continued my search amongst the machines. I didn't know precisely what I was looking for, but I knew I'd recognise it when I found it.

'If we can't go up on the inside,' I heard Jake remark, 'we could try the outside.'

'Out there?' asked Marty. 'You crazy? We're over a thousand feet up. The tower is clad in glass. What are you going to tie your rope to?'

I found it. A heavy, steel starting handle to activate a generator in the absence of electrical power. I carried it back to the others.

'We're going outside,' said Jake.

'No we're not,' said Marty. 'I never agreed to that. What do you think, Iggy?'

'Going outside is the dumbest idea. Forget it. I have another way.'

'What's that?' asked Jake.

'The elevator shaft,' I replied.

'The elevator?' he echoed.

'No, the shaft. Forget the elevator. We know that's booby-trapped. There are cables inside the shaft. All we have to do is force the doors open with this and climb up two levels.'

'What's that?' asked Marty, looking suspiciously at the metal object in my hands.

'It doesn't matter,' I told him. 'It's just something to get the doors to open.'

'Well it won't get the job done,' he said.

'Why not?'

'Because I've seen something better. Follow me.'

He took us to a closet where he had earlier found the ear protectors. It was packed with first aid and safety equipment. Amongst the items was something I had only ever seen on television: the Jaws of Life. Designed to cut through cars, this power tool could chomp its way through the doors of the elevator shaft. Marty unplugged it from its charger. A light glowed, confirming it was ready to use.

'Hey guys, look at this!' called Jody. He was standing by a window, pointing outside. Something was suspended on the dark exterior of the tower.

'Robotic window cleaning rig,' said Marty. 'Guess it's been sat there for years.'

'We could use it to get to the higher floors,' said Jody.

'It will be booby-trapped,' I said. 'Just like the internal elevators. Only you'll be stranded a hundred floors up in the open air.'

'Marty, what do you say? We give it a try?' Jody

271

asked.

'I don't know. Don't you find it odd that it's been left on this floor? Like it's been waiting for us at the highest level we can get to from inside?'

'It's got to be safer than the elevator shaft,' said Jim. 'All we do is cut through the glass here, climb onto it, and see if the thing can be made to rise a couple of floors. If not, we climb the cables. At least the drop is only a few feet back onto it if we fall. Not like in the elevator shaft.'

'I don't like it,' I protested. 'It's too obvious. All the traps have been triggered by us doing obvious things. I think we should stick to the elevator shaft. It's less likely that they set up a trap in there.'

'I agree,' said Marty. 'And if you send glass smashing to the sidewalk, it's going to be heard across lower Manhattan.'

'I didn't say smash the glass, I said cut it. Jody knows how to do it neatly and silently. Nothing will fall.'

I looked at Jim doubtfully. Jody nodded agreement and held out the finger upon which his mother's diamond ring still sat.

'Watch this,' Jody said, and walked up to a glass-panelled door. 'My new party trick.' Without even removing the ring, he scored a reasonably neat circle in the glass. Jim passed him a roll of duct tape from their bag. He used the tape to create two handles on the glass, inside the circle, and clasped them with both hands. 'Jim can now knock out this circle while I hold on to the glass to stop it falling.'

With a degree of nonchalance that implied the pair had done this several times previously, Jim knocked at the glass circle with his fist. The window exploded. Jody was left holding the few shards that remained stuck to the tape.

'Come on Marty,' I said with a sigh. 'We'll take the

elevator route. You kids can wait on this floor if you don't want to join us.'

Marty was eager to use the Jaws of Life. He selected one of the dozen pairs of elevator doors and set the powerful mechanical claws to work. It cut through the steel like paper. Made Marty feel superhuman for a few moments. Soon the smell of stale air and oil wafted into the corridor from the shaft. The hole was large enough for us to crawl through. I shone a flashlight into the space. A set of cables hung in the centre, just out of reach. Marty walked off, and returned moments later with a broom.

'Can we use that to hook a line around the elevator cables?' he asked.

'I don't know how we get it back to us,' I told him. 'But there is some gridwork holding the elevator tracks. If I can reach it, I can probably climb it.'

'Probably? It's not like you have a second chance, Iggy.'

'Just tie the rope around my waist, and fix it to anything that's too big to get through this hole you've made. Maybe an office chair. That should give me all the chances I need.'

'You got it,' said Marty.

Once I was satisfied that the chair he had selected would not squeeze through the rough hole in the elevator doors, I climbed through. Despite the altitude, I felt no sense of true danger. A drop of a thousand feet was only an intellectual concept. My little flashlight could not hope to send its beam far enough to illuminate whatever lay in wait for me if I were to fall. Facing mere blackness below me, I remained calm. I found a small toe-hold and reached out to the side. The steel support for the guide rail remained just beyond my fingertips. A small jump was all it needed.

I pointed the flashlight at my target. I checked the knot that secured me to the safety rope. I jumped into the void. My hands made contact with icy steel. Fingers grappled against the smooth surface. Sweat lubricated my skin. Grip became impossible. An indifferent and deadly force dragged me from glory into the darkness. Arms flayed, seeking the safety line and finding only air. Then came the jolt in the stomach, like I had been punched hard. I folded in two. I swung and hit my shoulder against an unseen wall. The flashlight fell from my pocket. Movement slowed. I hung in silence.

What seemed like an interminable while later, I heard the faint echo of the flashlight exploding on impact. Panic enveloped me. I had nothing to hold on to. I was terrified of slipping out of this hastily arranged loop in the rope. I thought of the office chair that held me a thousand feet above certain death. I needed to right myself and get out of that situation. I wiped the sweat from my hands and reached for the rope. The knot was at my back, and above that I found the taught cord and pulled myself upright. About thirty feet above me was a chink of light. Marty's head appeared in it.

'You OK?' he shouted.

'Sure,' I replied. 'Just testing the safety line.'

His silence confirmed to me that he'd understood my attempt at a lighthearted bluff. I was in a surreal environment. I hated it in there. I just wanted to get the job done and get out. Marty shone a light down at me. I reoriented myself to the support grid for which I had been aiming. With a gentle kick I could now swing across the shaft, and at the second attempt I gained a secure connection to the steelwork. Other than the pain from my bruised shoulder and winded stomach, the climb from here was straightforward. When Marty's head was as far below me as it had been above me, I lashed myself to the frame and convinced myself that I was safe. The light from his torch showed me the doors I needed to get open. The floor above the sealed staircase lay behind them.

'Tie the Jaws of Life to the rope, Marty,' I called down to him. 'Once I'm through I'll tie the rope to something and send it down to you.'

I hoisted the device up to my hands and attempted to reach across to the doors. The machine gave me the extra inches I needed, and without moving from my position I was able to begin the task of cutting through the doors. The jaws ate their way through the metal structure with an apparent ease that was short-lived. The ageing battery was draining fast. Two sides of my intended square hatch had been cut. Marty confirmed the absence of a spare battery, and there was no way I was going to remain suspended above this bottomless pit waiting for a recharge. I had to finish the job fast. The hole would be smaller than planned. A triangle instead of a square. Just one more line to cut. Every inch now required more of my own muscle power to complete. Progress slowed. My bruises hurt like mad. I hoped to hell that this effort was going to pay off somehow.

Just an inch left to cut, and the jagged triangular hatch would fall open. The jaws slowed further. I knew they would fail me on this last cut. I moved them to the lowest point and used every last drop of juice in the battery to close the jaws tight upon the metal, leaving it sticking out towards me. It felt solidly attached. It had to be, because my life was going to depend on it.

I untied myself from the elevator track and committed my full weight to the protruding Jaws of Life. The metal of the elevator door to which the machine was attached began to bend and curl. I felt the jaws sag, but the hatch was in reach. I punched it and it bent inwards. I hit it repeatedly until it looked like I could crawl through. I dragged my hurting body up, over the jagged metal, through a gap that crushed and grazed my hips, and flopped, battered and bleeding, onto the lobby of the hundredth floor.

A fanfare sounded through speakers in the ceiling. Trumpets rose in a pompous crescendo. Then the music ceased abruptly.

'Congratulations,' said a loud voice.

Chapter 24

I had seen footage of the interior of the International Space Station, presumably now uninhabited and drifting in frozen silence: cables, pipes, technical complexity everywhere. But the space station was always spotlessly clean. The sight that greeted me on the hundredth floor of the tower was like a dust-encrusted version of man's final foothold in space.

I stood up. Cabling snaked across the floors and through the doorways, laid by hands that had no concern for the niceties of aesthetics. This was pure utilitarianism. No human eyes were intended to view it. There was a sense that these wires were more than networks and power supplies and data connections: they were veins and arteries. There was a hum in the air. The place was alive.

The recorded music and speech began again.

'You are the strongest,' the voice said, to a background of soft violins. 'You are the fittest. You have earned your place on this floor, and you have earned much more besides. Please look into the nearest security camera and state your name.'

That sounded crazy. Like I'd be stepping into the next trap they had lined up for me. Whoever *they* were. I looked down at the dust on the floor, amid the cables. Apart from the signs of my own chaotic arrival, it was undisturbed. There was no one here. Even so, I wasn't dumb enough to state my name to an anonymous electronic surveillance system. There were cameras everywhere. Not like the other floors. I looked up at them in turn. Four in this elevator lobby alone.

'Thank you,' said the ghostly voice. 'You have been identified as Ignatius Inuus. Transfer of executive power is complete. All building defences are disarmed. Awaiting your instruction.'

I didn't really take in any of what I was hearing. I was too bruised and too tired to think about the nonsensical words that boomed at me on that floor. I needed to get Marty up here. I returned to the gash in the elevator door and picked up the rope. I needed something to tie it to. As I looked around for a chair or something else big enough not to fall through the hole, some of the words I had heard sunk in. 'All building defences are disarmed.' Surely it couldn't be that simple?

I went to the bank of elevator doors opposite the one via which I had arrived. I pressed the button on the wall. Moments later the doors whooshed open and a bright elevator car sat there, waiting for me. I stepped inside cautiously, pressed the number ninety-eight, then jumped back out again. The doors slid closed. I went to the hole and stuck my head through.

'What the hell?' I could hear Marty shouting.

'Don't go in,' I told him. 'Send it back up to me, and let's see if it's working. If it is, you guys can join me.'

Twenty seconds later the elevator returned to my floor and opened its doors again. I sent it back to Marty and shouted through the open shaft that it was safe to use. He arrived alone.

'Iggy, we have a problem,' he announced.

'The building is disarmed,' I replied. 'There was an announcement. They know who I am. It's like I've won

278

something. But what happened to the J Team?'

'Kids always think they know best,' said Marty. 'They're on the rig.'

'Why didn't you stop them?'

'I didn't hear it. There were two doors between us. Now they're outside and they're stuck. We need to go back down to ninety-eight.'

I followed him back into the elevator. The blast of cool night air was noticeable even before we opened the second door. A neat hole had been cut into the window. The missing section lay on the floor, undamaged. It seemed they had perfected their technique in this second attempt. I grabbed Marty's arm for stability and poked my head outside. A few feet above me was a dark shape that had to be the cleaning rig.

'Looks like they've made it to ninety-nine,' I said. 'Let's go up a level.'

I was right. Three cold-looking youths were clinging to the robotic window cleaner. One of them tapped pathetically at the window.

'Why don't they cut the glass like before?' I asked.

'Beats me.'

'So we have to do it. Or we find a way to move the robot down a floor, back to the hole they made.'

'Would you have a clue where to go to do that?' asked Marty.

'Of course not. Let's find a fire axe.'

'If we smash the glass we risk telling the world that we're here.'

'I'm not so sure that matters now,' I told him. 'Find a roll of tape.'

The axe was located near one of the staircases. Marty located a pristine roll of duct tape and spread it all over the glass. He then ran strands of tape from the window to the nearest wall. As I knocked the glass with the blunt end of the axe, the pane shattered and remained in place until we pulled the tape hard and the entire window fell harmlessly inside followed immediately by Jake, Jim and Jody.

'What the hell happened to you guys?' I asked them.

Jody looked sheepish. I looked at his hands and noticed the ring was absent.

'There are no controls on the rig,' said Jim. 'Once we were on it, the damn thing went up just one floor and stayed there. Must have been its booby-trap system. Climbing up or down seemed impossible.'

'And you couldn't cut your way back in with the ring?' asked Marty.

Jody took it off to get a better grip,' said Jim.

'And dropped it?' I asked.

Jody nodded.

'Come on guys,' said Marty. 'Iggy's disarmed the building's defences. We can ride the elevator now.'

'Is anyone up there?' asked Jim.

'You'll see,' I told him, guiding everyone back into the elevator.

'You sure it's safe now?' asked Jake.

'Completely,' I said.

I pressed the button for the hundredth floor, and the elevator delivered us there without fuss. The doors opened.

'You came through that hole?' asked Jody, aghast that I had pulled my body through such a small and ragged hole in the door of the elevator opposite.

'Welcome back Ignatius Inuus,' came that weird voice again from the loudspeakers. 'Awaiting your instruction.'

'What the fuck?' asked Marty.

Everyone watched me with an expression of awe.

'Who the hell are you?' asked Jake.

'Me? I'm nobody.'

I stepped over the cables on the floor and led them from the elevator lobby through to one of the main spaces on this floor. The ceiling was double-height, while the centre of the floor was dominated by a mezzanine level.

'Welcome to the observatory deck,' said Jody.

Computers were piled in racks where tourists should have been admiring the view across Manhattan. Solar panels hung at most of the windows. Fans kept cool air flowing across the warm machines.

'Look,' I said, pointing at the floor. 'No footprints in the dust. We're perfectly safe.'

'What the hell is this?' asked Marty. 'It's like a high-tech version of the goddamn *Mary Celeste*.'

'Who was she?' asked Jake.

'Before your time,' I told him. 'Let's see if we can work out what all this stuff is doing up here.'

'Someone abandoned this in a hurry,' said Marty. 'Didn't even switch anything off.'

'I don't think so,' I said.

'Iggy's right,' said Jody. 'This wasn't abandoned. It was never meant to be populated. There are no chairs.'

'Exactly. It's a pure machine room,' I explained. 'Set up to run without human interference. Probably configured for multiple redundancy.'

'Multiple?' asked Jody. 'That's an understatement if ever there was. Look at this stuff. There has to be at least a thousand of everything. That kind of redundancy could last for a century.'

'But what's it for?' I asked.

'We'll find out,' said Jody. 'Come on guys.'

Jody and his two friends began to inspect the hardware, tracing the connections and noting what they

281

found. When they disappeared round the corner I removed a solar panel from where it hung by a window and placed it gently on the floor. Marty joined me at the window. We stared into the void, looking down upon the primeval darkness beneath which America slept.

The J Team were absent for what seemed like hours. We didn't know if they were still on this floor, or whether they were checking the situation on other floors above, but Marty and I remained transfixed by the invisible view from the window.

When the first hint of an orange hue hit the tops of the towers in Hoboken, I knew we were facing west. The angular outline of the city across the Hudson began taking shape. We had heard nothing from our team of whiz kids for hours and I was beginning to be concerned for their well-being.

Loud footsteps tramped through the dust towards us. I controlled my urge to hide. There was no reason to suspect it was anyone other than those boys.

'We did it!' shouted Jody, arriving with Jim.

'We did?' I asked.

'We found the source of the Government. The spring from which everything flows.'

'Where's that, then?' asked Marty.

'Here, of course,' said Jody. 'You're standing in the middle of it.'

'But it's just a bunch of computers,' said Marty. 'Where's the Government?'

'What is government?' asked Jim. 'I mean, what does it do? It receives money through taxes, pays people to do stuff, and issues laws telling everyone what they can't do. Is there anything in that list that can't be automated?'

'Are you trying to say that the whole goddamn nation is being run by a stack of ageing Dells covered in dust?'

asked Marty.

'They're not all Dell computers,' said Jody, 'but we found a terminal and hacked into its operating system.'

'Don't be absurd,' said Marty. 'This is weird, sure, but it's not our government. I haven't been getting paid these last few years from a computer.'

'Of course you have,' said Jody. 'You were paid by a computer even before the plague hit. Nothing really changed. Except now there's no one around to polish the boxes.'

'How do you get paid, Marty?' asked Jim.

'Bitcoin,' Marty replied. 'Just like all public employees. Cops and military and everyone paid directly by government, we all get Bitcoins put into our accounts.'

'Exactly,' said Jody. 'And where did you think they were mined?'

'Are you saying all these computers are mining Bitcoins with which to pay the police and the army?' I asked.

'Not all, no,' said Jody. 'The mining takes place two floors up.'

'Mining?' I asked. 'What does that mean?'

'Oh, right,' said Jody. 'Guess you slept through most of the Bitcoin revolution. Units of the currency have to be digitally mined by computers. They have to solve complex algorithms before they can unlock another coin, so the supply is limited. But with enough computing power you can mine enough to pay the assholes whose job it is to murder our citizens.'

'I thought there was no Internet, though,' I said. 'How do the payments get sent?'

'Just like they were sent for a hundred years before the Internet. The physical wires are still there. Computers can still communicate on the phone system. It's slow, but it

283

works.'

'So, Jody, what else is there?' I asked.

'Administration of payments. In and out. Whole block of servers dedicated to that.'

'Anything else, Jody?' asked Marty.

'We also found the computers from where the random text message challenges were sent,' he said, with a glint in his eye.

'What do you mean, *were* sent?' I asked him. 'Have they moved it?'

'We, er, disabled it,' said Jim, grinning.

'It was a big job,' said Jody. 'A system like that with a thousand levels of redundancy took a bit of effort to disable, but we did it.'

'How?' asked Marty.

'With a fire axe,' said Jody.

'So you mean no one will ever receive another text message challenge?' I asked.

'Never,' said Jody. 'There were three parts to the system. One generated the challenge based on a database of topographical and architectural features related to the person's home and work address. Another part tied up this information with a triangulation of the person's cellphone signal to work out where they were. It then contacted a known police operative in the location, and gave them a half hour's notice to get into position before the challenge was delivered by the third part of the system. We smashed all three. No one else will die from that sick policy.'

'But won't that trigger a reaction from the cops?' asked Marty. 'Breaking into this place is one thing, but once you interfere with the signals going out from here, someone's going to find out.'

Jody shrugged. I guessed it didn't matter what happened to us now. Even if we were shot by the cops, his actions would have saved thousands of lives today.

'Anyway,' continued Jody, 'the really cool stuff happens right here on this floor. This is the closest thing to a government that we have. The computers on this floor are programmed to issue laws. They can make broad policy decisions based on information received.'

'Computers are making laws?' asked Marty. 'We're being governed by goddamn robots?'

'Perhaps this is just where they archive their rulings and decisions,' I suggested.

'No, it's a closed loop,' explained Jody. 'It's capable of making its own rulings based on its general objective.'

'And what's its general objective?' asked Marty.

'The preservation of mankind. At all costs.'

'And what kind of power does it have to implement its objectives?' I asked him.

'Total,' said Jody. 'It has the police, the army, the navy and what little remains of the air force in its pockets. It could order a war to be started if it wanted to. It could issue new laws or revoke old ones. This is more powerful than the President used to be. There's no Congress to stand in its way.'

'How does anyone know what it decides to do?' Marty enquired.

'New laws are sent by wire to all police units. That's enough.'

'Does that happen often?' continued Marty.

'Not at all. Not since the law of the jungle came in. Once survival of the fittest became the law, it negated the need to bring in many others.'

'So the law of survival of the fittest really had been a catch-all statute?' I asked. 'The law to end all laws. The end of true governance.'

'Pretty much,' said Jody. 'Even if you killed someone

in a fight, you would be covered by that rule. No prosecution necessary.'

Far from protecting humanity, it seemed to me that this law had shoved it to one side: a backwards step, into the goddamn Dark Ages.

'Well, Iggy,' said Marty, 'you've made it.'

'Made what?' I asked him.

'According to the law of the jungle, if you have seized control of these computers, you have won the right to change their programming. You have control.'

'Like, I'm the President?'

'Better than that,' he replied. 'You're a dictator. At least, if that's what you want. You can change your status. You can bring back democracy. You can heal this goddamn nation by bringing back the old laws, Iggy.'

I let that sink in. The computer's voice had told me that the transfer of executive power was complete. Did it really mean that it had transferred the executive power of the whole nation onto my unworthy shoulders?

'What about bigger decisions?' I asked.

'What do you mean?' said Jody.

'Like the outbreak of the plague in Brazil. Are these computers going to make the decision about what to do?'

'Of course. They're programmed to monitor the spread, according to the reports they receive via police and military networks. When it gets to a critical mass they'll probably order a strike to neutralise the threat and save our asses.'

'Can you stop them?' I asked.

'Stop the computers annihilating Brazil? Why would I do that?'

'Jody, we have to stop that from happening.'

'Hang on,' said Marty. 'Let's just think about this, shall we? We don't want to risk the whole of North

America getting infected by refugees from the south. If the computers calculate that mankind's chances as a species are improved by sacrificing another continent, then that's what we must do.'

'No, it doesn't make sense,' I countered. 'You'll be slashing the population again by doing that. We'll be weaker as a species. We annihilated Asia, and still the plague made it across the Atlantic. Ultimately the sacrifices in Asia were futile. And now we have kids in South America who can get through this.'

'Ah, yes, your kids, Iggy,' said Jody. 'Don't you think that's making you a little too biased to be able to make a decision?'

'Iggy, forget the goddamn kids,' added Marty. 'You have millions around the world. You can't possibly even meet them all, and if a few have to die then they have to die. It's for your own good.'

'What kind of parent sacrifices his kids to save himself?' I asked.

'That's not relevant to this situation and you know it,' said Marty. 'You've never even met them and you never will.'

'Am I really in charge now?'

'Sure, Iggy. But if you go and do something stupid like trying to dilute the defence of our country, I might have to invoke the law of survival of the fittest and take over from you.'

'Well in that case I hereby revoke that law.'

'You can't just do that,' said Marty.

'The law of the survival of the fittest is revoked,' boomed the computer. 'All police units are being informed.'

'He just did,' said Jody.

'Shit,' I said, overwhelmed. I felt like a magician. I

287

only had to point my finger and stuff would happen. The sense of power was euphoric. Until I remembered Tania and realised how utterly powerless I was when it came to the things that really mattered to me. Even presidents couldn't reanimate the dead.

But they could do something to prevent further deaths, and I wasn't prepared to destroy an entire continent. Besides, annihilating South America wouldn't actually save the north. The result might be nothing more than a delay before the plague eventually hit.

'Iggy, you have to do something about the plague. Seriously,' said Marty.

'It's gonna have to wait,' said Jim.

'Why?' asked Marty.

'We got visitors. The elevator is moving and we didn't order it to move.'

'Can you stop it?' asked Marty.

'Not from up here. And there's nowhere we can hide,' added Jim. 'Our footprints in the dust will lead us them to us.'

'Not if we go where there's no dust. On the roof,' said Marty.

'Are you out of your mind?' asked Jody. They'd still find the trail that led there.'

So in the absence of workable ideas, we did nothing other than shuffle back behind a bank of computers. Hardly the work of masters of concealment.

I heard the elevator doors open. There were voices and footsteps. I wondered whether we might make it to the elevator or the stairs before they found us, but when the feet of the intruders shuffled nearer, I thought of something else. I stepped out from behind the computers.

'Welcome,' I said to the two police officers.

They eyed me suspiciously. They both appeared older

than me, which made it all the more difficult to deliver the words I intended to say.

'Who are you?' asked one of the officers, his hand poised an inch or two from the gun on his holster.

'My name is Ignatius Inuus. I have survived the plague. I have fathered the children who will help humanity through the next outbreak. Under the protection of the legislation relating to the survival of the fittest I have taken executive power from whoever abandoned it to these machines. I have revoked the policy of cellphone challenges, and I have revoked the law of the survival of the fittest. Gentlemen, please stand by for further orders.'

I felt the handcuffs click around my wrists before I saw them.

Chapter 25

It was difficult to get any sleep in the cell. The station was bursting with cops, and the noise of their excited chatter echoed down the corridor. Capping that sound were Marty's shouts of abuse aimed at me from the neighbouring cell, but I had been awake for more hours than I could remember, and when the voices in the building finally merged into a white noise I gratefully passed out.

The clunk of the key in the lock didn't wake me. It took a vigorous shaking of the shoulders to force my heavy eyes to open.

'Time to wake up, sir,' said a female cop who was leaning over me.

I hadn't expected politeness.

'What's going on?' I asked her.

'The legal updates have arrived. Sorry it took so long. We're ready for you now. Please come with me.'

'What legal updates?' I asked as she removed the cuffs.

'Your new laws. It took a few hours to get the message out to all our officers.'

She slid the steel door open. I followed her to the source of the hubbub, dragging my heels. I had been conned too many times before. This could be a sick joke to alleviate someone's boredom prior to my execution.

I walked into a large room and was greeted with a

barrage of gunshot noises.

I closed my eyes and tensed, waiting for the bullets to impact my flesh and my organs, preparing myself for the pain followed by the welcome release of death.

There was no pain. The only sensation was a gentle tickle on my face. I opened my eyes and saw multi-coloured streamers floating down onto the heads of everyone present, and the sweet smell of cordite from the tiny explosive charges that had triggered the party poppers.

'We've been saving these for a long time,' said the policewoman. 'Been nothing worth celebrating these past years. Would you like to say a few words to everyone?'

'Huh?' I said. 'What about?'

'Your new laws,' she told me. 'I gotta say, mister Inuus, this is quite an honour for all of us here. Hey you guys, quiet. The President's gonna speak to us.'

I performed a double-take at that introduction. Expectant faces looked at me. Toughened cops, years of exposure to blood and violence etched on their cynical faces, all turned to me for guidance. I heard more arrivals behind me. Over my shoulder I saw Marty give me an encouraging nod. Jody and Jim stood beside him. For the first time I wondered what had happened to Jake. He hadn't made it back to our floor on the Freedom Tower before the cops arrived and I hadn't seen him since.

The hush became strained. I needed to say something to these people.

'Er, hi guys. How's it going? I don't know what to say. I just woke up and everything's pretty strange right now. My name's Ignatius Inuus. Some of you probably heard of me already. Apparently I've been sowing a lot of oats, if you know what I mean.' I paused to allow them to laugh, but the occasion seemed too important to them. No one so much as grinned and my discomfort deepened. 'I, er, know I missed out on pretty much everything that's happened since the plague. All I know is that some pretty bad shit went down after it broke out. Some think the changes to our laws were necessary. I heard some bullshit about needing to evolve to a stronger species or something. I'm no doctor, so I know nothing about this stuff, but I am a human. And as a human, it seems to me that we lost our humanity when the law of the jungle was passed. It was like a kind of over-reaction to the situation. Since I got out of hospital and discovered how things are in the world today, I've been wanting to change it. Maybe you've all wanted to as well, but didn't know how. I didn't really know either, but with the help of some great guys I managed to get to the source of the laws and you know what? It turns out we've all been screwed over. Whoever took power eleven years ago isn't around any more. They set up some kinda computer system and disappeared into the sunset. There's been no one running this country for years. It's like some kinda sick joke. The population is scared shitless and for what? Because a computer is paying you guys to maintain rules that aren't needed, and no one is keeping watch on things. No one was looking at the big picture. I know your colleague here introduced me as the President. That's bull. I'm not your President. I'm not qualified and I don't want the job. There are far better people than me who could run this place. All I want to do is to put things back to normal. The text message challenges have ended; survival of the fittest is no more. I will bring the old laws back, and democracy. You will run elections for a new President. You will do your job of protecting the people, especially the weak and the vulnerable.'

I stopped. I was proud of myself. I didn't think I was

capable of a speech like that. But somehow all of the anger and frustration that had been brewing inside me, all of the rage against the injustice and evil that I had witnessed, all came together to guide me through it. A hesitant applause began to break out, gaining in strength and accompanied by cheers. These cops were humans too. They had yearned for the old ways as much as anyone. But it was a matter of obeying the law, obeying orders and surviving. I understood.

'What is your policy on the plague?' asked an officer close to me.

'What do you mean, policy?' I asked.

'There are reports that it's reached Honduras. We need another Annihilation. Have you given the order?'

The Annihilation. I'd forgotten. An automated process, liable to be instigated by the computers in the tower at any moment. I had to get back there with the J Team. I had to look at the evidence. Monitor the progress of the pestilence. Ultimately I would have to make a judgment that would affect the planet. I had been instinctively against another Annihilation. It was inhuman. No sane person could authorise such a procedure. But that was before. Marty was right. Everyone now looked to me for guidance. Innocent Americans depended on me to defend them against the disease, no matter what it would take. I knew I could order increased border security, bans on imports and international travel, all that kind of stuff. I could also order quarantine centres to be set up, especially in the southern states. I could divert whatever resources the nation had towards a peaceful resolution of the crisis.

What if that wasn't enough? What if the plague spread close enough to get a foothold in our country? Would I choose to annihilate anyone at that point? Would it be a kindness to end the suffering of the millions in South

America who were either dying already from the plague or about to catch it? The power was in my hands. There was no room for idealism in my soul. My duties were real. My people needed the right choices made for them. This job was not going to be an easy ride.

'Take me to the hundredth floor of the One World Trade Center,' I ordered. 'I have unfinished business there.'

A path cleared through the crowd of officers. I walked out into the street, still half-expecting to be re-arrested or shot. An electric car whisked me to the base of the tower, and I journeyed alone to the computer installation at the top.

'Hey, computer,' I said, feeling self-conscious. 'I don't know what I'm supposed to call you.'

There was no response.

I moved from the elevator lobby to the double-height observation deck where the majority of the computers were located. I repeated my greeting. The machines were running, but not responding to me.

'My name is Ignatius Inuus,' I continued. 'Yesterday you granted me executive powers. I need to discuss the progress of the plague.'

Still nothing.

'Look, computer, I don't want to rush headlong into another Annihilation, and I don't want to leave the decision until it's too late. I need to see the evidence.'

'Yo, Iggy,' said a voice. Either this computer had received a personality update, or someone else was addressing me. I glanced up at the mezzanine. Jake was leaning over it.

'Jake? You still here?'

'Guess so. Been trying to sort something with these computers.'

294

'Is that why it's not talking to me?' I asked.

'Sorry, Iggy. I switched it to keyboard input only.'

'So what were you trying to sort?'

'The location of Tania's kids. I know you wanted to find them, Iggy. I've been searching the databases. I found out where they went.'

'Great! Tell me!'

'They've been exported.'

'Where to?'

'I'm real sorry, buddy.'

'Just tell me, Jake.'

'They were sent to Brazil.'

Chapter 26

The ball hung above Times Square, lit by a mere fraction of the number of bulbs that used to dazzle revellers in the New Year's celebrations in pre-plague times. In the five months that followed the end of the automated regime and the return to democracy, power was still rationed; billboards still lacked the neon gaudiness of generations past, but hope had returned. People now had a reason to celebrate the future. Knowing that I had played my part in giving them that hope provided me with a sense of warmth that countered the chill of the December night. There must have been a quarter million people gathered tonight. They were mostly young, as had always been the case, but it pleased me to see a few older people who had only made it through the years of oppression thanks to the generosity and bravery of those who sheltered them from the police in their community. And there were children, too, many of whom I knew would be my own, recently reunited with their mothers.

My own fame was diminishing. I had stood aside from politics as soon as possible, but not before I had ordered the return to their parents, where practicable, of all children in state care. I had also ordered the return of some of the children exported overseas, although many could not be traced. And, to my shame, this included Tania's kids. Amid the chaos of a Brazil on its knees due to the plague outbreak, no records were kept of the final destination of Scarlet and Bert.

My decision not to initiate an Annihilation of South America was my Cuban Missile moment. Like Kennedy before me, I had refused to pander to panic, I had refused to over-react, and my steadfastness had been rewarded. The plague spread slowly, then stopped. Brazilian doctors didn't possess a cure, but they had been working for a decade on ways to mitigate the symptoms and control the contagion. It worked. Was I aware of their medical advances? No. Was I influenced by the knowledge that Tania's kids were in Brazil? Of course. I'm human. I'm flawed. And I intended to remain that way.

When the formal transition of executive power to the acting president was complete, I spent some days investigating the circumstances surrounding Tania's incarceration and execution. The sentimental side of me wanted to know if she had written or said anything about me in her final hours. I started at Norfolk naval base and followed the trail to the military correctional facility where she had been sent to face the death penalty, but there were no records of her arrival there and no records of her execution. I assumed a cover-up. After all, if she had, by some miracle, engineered an escape on the way to the place of execution she would have made contact with me by now. There was no way she could have avoided hearing about me if she had lived.

And so I found myself alone, avoiding eye contact with the celebrating hoards, walking slowly around the edges of Times Square on the night that Tania and I had arranged to meet if we were separated. Our separation could not have been more complete. I knew that when this night was over, I would need to start to rebuild myself. My own life had been on hold for too long. I was mourning Tania and I was mourning my father and, it seemed, I was even mourning the eleven years that had been stolen from my life. When the ball dropped I planned to leave Times Square, leave New York altogether. I didn't know what I would do with the rest of my life, but I didn't plan on spending it in the accounts department of a repair company.

The ball began to fall. The energy of the crowd surged through me. I felt privileged to witness their anticipation of a better life. Despite my loneliness I managed to smile. These were my people. In some cases, quite literally. We were family. The ball finished its journey. The year was done. People screamed and started kissing. At the fringes of the crowd, where I was standing, it was a free-for-all of embraces. A young woman kissed me on the cheek. Another grabbed my head and kissed my lips. Someone hugged me. None of them recognised me. All immediately went on to kiss other random people.

More lips met mine. They kissed with a strength that shocked me. More than the others, this woman was invading my personal space. The kiss continued. I felt her arms surround me. Then, bizarrely, I could feel tiny hands clamping on to mine.

Finally, she paused for breath.

'Just made it,' she said. 'Brazil's a long way by horse. Thanks for stopping the Annihilation. Bert and Scarlet always believed in you.'

The End

Proudly published by Accent Press

www.accentpress.co.uk